Rootbound

A *Tangled* Novel

New York Times bestselling author
MARGARET OWEN

Random House New York

Random House Books for Young Readers
An imprint of Random House Children's Books
A division of Penguin Random House LLC
1745 Broadway, New York, NY 10019
penguinrandomhouse.com
rhcbooks.com/disney

Jacket illustration by Noor Sofi
Designed by Gegham Vardanyan

Library of Congress Control Number: 2024949418
ISBN 978-1-368-10104-2 (trade)—ISBN 978-0-7364-4793-5 (ebook)

The text of this book is set in 13.3-point Perpetua MT Pro.

Manufactured in the United States of America
2nd Printing

The authorized representative in the EU for product safety and compliance is Penguin Random House Ireland, Morrison Chambers, 32 Nassau Street, Dublin D02 YH68, Ireland, https://eu-contact.penguin.ie.

Random House Children's Books supports the First Amendment and celebrates the right to read.

For the ones outgrowing their gardens:
There's so much more waiting
beyond the walls.

Part One

White Shells

One

Rapunzel

Rapunzel's neck is too cold.

It's a silly thing to be hung up on at a ball. Not just any ball—a ball in the royal palace. A ball thrown for *her.* The hushed grand ballroom looks like a dream she would have painted back in Gothel's tower only a month ago, with glittering chandeliers swaying above and echoes of candlelight in the gold-flecked marble floor, its smooth tiles pressing through the soles of the satin slippers she's almost tripped on twice tonight.

It's just that everyone is watching her cross the mostly empty dance floor, arm in arm with the queen, bound for where the king—no, *Father*—waits at the heart of an inlaid golden sun.

And it's just that she's still not used to hems that skim the floor instead of her calves, or a bodice of barely too stiff brocade, or even a gown she didn't sew herself.

And it's just that for eighteen years, birthdays meant hazelnut soup and tiptoeing to the window to watch the lanterns once Mothe—no, *not* Mother; Gothel—fell asleep.

Not ball gowns. Not feasts. Not fireworks. And certainly not a waltz with Father in front of the most important people in the realm.

And to top it all off, every time the short strands of her now-brunette hair tickle the back of her (cold!) neck, she has to hide the shiver zipping down her backbone.

"You're going to do wonderfully," her mother whispers, hand snug on Rapunzel's elbow. Rapunzel doesn't know how the queen does it, gliding over the floor smoother than paint under a palette knife, as if no one is watching and she does this every day. (Not "the queen." *Mother.*) "Madame Frangeline says you have a gift."

Madame Frangeline was saddled with training Rapunzel to dance like a courtier instead of a feral princess for this ball. After the last two weeks of jabs from the madame's training baton, Rapunzel suspects her only gift is kicking her partner in the shin.

"I won't let you down," Rapunzel promises.

Her mother slows just before they reach the king. Her arm unwinds from Rapunzel's, but her fingertips graze the side of Rapunzel's cheek, a faint line digging between her brows despite the reassuring smile. "Sweetheart, just having you here is a miracle. This is your night. All you need to do is enjoy yourself."

Over her mother's shoulder, Rapunzel finds Eugene in the waiting crowd. His tilted smile grows when their eyes meet, his chin dipping in a nod. Somehow he looks even more at ease in this sea of dignitaries than she feels.

Maybe, if they can get a dance later, she'll ask how he does it.

"Thank you for all of this, Mother," Rapunzel says, and walks the last few feet to the king.

She's practiced the formal curtsy nearly as much as her dancing, with marginally the same outcomes. Now, in front of the whole ballroom, it's halting and ungainly, and her knee wiggles a little as she rises, but at least she manages not to kick the king in the shin. (Rapunzel thinks that *may* be a hanging offense.) Her father's mustache wobbles at the ends as he bows in return and offers his hand, and the orchestra finally looses the first notes of the waltz.

Rapunzel takes his hand. She's learned Father's mustache wobbles that way when he's holding something back; she's still trying to sort out if it means the same thing as when Gothel's footsteps on the stairs creaked a little too fast. "I'm going to keep practicing my curtsy."

"You were perfect," he says as the dance begins, but his mustache wobbles again when she can't keep the doubt off her face. "It's just . . . remarkable," he tells her. "When I first met your mother, she had a devil of a time keeping her knee steady in a curtsy, too."

"Really?" Rapunzel blurts out.

"Really." Her father's face softens even more as he glances toward the queen. "And she practiced for—"

He sucks in a breath. Rapunzel realizes she's stepped directly on his boot toe.

But before she can squeak out an apology, her father shifts his feet and keeps leading them through the waltz.

"Practiced for years," the king finishes with an astonishing wink. "Remember, tonight is *us* making up for eighteen years of lost birthdays, not you. Now here comes the spin—"

Rapunzel is a little surer in a twirl. It's only been a month since she left her tower, and some of this whole new life is better, and some of it is harder, and some of it is just—different. She still holds her breath when she wakes up, ready to gauge Gothel's mood by how she bangs around the kitchen, only to hear birdsong and a bubbling fountain in the garden below her window. She can't stop tugging on her sleeves, only to remember her dresses actually fit now.

And she knew how to twirl despite seventy feet of hair, but even in a ballroom, in front of her new family and all these important people, it's so, so much easier to move without that weight.

The ballroom whirls around her almost like the floating lanterns, and when Father catches her hands again, he's beaming. "Just like that."

The steps come easier, back, left, *close* the box, even as eyes bore into the back of Rapunzel's neck. "Do you ever get used to the staring?"

Her father's brows rise. "Yes and no," he admits. "I hated it when I was younger."

"What changed?"

"I met your mother," he says with a rueful laugh. "And I realized sometimes people stare because they like what they see."

Rapunzel finds Eugene in the crowd again. His eyes are still on her. The knot in her stomach dissolves into pleasant butterflies. "Oh."

Then she's spinning again, and if she lets the faces and lights blur, she can almost believe she's back in the boat last month, swaying on the bay in the galaxy of lanterns. For a few more breaths, it's just the box step and twirl, back and forth, left and right and spin, and then—

The music sweeps to a grand finish. The king lets her go with a smooth bow, and this time, when she curtsies, her knee doesn't falter at all.

"Well done," he says as the ballroom rings with polite applause. "It's all easy sailing from here, so go have fun."

For exactly four and three quarters of the next dances, the king is right.

She dances with an earl, a councilor, the mayor, a brigadier general, and now jolly old Duke Louis of Maenvale. He's spent most of the lively gavotte extolling the virtues of his nephew's vineyards. All Rapunzel knows about wine at this point is that it typically comes in red and white, but the duke is delighted to carry the conversation himself, and she can smile and nod and concentrate on the footwork.

And then they enter the final turn.

". . . unless it comes from the Campina region, otherwise it's just sparkling wine," the ruddy-faced duke is saying. Then: "I say, what an extraordinary brooch, Your Highness."

"Brooch?" Rapunzel looks down at her bodice.

There's a coil of gold there, one she doesn't remember pinning on. Just as she registers the pebbled surface, Duke Louis adds, "I can't believe I didn't spot it before. Is it a . . . dragon?"

"Pascal," Rapunzel gasps. The duke blinks at her, bemused. She hastily fibs: "The jeweler! Her name was Pascale."

"Wonderful craftsmanship," says Duke Louis with a stout nod.

The gavotte bounces to an end. The duke bows and steps away. Rapunzel hisses, "Pascal, we *talked* about this! You can't be here!"

The chameleon cracks an eye open and lets out a stubborn *bihrrrr*.

"May I have the next dance, Your Highness?"

Of all the people here that Rapunzel doesn't want seeing her talk to herself, Minister Cressien is probably at the top of the list. Minister Cressien is one of her parents' most trusted advisors. Minister Cressien is in all things composed, polished, and unflappable; tonight, his peacock-blue velvet doublet perfectly sets off his cool brown complexion, the silver trim precisely calculated to complement his short-cropped gray hair. Minister

Cressien, it is rumored, has been summoned for emergency meetings in the middle of the night and never answered the door in anything more casual than a three-piece suit.

And Minister Cressien, in particular, looked like he'd found a snail in his salad the moment her parents introduced her to their council of advisors.

"O-of course," she stammers, her swift curtsy teetering precariously.

When she straightens, the minister has already risen from his bow. A dour pinch to his line-framed mouth defies the merry bourrée now soaring from the orchestra. The contrast is even starker as they skip sideways and back, his long silence making her wonder if he's spied Pascal after all. But when Rapunzel sneaks a look, the chameleon is gone.

"I understand you've"—Minister Cressien glances down briefly—"accustomed yourself to shoes."

In fact, the slippers may be giving her blisters. Rapunzel can't help an awkward giggle as she tries not to panic. "It's, uh, a work in progress, I guess?"

"Mm." The minister's slender mahogany fingers close around hers as they move forward one step, two, three. "I would encourage that progress to continue, Your Highness."

They let go and face each other again. Rapunzel's hands slip on the silk of her skirts as she briefly fans them out. *Where* did Pascal go? "I'm—I'm planning on it."

Cressien fixes a grave hazel stare on her. "As minister of diplomatic affairs, I have found that the key to understanding is a common language, not just in words, but in deeds. Every member of nobility speaks etiquette. It would be in your best interests, Your Highness, to strive for fluency. *Quickly.*"

Rapunzel isn't even sure how to respond to that.

The words evade her entirely, though, when she realizes Pascal is now clinging to the front of the minister's velvet doublet.

"I—I agree." She falters, trying not to gawk at the chameleon. "I would hate to be *seen*"—Rapunzel leans on *seen* as a load-bearing warning to Pascal, and his hide shifts to match the doublet's deep teal as she tries not to frown—"as a step *back* for my family."

The bourrée calls for them to split and walk in tight circles. When Rapunzel returns to the minister, Pascal's not on the front of his doublet anymore. For a beautiful moment she thinks he's picked up her plea to return to her bedroom, *where they agreed he'd wait*—

And then, as she and Minister Cressien turn, Rapunzel finds Pascal scaling the minister's spine.

"Don't—" she sputters. The minister's face stiffens with alarm. "Don't, er, worry," Rapunzel stumbles. "I know tonight is *very important* for us, and I don't want *any surprises* to *cause a scene.*"

"I am delighted we concur," Cressien says tonelessly. Pascal scuttles up to his shoulder, head tilted, and mottles his hide with silver to blend in with the doublet's trim. "Matters of diplomacy are of the utmost importance to the kingdom's security and prosperity."

One

Rapunzel forces an uneasily toothy smile onto her face, only listening with half an ear. Pascal has always kept close, but for the last month, he's been even clingier, rarely letting her out of his sight. Even now, he's giving her the look that says Minister Cressien is perilously close to the once-in-a-lifetime experience of being slapped by a chameleon.

"I do hope Her Highness doesn't find the kingdom's security an amusing matter," the minister says thinly.

Rapunzel decides it's time for more direct methods. "No, no, I'm sorry—I was distracted. I think there's a, er, flower petal on your epaulet." Before he can look, she swipes for Pascal.

The chameleon is unfortunately two steps ahead. He scurries around the minister's shoulder, out of Rapunzel's sight. She tries not to scream with frustration.

"How odd." Minister Cressien glances at his doublet, clearly unconvinced. The music slows as the bourrée winds down, but to her surprise, he stops in place entirely, voice lowering. "Your Highness, no matter the intentions, an unprepared sovereign is a catastrophe waiting to happen."

Rapunzel can only stare.

Cressien continues speaking quickly. "It's been my life's work to strengthen this kingdom's alliances, but many of our neighbors are simply waiting for a weakness to exploit. For the sake of everyone, I would urge you—"

"Don't mind if I cut in."

Rapunzel starts. Eugene sidesteps in front of the minister and briefly clasps the man's shoulder, giving him a broad, cheeky grin. "Suitor privileges, you know how it goes. Shall we, m'lady?"

"Your Highness," Minister Cressien grits through his teeth. Rapunzel can't tell if he's correcting Eugene or excusing himself.

Eugene links their arms and sweeps her away before she can find out. "Everything all right? I've seen happier chats at the dentist."

"Wait," she whispers frantically, "I need to go get—"

"Your frog?" Eugene drops a nonplussed Pascal onto her elbow with a flourish.

Rapunzel almost falls over with relief. "Pascal! You were supposed to go back to my room!" The chameleon trills an objection that, per usual, only Rapunzel can parse. "Of course I couldn't just tell you that. Didn't you see I was dancing with someone?"

"You still haven't told your parents about him?"

Rapunzel can't make herself look at Eugene, even though she knows he won't pry. All she mumbles is "Not yet."

Sure enough, Eugene doesn't push the issue. Instead, as a minuet starts, he bows. "Well, *Your Highness*, I'd be happy to smuggle him out after this dance."

"Thank you, Eugene, that would be wonderful," Rapunzel says. Pascal *brrs* another protest, and Rapunzel sneaks a head-shake into her curtsy. "I'll be fine, Pascal."

"You're doing great, you know," Eugene whispers, taking her hand as they fall into lines for the minuet.

Rapunzel wants to believe it. Unfortunately, within the first measure of song, she collides with the woman to her left and trips the woman on her right. The minuet is so *fussy*, but after maneuvering around her hair so long, shouldn't this be a breeze?

"How do you do it?" she finally gets a chance to ask once the dance brings her back to Eugene.

"The minuet? The trick is to follow the person in front of you and just sort of crouch every six steps." He deftly catches Pascal before the chameleon can climb back onto Rapunzel. "Or did you mean something else?"

"Doesn't all of this make you nervous?"

They have to split off again before he can answer. *Three, four, five, CROUCH*—Rapunzel is surprised when it actually works. Madame Frangeline would be livid. Her shoulders relax as she circles and returns to Eugene. The warmth of his hand around hers breathes sparks up her arm, through her chest, until she'd swear she'll float if he lets go.

"You have the hard job tonight," he says under his breath, like he's getting away with something. "Eventually you'll have to work with most of these people. But me? They're never going to like me. So if you need a rude suitor to barge in and bail you out, I'm just one desperate look away."

The strange thing is it sounds like a joke, and Rapunzel *thinks* it's a joke . . . but something about it bothers her, and she has no idea what. Four, five, and *crouch*, then they're letting go and weaving around the other couples.

Eugene winds up averting no fewer than five further Pascal-related incidents before it's his turn to be cut short; as the minuet settles down, the queen herself arrives.

"We have a little surprise for you," the queen says over the tolling of the hourly bells as she reaches for Rapunzel's elbow. Somehow it's already eight o'clock.

"Oh—okay—" Rapunzel looks to Eugene, who appears the picture of serenity, as if he hasn't just fished Pascal out of another man's wig.

"Thank you for the dance, Your Highness," he says gallantly, and bows. "Your Majesty."

Rapunzel's mother tugs her away. Rapunzel herself glances over her shoulder and mouths *thank you* to Eugene, giving Pascal a stern look.

"Are you having fun?" the queen asks as they cross the floor.

Rapunzel catches herself waiting for the second half of the sentence again. Usually, Gothel would follow a question like that with *because you left me all on my own*, or *it was so nice of that gentleman to humor you*. It's not easy to adjust to questions just being . . . questions.

"Everything is wonderful," Rapunzel offers. She's conveniently painting over the fact that her secret chameleon is waging a one-lizard campaign to crash the ball. And that the minister of diplomatic affairs more or less told her to come back when she's ready to sit at the grown-ups' table. And that the slippers make her feet feel like two enormous blisters.

Everyone's worked so hard to make this night perfect, and it's so much more than anything Gothel ever did for her birthday. The last thing she wants is her parents thinking she isn't grateful.

She'd toss her sketchbook out a window before she'd admit that it might be too much. Maybe if she'd been raised as a princess, she'd be used to the pomp and grandeur, but right now it feels like starring in an opera she's never heard of.

As she and her mother clear the crowd, a herald brays across the floor, "We shall now commence with the presenting of gifts!"

Oh no.

She's led to a dais where guests are already queueing up. The line seems impossibly long.

The king's hand falls on her shoulder. "Nothing can make up for eighteen years," he says quietly, "but we hope this is a start."

Duke Louis of Maenvale is first. "My finest rosé," he announces, gesturing to a wine cask trimmed in gold and purple. "Five barrels. The rest have been delivered straight to the cellar, Your Highness, but perhaps we might tap this one tonight?"

"Perhaps later," the queen says firmly.

Rapunzel makes a note to ask what a rosé is, and what she's supposed to do with five barrels of it, later. "Thank you so much, Duke Louis, this is so thoughtful."

Next comes a countess with a beautiful string of pearls ("How lovely, thank you!"). Then a marquis presents her with a fine mare who seems, incredibly, more at ease in the ballroom than Rapunzel ("She's perfect, thank you!"), and an earl somehow manages to fit an entire new carriage through the doors ("I'm . . . speechless! Thank you!").

By the fifth present, Rapunzel is beginning to sweat.

By the eighth, she's trying to find new and creative ways to say "I love it, thank you" while Minister Cressien looks increasingly unimpressed. It's not that she doesn't mean it—it's just *so much.*

It's all for her, all this treasure, all this fanfare. After eighteen years of hazelnut soup, it's . . .

It's not just *so* much. All of it—it's *too* much.

Finally, after a present Rapunzel actually knows what to do with—yards of gorgeous silks and velvets from the head of the merchants' league—it seems like a reprieve is finally at hand, the end of the line at last.

Then a tall woman steps from the crowd. She's wearing a curious midnight-blue silk robe, embroidered in silver and gold patterns that look strangely familiar—

Stars, Rapunzel realizes. Stars charted in thread, the way she painted them in her—*Gothel's*—tower.

The woman approaches the dais and bows deeply. Her hood falls back as she straightens, revealing a pale lined face and silver hair glittering with crystal pins. When she speaks, her deep voice lilts in a way that makes Rapunzel think of incense smoke. "Greetings, Your Highness. I am Councilor Teophine Trahan, emissary of the kingdom of Astera. I bear a gift from His Majesty King Enver."

Astera. Rapunzel knows next to nothing about Astera, other than that its white seashells make her favorite pigment. And that it's three days there and back, but only because of how Gothel had griped when Rapunzel asked for those shells. Gothel was careful to keep any maps or history books far from their shelves.

But judging from the murmurs leaping through the ballroom, there's more to Astera than its seashells. Queen Arianna draws a sharp breath behind Rapunzel. Minister Cressien's brow has furrowed, eyes darting to the king. Rapunzel fishes ". . . ever seen an Asteran?" and "hundreds of years" and "forbidden" from the darting whispers.

Teophine's smile doesn't quite reach her eyes. "Our crown princess, Verette, is coming of age in ten days. To forge a new working relationship between our two nations, for the first time in our history, King Enver has extended a royal invitation to attend the celebration"—her slender hand emerges from her robes, extending a golden envelope—"to Her Highness Princess Rapunzel."

Rapunzel gulps. Didn't Cressien say diplomacy was critical to the kingdom's safety? He's already elbowing his way through the crowd—it would be rude to refuse, and Councilor Teophine is waiting for an answer—

"Thank you," Rapunzel says automatically, taking the envelope. "I'm honored to accept—"

"—consider it," her father interjects as Teophine's smile widens and half the room gasps. "We'll need to—"

Rapunzel swings around to look at him, startled by the urgency in his voice.

Unfortunately, the king was stepping forward, halfway to dropping a hand on her shoulder again. He tries to jerk back, loses his balance, lurches to the side . . . and misses the top step of the dais.

There's a scuffle, an ugly crunch, and a muffled string of words Rapunzel's pretty sure a king's not allowed to know.

"Oh dear," her mother sighs. "Can someone get the doctor? He's done it again." As she hurries past Rapunzel, she says under her breath, "Don't worry, sweetheart, this dais always trips him up. If we're lucky, it's his fourth sprain; his second break if we're not. I *told* him we need railings."

Rapunzel reaches for her hair, ready to say that for once tonight, she knows what she's doing—

And comes up short. Her hand closes on empty air.

There's no denying it's easier to move without seventy feet of hair. But if she still carried that weight . . .

A quick little song, and all of this would be fixed.

The queen crouches by her husband, who sits red-faced on the stairs, one leg outstretched. They insisted she need only have fun tonight. Rapunzel's fairly certain they're regretting that now.

There's a firm cough at her elbow. "I'll handle this, Your Highness," Minister Cressien says stiffly, and plucks the golden envelope from her grasp.

"Oh—sure," Rapunzel says hesitantly. She turns back to look for Councilor Teophine—

But there's no sign of midnight-blue silk or crystal-studded hair anywhere in the ballroom. All that she's left behind are the invitation and whispers trailing like stardust in her wake.

Two

Eugene

"Oh, it's not just you," Eugene tells Rapunzel, watching her brush a streak of violet across the wall as he perches on her ladder. It could be a garland, or a decorative flourish, or, as he's learned, the dark base she'll build lighter layers into. And heaven knows she won't tell him; it's a game they like to play, seeing how long it takes him to guess what she's painting. He'd like to think he's gotten better at it, but then she goes and does something like turn a purple line into patina-green rooftops. "Nobody knows anything about Astera."

Rapunzel frowns and blows a hair out of her eyes. Eugene's witnessed her various attempts to keep it away from her face;

today's handkerchief is just this side of peasant quaint, but it seems to do the job better than most.

Which is good, because after last night's invitation fiasco, Rapunzel's spent most of the day painting through her feelings in her nursery. Well, nursery turned painting studio. From what Eugene's eavesdropped on, the king and queen had the room locked fourteen years ago, once they accepted that if their daughter was ever found, she'd be too big for her crib.

One thing Eugene *will* give himself credit for, though, is noticing how Rapunzel kept staring at the relatively plain palace walls, and discreetly telling the king how Gothel's tower bloomed with Rapunzel's work. Her parents were all too glad to open the nursery and clear those fourteen years of dust just so she could paint new life into it.

"I thought it was only a day and a half away." Rapunzel steps back from the wall. By now Eugene knows the tilt of her head when she's assessing a painting's composition. Pascal, in his semipermanent post on her shoulder, tilts his head too. Then she swallows. "At least . . . it was for Gothel."

Eugene squints, trying to piece together the blocks of color and see what she sees. Still no dice. "At least three days by ship, with good wind and good seas, and another three back. But she was a creepy old witch—maybe she just turned herself into a bird and flew? I could see her as a seagull."

He's never sure how jokes about Gothel will go over. Sometimes Rapunzel laughs, and sometimes she looks like she bumped a bruise. This time, he can see her ears lift with her smile, which means it landed well. "Maybe. That's still not that far, though. Why don't we know anything?"

"Well, for one thing, they don't let outsiders onto the mainland. May I?" Eugene hops off the ladder and picks up a stick of chalk. Sometimes Rapunzel will use it to sketch her paintings out first. When she nods, he moves to an empty stretch of wall and draws the outline of Astera—or at least, his best recollection of it, which looks like a fried egg being orbited by other, smaller breakfast foods. "It's an archipelago. Most everyone lives here on the mainland"—he taps the fried egg—"but foreign ships can only dock here." This time, he indicates a tiny croissant to the south. "It's called Merchant's Crescent. Asteran traders will cross the bay to do business with foreigners there and then sail right back. Guards even observe the trading to make sure no one spills Asteran secrets."

"How do you know all this?" Rapunzel asks as she studies his crude map. A blob of pale yellow waits precariously on the tip of a brush in her hand, abandoned for the moment. Candle-flame yellow, he realizes, and finds she's already sprinkled it over the upper half of her painting, the earlier purple now the folds of a velvet drape. It falls into place: She's painting last night's ball, before everything went sideways.

"Solena, one of the caretakers at my orphanage, wanted to see the world before she retired. She joined the crew of a trade ship but wound up falling for an Asteran. She came back to say goodbye, because once you set foot on mainland Astera, you can't leave the archipelago. I'm assuming they make exceptions for royalty. And royal emissaries." Eugene dusts the chalk off his hands and jerks his thumb at the couch, where a worn book lays half under a throw pillow. "Flynnigan Rider's supposedly Asteran, you know. Got his start as a royal guard, even. But I think the author was just making things up, since no one outside of Astera . . ."

Familiar voices seep from the hallway beyond the door.

". . . too harsh on her," the queen is saying.

". . . knows the truth," Eugene finishes. Rapunzel goes still; Pascal *brrrrs* a protest as Eugene quickly plucks him from her shoulder.

The echoes in the hall distort the words, but he catches *still learning* and *doing her best.*

Eugene likes the queen. It's hard not to like a woman who saw him standing on the outskirts of their reunion with a long-lost daughter and pulled him quite literally into their family.

The thing is . . . princesses don't marry criminals. Not even pardoned ones. He remembers that every time he passes the guards' barracks and sees the gallows still waiting in the courtyard.

So Eugene has no doubt that, sooner rather than later, the queen will be every bit as understanding and gracious when they make it clear it's time for Rapunzel to move on from him.

The other voice belongs to Cressien, minister of diplomatic affairs, currently running neck and neck with the captain of the guard for Eugene's number one hater. *". . . see the consequences herself,"* he's insisting. *"She must understand what's at stake."*

Two

Eugene and Rapunzel trade looks. He sets Pascal on the couch to blend into the cushions.

"I just didn't want to be rude," Rapunzel whispers.

There's a beat filled with slowing footsteps, close to the door now, not quite at the threshold. Then the queen asks gently, "How are you doing with the separation?"

"Thomas returned his wedding ring two days ago," Cressien says shortly. And after a moment: "Always had a rotten sense of timing."

"You know we can manage if you need to step away for a bit."

"I need no such thing," Cressien replies almost immediately.

The pause stretches a little too long. Eugene realizes the silence on their side of the door is betraying their snooping too. "It occurs to me," he all but brays, "that we need a new nickname for you, since Blondie is a bit, oh, obsolete now. How do you feel about Blossom?"

Rapunzel wrinkles her nose. "Okay?"

" 'Okay' is code for 'no thank you,' " he surmises.

She grins sheepishly. "It's too close to Flower."

"Good point. Florals are completely out." He rubs his chin. "Something flashier? Razzmatazz?"

"That's just as many syllables as Rapunzel."

"True, true. Punzie?"

She doesn't have time to shoot that down before there's a knock at the door. "Rapunzel? May we come in?"

"Of course!" Rapunzel's face tightens as her mother and the

minister enter. "I'm so sorry about last night—I didn't mean to cause any problems—"

The queen crosses over to her. "We know, dear. No one expected you to be in that position—oh, wait." She catches Rapunzel's chin and wipes a fleck of purple paint off her cheek. Eugene wonders if Rapunzel's aware of how much she lights up at the simple gesture. "Cressien can explain better."

The minister straightens, tugging at his cravat. "The fact of the matter is, we know very little about the kingdom of Astera."

"Eugene was just telling me no one ever leaves," Rapunzel says.

Cressien's gaze briefly flicks to Eugene as if he's a dog who jumped through an unexpected hoop. "Correct," he says mildly. "The last record we have is of a wedding announcement between Queen Gaelle and a Duke Enver over fifty years ago. King Enver is presumably their son, and Verette their granddaughter. We've sent customary invitations to neighboring kingdoms, including Astera, for all significant events as a matter of courtesy, including the ball last night. But it is unprecedented for Astera to actually make an appearance. And it is even more concerning that they've singled you out this way."

Rapunzel pushes the paintbrush into a blob of reddish pink that's increasingly matching her cheeks, her eyes on the palette. "I didn't want to insult them by refusing."

"A skilled leader is able to receive an invitation without committing to attend," Cressien says. "Express gratitude in public, decline later in private, send gifts, soothe egos. But because you accepted, no matter the excuse we give, Astera will know we're suspicious of them and be insulted nevertheless. Something of a minor"—he clears his throat—"catastrophe."

Eugene doesn't miss Rapunzel's flinch. Yet a month's distance from his life of crime has not dulled his eye for a scam, and this is checking all the boxes: vague terms, forced urgency, targeting someone too new to know better. "Is it me, or does that sound like a setup?"

The minister only shoots him another *good boy, now shake* look, but the queen's lips purse. "I don't disagree. The Asteran ship only arrived right before the ball last night, and Councilor Teophine delivered their invitation in the most conspicuous way she could. It suggests they wish to strong-arm us into a visit."

Rapunzel still twists her hair when she's anxious, even if it's harder with it cropped short. "So . . . when am I leaving?"

"You aren't," Cressien says, at the same time her mother says, "Oh, no." The minister bobs his head in deference to the queen, and she continues, "You've barely been here a month. We just want you to be aware of what's happening, since this is a very delicate situation. No one expects you to navigate it yourself."

Rapunzel sets her paintbrush down.

There's a look in her eyes that Eugene recognizes. It doesn't show up often, but he pays attention when it does, because the first time he encountered it, Rapunzel was threatening him with ten pounds of cast iron and a likely concussion.

Sometimes he thinks people focus more on the tower, and less on the fact that Rapunzel spent eighteen years playing chess against herself.

"Right," she agrees, "so why don't we use that?"

Minister Cressien frowns. "I don't follow."

Rapunzel's chin lifts. "They expect me to be completely naïve, don't they? So they won't bother trying to hide what they want from us in front of me."

Eugene's belly flops as the queen steeples her fingers, considering. Rapunzel's right—it's risky, but she's right.

And the moment her ship clears the horizon, he has no doubt he'll be kindly and firmly escorted out the back door.

"I could go with," Eugene volunteers quickly. "So you're not on your own."

Two more weeks; one more adventure with her. Then maybe, once he's asked to go, he'll be ready.

"I would consider *alternative* courses of action, Your Majesty." Cressien looks like he's barely repressing a lip curl.

"But Eugene's more . . . unorthodox skills could be quite useful, I think," the queen muses.

Right. That clinches it. Pardon or no, this is how they're always going to see him. Eugene forces a laugh. "Ah, yes. I can spy, steal state secrets, keep an eye out for any traps, you know. Rogue things."

"That's not all." To his dismay, Rapunzel is picking up *The Tales of Flynnigan Rider* from the couch and handing it to her mother. "Eugene's favorite book is about a man from Astera. He might actually know more about the customs than we do."

As the queen flips the pages, Eugene's face burns. "Well," he blusters, "maybe . . . it's just a kids' book, and the author could have made it all up."

The queen's hands go still. "Cressien . . . do you have the invitation with you?" When he passes the envelope over, she flips it and lays it against the book's first page, then turns it around to show them what caught her eye.

There's an old mark embossed into the inside of the front cover, one he always assumed to be simply ornamental: a crown surrounded by four stars, like the points of a compass rose.

The same symbol that's pressed into the envelope's wax seal.

The seal of the king.

"How did you get this book, Eugene?" the queen asks.

Sometimes you can hear the asterisk attached to a question. This asterisk's annotation reads, *Do we need to draft an extradition treaty?*

"The orphanage," he answers, bewildered. "It was just—always there."

To his surprise, the queen shuts it and hands it back to him. "You may just be an accidental expert after all." She thinks for a moment, then shakes her head at Rapunzel. "I appreciate your initiative, dear, but it's not worth the risk. We'll decline and say it's just too soon."

"And since they won't believe it, I will handle the aftermath," Cressien says stonily.

"But—" Rapunzel's hands ball into fists. "But I made this problem. I should help fix it."

Her mother squeezes her shoulder. "Believe me, there will be plenty of opportunities to help in the future. For now, let us deal with it. And if this Teophine tries to seek you out directly, tell her I summoned you, and come straight to me."

It's the tone Eugene's heard a thousand times from mothers sending their children down to the market with a very short list and exact change. From the look on Rapunzel's face, she has no idea how to parse it.

"Okay," she says, almost confused. "If that's what you want."

"Everything will be fine," the queen tells Rapunzel with one final squeeze.

As she and Cressien leave, he flips *The Tales of Flynnigan Rider* open once more and studies the seal. Now that he thinks about it, the orphanage had a bookshelf . . . and this book was never on it. Even when he left it in another room, somehow he would always find it later on the foot of his bed, or under his pillow, or resting on the crate he used for a nightstand.

And for a book that was always *there*, it's even stranger that he's never come across another copy.

How *did* he get this one?

Rapunzel waits, head cocked, until the footsteps in the hall fade. Then she picks up her paintbrush again, eyes narrowed, and says, "Pascal, you can come out now."

And as she dips the brush in a dollop of midnight-blue paint, Eugene knows one thing for sure: Even if the queen thinks everything will be fine, it's certainly far from over.

Three

Rapunzel

Really, Rapunzel thinks, it could be worse.

For example, this could all be happening in the dead of winter, when the sun would have already set hours ago. Years of late-night sketching by the light of a secret candle mean she can tell the royal library's lamps would be direly insufficient for her search. Instead, even though it's well after dinner, the low summer sun gilds the sea, lighting the shelves and their contents with a reflected amber glow more than equal to the task.

Rapunzel survived a pub full of brigands, nearly drowning in a dam collapse, and eighteen years in Gothel's tower. She's pretty sure she can survive a birthday party. But if Minister

Cressien doesn't think she's ready to go to Astera, then she'll just have to *make* herself ready.

There's just one problem: The library is not cooperating.

Brandleton's History of the Northern Kingdoms. Maybe this one? She pulls the book down and skims the table of contents. Nothing specific to Astera, but . . . Rapunzel flips to a section on island kingdoms, skims, finds one line:

As for the archipelago of Astera, due to their strict isolationist policies, little is known about this kingdom's past.

Pascal *brrs* on her shoulder.

"Not this one either," she says with a sigh, and slides the book back into the gap left on the shelf. She hasn't found a single volume yet with any more information than this, if it even mentions Astera at all.

It could be worse, Rapunzel tells herself. She could be without access to the royal library entirely.

Pascal suddenly scuttles down her sleeve and into her pocket. A moment later, a librarian passes the end of the row of shelves, double-takes, and bobs a curtsy. "Your Highness! Can I help you find anything?"

"Oh no, don't worry about it," Rapunzel says in a rush. "Just looking! Haha!"

Before the librarian can offer again, she hurries away from the history section. Rapunzel is sure the librarian is very good at her job and might actually possess a trove of Asteran lore; she knows it makes very little sense, but for reasons completely beyond her, the idea of asking for help makes Rapunzel want to march into the sea.

Lore. There could be something in the legends and folklore section, at least about beliefs? Something about Asteran culture? Rapunzel spends another ten minutes scouring those shelves . . . but comes up empty-handed once more. When she tries the law section, she finds only a stray note in a tome of international legal codes about the limited documentation of Asteran regulations. She tries naval history—they have boats, right? (Of course they do; how else could Councilor Teophine have gotten here?)—and agriculture and, in desperation, a compendium of international recipes.

Nothing.

It *still* could be worse, Rapunzel internally insists. She could be in the tower, with a grand total of three books for reference.

But at least you knew those books by heart, a mutinous voice returns to remind her.

"Please let me know if you need anything, Your Highness." The librarian hums a drive-by hint, pushing a notably empty cart past the aisle.

Rapunzel contemplates the walking distance to the sea beyond the windows for a moment, decides it's too far, and caves. "Actually, yes. Do you know where I can find *anything* about Astera?"

A few minutes later, the librarian is pulling *Systems of Government of the Modern Age* from a shelf in the political arts section. "It's not a lot," she warns. "More than the rest of our collection, but that's not saying much." She hands it to Rapunzel. "May I ask, Your Highness . . . is this about the invitation last night?"

"My mother doesn't want me to go," Rapunzel says, trying not to let her glumness show.

The librarian's shoulders droop. "That's too bad. There must be so much for outsiders to learn there. Not that I'm questioning Her Majesty, of course. I wouldn't let my daughter go alone either."

Rapunzel's smile feels a little tight. "Of course. Thank you for your help."

She retreats to a nearby table and, once the librarian is out of sight, sets Pascal on the oak planks, then takes a seat and cracks open the dusty tome. The section the librarian promised is also just as brief as she warned, and it starts like most of the other books:

Little is known about the current regime in Astera.

Judging by the book's brittle leather, that regime was decades ago. Rapunzel's mouth twists, but she keeps going.

As of this writing, limited import trading is allowed on the main island by day under the watch of the guard, but every foreigner must return to Merchant's Crescent at sunset or remain on Astera as a permanent resident. Similarly, Asteran citizens are forbidden from leaving the archipelago, and surprisingly few attempt to do so. This makes gathering and confirming information about their society difficult, and the rulers at present seem inclined to further restrictions.

Eugene did say all trading happened on Merchant's Crescent now. The author's instincts seem to be right on the nose.

From what I have gleaned, Astera is led by a monarch and their consort, with the monarch's authority taking precedence. There is also a council of five advisors, and in the event that a monarch is incapacitated before their heir is of age, the council assumes governance of Astera in the interim. I believe there is some correlation between the cardinal directions and the jurisdiction of each councilor, for my admission papers bear the seals of the Councilor of the West and Master of Seas, as well as that of the Councilor of the East and Master of Prosperities. From my best estimation, the Master of Seas is responsible for Astera's navy, while the Master of Prosperities seems to be in charge of economic affairs. I have yet to determine what the North and South administrations cover, or what the fifth council position is; when I inquired, the supervising guard said it was none of my concern. This is the full extent of my observations regarding the government of Astera.

Rapunzel blows out a breath, the chair creaking as she sits back. All this secrecy, and they're breaking it to invite her to a party. No wonder her mother's suspicious.

But . . .

That only makes Rapunzel want to go *more.*

If she can't study up on Astera, maybe she can dive into diplomacy. She descends upon the political arts shelves, and returns to the table with a wobbling stack of books with titles like *Theories of Arbitration* and *Duties of the Plenipotentiary.*

A few hours later, she's wading through a chapter of the rather silly and bloated *Art of the Bargain* when the chair across from her squeaks. Rapunzel jolts to attention as Pascal ducks behind the book stack and fades into the pages.

Her mother is lowering herself into the other seat. Somehow, it's already dark out. The library's lamps were sufficient after all.

"You're a little too old for me to enforce a bedtime," the queen says gently, "but it *is* late." She picks up a discarded book—*Rules of Engagement*—skims the title, and looks up at Rapunzel. "You really want to go, don't you?"

"I—I don't expect it to be a vacation or anything," Rapunzel blurts out. "I promise I'm taking it seriously. I know it could be dangerous. I just think . . . we should find out why me, why now."

"Sweetheart, what happened yesterday isn't your fault. You know that, right?" Her mother reaches across the table for her hand. "And it's not your mess to clean up. We'll manage it just fine. Truly."

Whenever a growth spurt hit and Rapunzel's dresses started getting too short, too tight, Mother—no, Gothel—would roll her eyes and sigh, *I suppose I'll just have to find you more fabric. No, don't worry, Flower. It'll be out of my way, but I'll manage it somehow.*

Rapunzel still feels like she's fourteen, trying to reverse engineer pictures of dresses into a workable pattern so she doesn't have to bother Gothel for that too, when she says, "I want to help. I *know* I can help."

"I know you can . . ." the queen starts.

"And it's part of being a princess, right? There's always going to be a risk." Rapunzel shuts the book. "Maybe this is an opportunity for a new alliance. Or maybe it *is* a threat, and we need to know how to protect our kingdom. I want to *do* something about it. It doesn't feel right for me to just stay in the"—she catches herself—"palace."

I can be the princess you waited eighteen years for, she swears but doesn't say. *I can't heal Father anymore, but I can do this. I can make you proud.*

When the queen finally speaks, her voice is hoarse. "Sometimes I forget you still have a whole world to see. I won't be the one to make this castle a cage. Just promise . . ." Her eyes glitter in the lamplight. "Promise me, Rapunzel, that you'll come back."

✧ ✧ ✧

The next morning brings one hitch to the plan.

Rapunzel and Eugene can't avoid eavesdropping while they wait awkwardly outside her mother's meeting parlor. It's almost fascinating to hear Minister Cressien try to wrestle vehement disagreement into a nice hat. "Your Majesty, I—I'm afraid I can't . . . rationalize this course of action. It doesn't seem . . ."

"You may speak freely, Cressien," the queen says dryly.

"I must be hallucinating," the minister erupts. "Surely we're not sending the *brand-new* princess, and her suitor with a pardon so recent the ink hasn't dried, as emissaries to a kingdom no one's heard from since before *any* of us were born. A kingdom that deliberately manipulated us into this situation! The king won't allow it, and he'll be right!"

Eugene grimaces and mutters, *"Ouch."*

The queen coughs. "The king is currently on the royal doctor's strongest painkillers, because he is a tremendous baby. He spent the morning in his bathtub convinced he's judging a pastry contest. But you're right, this is a risky move. At best,

King Enver does genuinely want to establish relations, and at worst, they have more sinister intent."

"Even the middle ground is unacceptable, Your Majesty," Minister Cressien insists. "They could have reached out to you or the king at any time. They almost certainly wish to exploit Princess Rapunzel's inexperience, and we don't know to what end."

Didn't I say we could use that? Rapunzel thinks a bit crabbily.

But the queen embodies serenity itself as she says, "I concur, Cressien. This calls for a shrewd, insightful, highly capable diplomat with decades of experience and familiarity with our kingdom's policies, who can see exactly what Astera's real goal is."

Eugene and Rapunzel have only a few footsteps' warning before the parlor doors open.

The queen ushers the two of them inside with a smile brighter than the sun. "And that's why you're going with them. Now, let's talk strategy."

✧ ✧ ✧

The call comes at midnight: *"Rapunzel!"*

Rapunzel pushes herself up from her bed, her head heavy. Suddenly it's jerked sideways.

Mother Gothel's voice scythes through the open palace window once more: *"Rapunzel! Let down your hair!"*

A sleek gold shroud falls around Rapunzel and slithers out the window, unbidden. There's another neck-straining yank, and another, as Gothel's weight drags her out of bed—Gothel is climbing into her bedroom, even though this is all wrong, this is the palace, she left the tower behind—

"Look what I made, pet," Gothel croons, fingers tangling in the ends of Rapunzel's hair. Suddenly a golden noose swings from her fingers. "Now where's the man who took you away?"

Dread and anger surge in Rapunzel's chest. She whips the noose out of Gothel's grasp. "I took *myself* away."

"Now, now, don't make me the villain here." Gothel seizes her by the shoulders and gives her a hard, strangely slow shake. "Stop fighting me, Rapunzel. That criminal is to be hanged. Stop trying to run—"

"NO!"

Rapunzel sits up with a gasp. Her head thunks against the low wooden ceiling.

Her neck is cold.

Her neck is cold, and it was just a dream.

Pascal lets out a sleepy chirp on her pillow, but only curls into a tighter ball.

For a moment, she just sits there, heart racing, trying to catch her breath. This isn't the palace; it's a royal galleon. She's in the middle of the ocean, and tomorrow they'll reach Astera.

Gothel isn't here. The rocking came from the waves. Gothel is gone.

Eugene was fine. *Is* fine. He didn't hang; Gothel's knife couldn't even finish him off. Sometimes she sees him showing off his stomach's scar to the guards and boasting he still has eight lives left.

They just don't talk about the gallows.

The moon slides over the water's surface beyond her cabin's porthole. Rapunzel's pulse isn't settling anytime soon. She makes an executive decision, throws on a dressing gown over her pajamas, grabs her sketchbook and pastels, and leaves the cabin. Even though the ship's creaking timbers cover her, she treads lightly as she passes Minister Cressien's door, then Eugene's. The sailors on night watch only bow their heads briefly when she climbs above deck and takes a post near the bow, bracing her sketchbook against the railing.

Councilor Teophine's ship leads them by a few hundred yards, its pearly sails almost glowing under the moonlight. It's a curious little craft—the captain said it was called a caravel—with gleaming jet-black sides and brass trim. Councilor Teophine insisted on serving as their vanguard lest the Asteran navy automatically bar passage into the archipelago. Now the ship is almost as good as a second moon bobbing over the waves ahead, bearing northwest.

It's exactly the sort of thing that she can draw to calm down—the moonlight's sufficient for blocking out shapes, even if she can't do detail work until the morning. Rapunzel flips to a new page in her sketchbook, wedges the pastel case into a niche in the railing, and smudges a swath of cobalt over the page. Between the rolling waves and the change from paint to soft pastel, it takes her a few minutes to feel really at home again—but then the world simplifies to salt air, moonlight, and the possibility waiting in the paper.

She never thought she'd see the open ocean, only read about

it. It scares her in a way nothing else outside her tower has; the whole world was bigger, fiercer, closer, but the ocean in particular makes her feel like a grain of sand on a beach. It's an enthralling, gleeful sort of terror.

And it's strange, having a home she's free to leave. It wasn't until after the highest tower of the royal palace vanished behind the horizon that Rapunzel felt it: the wild, awful joy of knowing—she could go.

When Eugene joins her at the bow, she's outlined the caravel and is searching for the proper slate gray for the base layer of the hull. "I didn't mean to wake you," she says as he leans against the railing next to her.

"Funny thing is, I'd probably sleep right through it if you were stomping," he admits, rubbing his face. "Sneaking by might as well be an alarm bell. Everything okay?"

"I had a bad dream." She finds her gray, but can't make herself set it to paper just yet. "Can . . . can I ask you something?"

"Fire away."

"Does it bother you that . . ." She swallows. "That if you hadn't been rescued in time . . . that you almost . . ."

His hand brushes his throat, and she knows he understands.

"Yes," Eugene allows. A layer of veneer strips off; Rapunzel enjoys his attempts at charm and bravado, but this is the Eugene she likes best. "But also—no. You don't do things like rob the royal palace without knowing the risks. There's no rush without them. And a month ago, my life was the only thing I really had to gamble." His voice catches. "So now the gallows just remind me how much more I have to lose."

Rapunzel stows her pastel stick as the ship crests a strong wave. Finding the words feels harder than picking the right blue. "It doesn't feel right," she says slowly. "You didn't even get a trial. You were almost killed just for stealing a—an expensive hat that belonged to the wrong family. I know everyone loves my parents. It just scares me that I'm going to have that kind of power to hurt people. That I might make a mistake. Especially since I can't . . . fix it anymore."

Eugene's hand catches hers, and she realizes she was picking at the ends of her hair again.

"I would like to remind you we're on a ship to fix something right now," he says, droll. "And the king and queen aren't liked because they're perfect. They're liked because they try to take care of their people, not just rule over them. They've opened and funded schools, libraries, clinics . . . even my orphanage would have shut down without the royal grants. You've only known you're a princess for a month. Maybe now is when you figure out what kind of princess you want to be."

Rapunzel moves his hand to her cheek. "Is this still your dream, Eugene?"

For a moment, he looks—almost like he's holding something back.

But maybe it's the kick of the breeze, the shift of the dark, the echo of Gothel sneering *Really, Rapunzel?*

"All of it and more," he says. Then he brings his lips to hers, and everything, even the doubt, fades away.

FOUR

EUGENE

The next afternoon finds Eugene back at the bow with Rapunzel, but this time in foggier weather and fussier clothes. He isn't sure if the mist they've sailed into is part of Astera's defenses, or just convenient; periodically, he sees the shadows of greater ships in the gray, but they vanish whenever a strange horn sounds from Councilor Teophine's caravel.

He *is* sure he'd rather be back in his pajamas. Rapunzel's parents have made sure he's properly outfitted for this trip, but the formal suit is meant for summer, and the breezy fabric isn't quite staving off the clammy mist. Rapunzel's not faring much better in a gauzy lavender gown and shawl; even Pascal has opted to stay in her cabin for warmth.

"So," Eugene says lightly, slinging an arm over her shoulders, "how do you want to play this? I can be your handsome and debonair consort, your handsome and thick-skulled admirer, your handsome and suspicious manservant . . . The handsome part is nonnegotiable, but everything else is on the table. Personally, I'm a sucker for an upstairs-downstairs romance."

Rapunzel mulls it over. "Just . . . be yourself for now. I want to go in open-minded."

"Prepare for the worst, hope for the best. Got it. Any other requests?"

"One absolutely *critical* thing." Rapunzel raises her hands palms out and hooks her thumbs together. "I need you to keep an eye out for white seashells connected at the middle like this. They almost look like butterflies."

"For . . . souvenirs?" he falters.

"For paint. The powdered shell makes an iridescent white pigment that mixes better than chalk powder, has higher opacity than zinc white, and *doesn't* slowly poison you like lead white."

"White paint is poisonous?"

"Lead paint," Rapunzel says cheerfully. "Any color, it'll all kill you."

After a beat, Eugene says with perplexed affection, "You frighten me."

"The shells could suffice as something of a code phrase," a dry voice croaks from behind them.

"Minister Cressien!" Rapunzel manages to convert her startled jump into an awkward turn. "Good—good afternoon!"

He inclines his head. He stands polished and immaculate in black brocade decorated with a badge of the royal golden sun emblem, hands clasped behind his back. If Eugene didn't know better, he never would have guessed Cressien had spent the first two days at sea violently ill, and the last subjecting them to three days' worth of protocol lectures crammed into one. (Though every so often, he'd pause in the middle of a diatribe, calmly excuse himself from the room, and proceed to be violently ill in the bucket outside.)

"Your Highness," Cressien says smoothly. "Before Councilor Teophine joins us, we would benefit from designating a code phrase to indicate to one another that we wish to converse privately. I believe bringing up your interest in these white seashells will suffice."

"That works for me," Eugene says, already compiling ways to shoehorn it into a conversation.

Rapunzel fiddles with the fringe on her shawl. "Me too," she says with a touch of reluctance, "as long as we *do* find the shells at some point." Cressien blinks slowly at her, almost catlike, and she adds, "It's *iridescent* pigment."

"I see," Cressien says with a notable deficit of conviction. "Councilor Teophine will be boarding soon, Your Highness. You will not have an opportunity to put on shoes once she arrives."

Eugene stifles a laugh at Rapunzel's near sulk; clearly she was hoping the minister wouldn't notice. She comes perilously close to stomping down to her cabin, and when she returns in slippers, he's pretty sure he catches a mutter of "don't know why everyone's so obsessed with shoes, anyway."

"Perfect timing," he tells her. The mist is thinning, and the luminescent sails of Councilor Teophine's caravel are peeking over the portside railing.

Councilor Teophine herself climbs aboard shortly after. *Extremely* valuable-looking crystals still dangle in her silver hair, but she's in fluttering seafoam-blue silk today, and amusement tinges her smile as she bows. "Good afternoon, Your Highness. Do you find this weather cold? Kourenne summer *is* somewhat warmer than ours."

Rapunzel's face is blank. "Kourenne?"

"The Asteran name for our kingdom, Your Highness," Cressien says in a *we-already-went-over-this* tone. (Eugene must have zoned out during that part of the lecture, given the sheer number of *Tales of Flynnigan Rider* subplots taking on an entirely new nuance.)

Rapunzel's laugh sounds forced. "Oh, right! I'm sure it'll be warmer in the sun. Is Astera always this foggy?"

"It comes and goes," Councilor Teophine says with the same catlike calm as Cressien. "Minister Cressien. Your reputation precedes you. And you, young man, I don't believe we've been introduced."

Eugene sweeps a gallant bow. "Eugene Fitzherbert, your ladyship. I'm the princess's companion."

Either sunlight's bouncing off the waves strangely, or a hint of a shadow just darted across Councilor Teophine's face.

Then it vanishes, if it was ever there at all. "I see. Lovely to make your acquaintance."

Eugene isn't sure what to make of that. Disapproval would seem fitting—after all, there's a conspicuous absence of "lord" or "baron" or "duke" before his name—but he'd almost swear that for a moment, he saw a flicker of . . . recognition.

"I've been meaning to ask . . ." Rapunzel's fingers pluck at her collarbone, Eugene assumes for a strand of hair that isn't there. "Are you the councilor of the north or the south?"

Teophine's eyebrows lift. "I wasn't aware Your Highness knew of the Cardinal Council."

"Nor was I," Cressien says warily.

"Is that what it's called?" Rapunzel's hand relocates to rub the back of her neck. "I just read an account from a visitor who heard of the eastern and western councilors."

Teophine's eyes crease at the corners. "I am the Councilor of the South and Master of Voices, Your Highness. The Administration of the South manages diplomacy and cultural matters. You will meet the remaining four councilors at the palace shortly, after my ship guides yours to the dock to be received by Princess Verette."

That strange, low horn bellows from the caravel again—somehow, the sleek boat has already reclaimed its place ahead of their ship. The horn sounds twice more as the fog continues to clear.

Then—

The ship breaks into the sunlight, and Astera sprawls before them. To the starboard, Eugene sees a narrow curl of land he takes to be Merchant's Crescent. It's cluttered with rooftops and docks, great trade ships moored on the south side, and squat barges either tied up on the north shore or ferrying their cargo across the bay to the main island. Another islet looms off the port side, its distant cliffs rising sternly above the waves.

But dead ahead swells the mainland, glittering like a dragon's hoard. Beyond the teeming harbor, sharp-angled rooftops and spires jab into the air over walls of pale stone and vivid painted plaster, the severe lines echoed by black fir treetops or softened by spills of ivy and billowing deciduous boughs. The city itself might as well be a heap of pearls cupped in hills like a titan's green hands, but a diamond of a palace sits at the island's peak, its white walls almost shimmering in the daylight, capped by spindly rooftops of gold and patinated bronze. Three great towers stand guard just downhill from it, and a fourth spears the palace's heart, all crowned with a windmill's slow-turning sails. Each arm is as long as the royal galleon, and wrought in crystal and iron instead of canvas and lattice.

Rapunzel is already pointing to the titanic structures.

"Sunmills," Councilor Teophine supplies nonchalantly, as if that speaks for itself. "I believe they'll be part of your tour tomorrow, Your Highness."

Eugene leans over the railing, squinting. *The Tales of Flynnigan Rider* mentioned sunmills, but in the same nondescript everyone-knows-this way you'd mention a wagon. "What do they do? Specifically, that windmills don't?"

"You will find many books on their construction and uses

in the royal library," Councilor Teophine says, giving him a sidelong look. "Perhaps you might visit it while Her Highness is engaged in affairs of state."

"Is Eugene not allowed to participate in those?" Rapunzel asks. Minister Cressien can't quite hide a wince.

Councilor Teophine pauses and finally says, "It will likely depend."

When their ship docks, the Asteran princess is waiting, just as Councilor Teophine promised. The pier bustles with crew and dignitaries alike, people of every size, shade, and gender, though one thing stands out to Eugene: every single head is gray. Some have pale silver locks, like Teophine, and some have dark slate braids, and hair of nearly every value in between can be found onshore, but he doesn't see a single redhead, brunette, or blond.

Princess Verette, in fact, is the closest to having a hue in her hair. Her loose curls are strange, almost like mother-of-pearl, seemingly lavender from one angle, periwinkle from another, near white in direct sunlight. A circlet of crystals wreathes her head, and her brown eyes appear hard in a pale round face made paler by the deep indigo brocade of her gown. If Eugene had to guess, he'd say she's about eighteen, like Rapunzel.

Unlike Verette, though, Rapunzel has a look of barely suppressed panic on her face that says she's forgotten Cressien's lecture on protocol for this moment. Instead, she just blurts out, "Hi, I'm Rapunzel!"

Verette bows, then touches her fingertips to her mouth, her

heart, and her forehead. "Greetings to you, Princess Rapunzel. I am Verette, Crown Princess of Astera. Welcome."

That gesture strikes a chord for Eugene, but not from Cressien's lessons—from *The Tales of Flynnigan Rider*. The book also described the gesture to respond with, and he figures it's worth a shot. He catches Rapunzel's eye, and she follows suit as he taps beneath his left eye, his right, and then his chin, and bows.

Verette's face stiffens as they straighten again. Her gaze flicks to Teophine, who gives a slight shake of her head.

"Sorry, that's just—how we thought we're supposed to reply," Rapunzel says uneasily.

"It was," Verette says, her tone unreadable, "a very, very long time ago. Please follow me. Our carriages are waiting."

She turns and strides down the pier, Councilor Teophine at her heels.

Even though Cressien emanates a considerable chill throughout the entire ride up to the royal palace, it's no match for Rapunzel's delighted wonder; her face is all but glued to the carriage window. Eugene's only marginally more composed. For him, though, the sights are measured against what his imagination painted as a reader—the curve of the bay is sharper than he thought, the palace stone paler, the sunmills taller—and yet it all feels uncannily familiar.

Almost too soon, the carriage is rolling through the gates, the wheels' clatter winding down as they slow. By the time they've climbed out, Princess Verette is already at the bottom of the palace steps, waiting as a tall, broad, decidedly kingly man descends from the open doors with a chamberlain at his heels. An immaculate midnight-blue cloak billows from the presumptive King Enver's shoulders, a spiked silver crown cinched around his pale brow. Even among the silver-haired Asterans, Enver seems to have gotten an early jump on going gray, because despite his long snow-white hair pulled back in a half-tail, he doesn't look a day over forty—younger even than Rapunzel's parents. Traces of gold dance through the near-black brocade of his doublet as his gaze sweeps the scene and alights on Rapunzel.

This time, Eugene is *positive* he isn't imagining the shadow that steals through the man's expression, even if it disappears as quickly as it did from Teophine's.

"Princess Rapunzel," he rumbles, "I am King Enver. On behalf of my kingdom, please allow me to welcome you to Astera."

Rapunzel's recovered her grasp on formal greetings, even if she hasn't quite eliminated the wobble from her curtsy. The words sound almost *too* formal, in fact, because Eugene heard her practice them for Cressien at least a hundred times. "Your Majesty, thank you so much for your gracious invitation. I'm truly thrilled to be part of your history."

When Enver strides closer, Eugene can see who Verette got her brown eyes from. "The honor is all ours. Your extraordinary story reached even our shores, and we are overjoyed the lost princess herself could attend Verette's celebration." He nods to Cressien. "And I see you've brought company!"

Eugene feels the prickle of a stare. As Rapunzel introduces the minister, he skims a glance over the steps and—there. It's the king's chamberlain, a narrow, angular man who somehow reminds Eugene simultaneously of a weeping willow and a hound dog. He's white as a sheet and almost gawking.

"—and my companion, Eugene," Rapunzel's voice cuts in.

That's his cue. Eugene steps up to Rapunzel's side and bows. "Eugene Fitzherbert, Your Majesty. It's an honor to meet you."

A taut quiet falls. The chamberlain isn't the only one pale as the grave now.

"All mine," King Enver says blankly. Then he swallows. "The—the honor's all mine, that is. I—I'm sorry, please excuse me."

He abruptly turns on a heel and climbs the steps, into the palace. After a beat, his chamberlain follows, and then so does Councilor Teophine.

Eugene leans closer to Cressien and mutters out of the side of his mouth, "For the record, I have absolutely no idea what's happening."

For once, Cressien doesn't hassle him, only murmuring, "Nor do I." Before Eugene can relax, he adds tersely, "Do *nothing* to make this worse."

Councilor Teophine reemerges to glide down the stairs. "I'm afraid His Majesty's lunch is disagreeing with him," she says smoothly. "He sends his apologies and wishes for us to proceed without him to the welcoming banquet."

Eugene doesn't buy the excuse. Even Princess Verette's frown is lightly salted with doubt.

FOUR

An hour later, the princess is doing a better job playing the composed hostess, but Eugene's misgivings are only compounding. They've been ushered to a banquet hall and introduced to the other four members of the Cardinal Council, whose names and titles Eugene did not retain past the appetizer course.

Save for one. Erwan Persevault, Councilor of the West and Master of Seas, which apparently means he commands the navy and controls the harbor. And even though Eugene has never seen this man in his life . . . he can't shake the feeling that he knows Persevault's face somehow.

But that should be impossible. Right?

Almost as impossible as a book with the Asteran king's seal winding up in an orphanage a sea away.

". . . and then following tomorrow's tour of the Northeast Secondary Sunmill, we will proceed to the Hall of Administration for a guided review of each councilor's wing," Teophine announces, reading off a dossier from her seat at Rapunzel's elbow. From here, Eugene can see *Friday* tastefully calligraphed at the paper's head.

Rapunzel, halfway through a crab puff, swallows and asks, "Is that when I'm supposed to address the council?"

Teophine's brow wrinkles. "No, I believe that's Monday—" She flips through densely packed pages labeled *Saturday*, *Sunday*, then, after a beat, *Monday*. "Oh, no, it's Tuesday. Monday is your tour of the Asteran Royal University with Councilor Laroux."

"Sounds like you'll be busy," Eugene remarks.

Rapunzel is frantically chewing the other half of the crab

puff. After a brief delay, she asks, "Can you see if Eugene can join me for anything?"

Cressien, the first human Eugene has ever seen eat a crab puff with a knife and fork, coughs in rebuke with a surgeon's precision. "It may be at our hosts' discretion, Your Highness."

Rapunzel turns pink, which Eugene would find adorable if not for the circumstances. (Nope, actually, it's still adorable.) "Ah." As servers begin filing in, bearing platters of butter-poached lobster, steaming mussels in cream sauce, strips of cold smoked bass, and more, she lights up—then pauses, looking at the empty seat by Verette. "Should we wait for the queen?"

Verette's fork clatters on her plate.

Another silence falls, this time over the banquet table. The servers hurriedly set their platters down and step back to the walls. Cressien looks like he's about to commandeer their galleon and return home on his own.

"The queen passed a very long time ago, Your Highness," Councilor Teophine says softly.

Rapunzel covers her mouth. "I'm—I'm so sorry!"

"Don't be," Verette says, betrayed by a clip to her words. "It's not as if we sent word out."

The lull nevertheless persists, until Cressien manages an excruciating pivot: "I believe we've covered tomorrow's plans. What does Her Highness's schedule look like for Sunday?"

"That will be the official reception ball in honor of your visit," Teophine says with a faint whiff of relief, and continues down the itinerary.

But the rest of dinner remains stilted, and Eugene isn't sure whether to be put off or happy that most of the attendees focus on Rapunzel and Cressien, not him. The king's chamberlain appears at the end of dessert, still as hound-faced as before.

"His Majesty conveys his apologies once more," the man drones. "He is still taken ill, and wishes to rest before joining you on the tour tomorrow."

"How unfortunate," Verette says stiffly. "Thank you, Hughes."

The chamberlain—Hughes, Eugene supposes—escorts them to the guest wing once the table has been cleared, carrying on about the masonry and architecture and other historical things Eugene has approximately zero interest in. Rapunzel's nodding along and studying the stonework, so for her sake, he at least tries to look like he's paying attention.

As they pass down a window-lined corridor overlooking the gardens, a dab of orange flame catches Eugene's eye below. Three figures are striding across a manicured lawn by torchlight: two in the gray uniforms of palace guards, and one . . . one in a cloak of spotless midnight blue, and a silver crown that gleams against snow-white hair.

It's not the lie that bothers Eugene, not really; anyone could see the king wasn't really sick.

What bothers him is that Enver lied for a *reason*. Just like he invited Rapunzel here for a reason.

The king is hiding something.

And if he wanted it to stay hidden, he never should have let Eugene through the gate.

FIVE

RAPUNZEL

Shawl? Check.

Shoes? Unfortunately, check.

Satchel full of art supplies just in case there's a lull in this morning's tour and she can sneak in an architecture study? Check.

Rapunzel runs a hand through her hair, wondering if it will ever grow long enough to tie back again, then takes one more glance at the mirror in her guest room and—

Gently pries the chameleon from her shoulder and sets him on the bed. "I'm sorry, Pascal, but you *know* it's too chilly for you."

The problem is the colder it gets, the groggier Pascal

becomes, so he only starts plodding sleepily across the bedspread toward her once more.

There's a knock at the door. She opens it to find Eugene waiting in the parlor that connects her quarters, his, and Cressien's. He points to her satchel. "Is he allowed to come with you?"

Rapunzel looks down. Pascal is doing his drowsiest attempt at blending in to the purple fabric, which renders him a mottled magenta. "No," she sighs. "How about you?"

"Apparently"—Eugene makes air quotes—"'Princess Verette prefers small parties,' so no. I'll keep an eye on your frog." Then he sobers. "Be on the lookout today. I think they're hiding something from us. After all that fuss about Enver being sick, I saw him trotting around the gardens last night, fit as a fiddle."

There's a creak from Cressien's quarters, though his door stays closed.

Rapunzel quickly passes Pascal to Eugene, speaking low. "I'll be careful. Can you try to figure out where your book came from while we're out? The royal seal has to mean *something*."

"I'm on it." Eugene hides Pascal behind his back as Cressien's door opens.

The minister steps out, regarding them both with faint misgiving, but all he says is "Good morning, Your Highness."

"Good morning!" Rapunzel chirps.

"Our schedule has us touring the city most of the day," Minister Cressien recites, apparently from memory, "and returning for a garden party in the late afternoon, where the three of us will be introduced to various Asteran dignitaries. Fitzherbert, I would suggest"—he says *suggest* like he means anything but—"that you stay within the palace grounds today."

"Maybe you can check on Max," Rapunzel offers. The white stallion wasn't exactly thrilled about the ocean voyage, but as a secret security measure, he seemed to understand his assignment.

There's another knock, this time at the parlor door. It swings open to admit Hughes, the king's chamberlain. "The king and princess are ready to depart, Your Highness."

"Have fun out there, you wacky kids," Eugene says blithely, waving with the hand *not* currently full of chameleon.

As Hughes leads them out of the palace, Rapunzel can't help taking a better look around, noting the architectural motifs, the propensity for geometric windows and arches carved with sun rays, floor mosaics patterned in charts of the seasons, all things Hughes highlighted last night but that only truly come to life in the day.

The daylight also reveals something she missed before: an iridescent glitter in the pale stone of the walls and columns, not unlike the shells she's looking for. And even more curiously . . . in some of the halls and corridors, the stone looks cloudy, almost mottled, where the surface's shimmer is subdued. Almost as if it's been repaired, but not quite good as new.

"Good morning and clear skies!" King Enver booms as they emerge into the sunlight. Princess Verette is by his side, wearing an icy blue dress and an icier expression.

"Clear skies," Verette echoes impassively, as does Hughes.

"Clear skies?" Rapunzel ventures, because that seems to be the proper response.

King Enver beams. "A quick study! Come, Teophine is waiting with the carriages."

"Your Majesty, if I may . . ." Minister Cressien produces a sealed letter from a pocket. "Her Majesty the queen requested that I send her daily reports via our galleon's messenger hawk. Might we visit the docks so I can hand this off?"

Rapunzel's heart leaps into her throat. The little folded paper might as well be a sword over her head. No one said anything about reports before. What is he telling her mother—that she flubbed her introduction to Verette? That she keeps sticking her foot in her mouth?

That she isn't ready to be a real princess after all?

"No need. Hughes will send a courier." Enver waves his chamberlain over.

"Right away, sire," Hughes says, taking the letter. Rapunzel's gaze catches on a mark on the back of his hand, almost like a rusty sunburst of scar tissue just south of his prominent knuckles.

Verette's lips thin. "Teophine is waiting on us, Father."

Enver's hand lands on her shoulder. "Right you are! Let's be off!"

The tour takes them all over the main city of Astera, starting with grand glimmering pavilions of the same pale stone as the palace, where Teophine and a high priestess explain their solstice and equinox ceremonies. Then it's off to the lavish opera house for a performance of King Enver's favorite arias, and then a public amphitheater to watch a troupe of traditional Asteran dancers. A crowd gathers everywhere they stop, kept at a safe distance by a line of guards. From the shouts and cheers, Rapunzel assumes the fuss is just for King Enver and Princess Verette, until she spots one citizen at the amphitheater slashing a finger in the air by their chin as they confer with another onlooker, and mouthing what looks like *heard it was longer.*

"This way, Princess." King Enver steps between them, tossing out a quick wave to his subjects as he ushers her inside.

Rapunzel can't quite put her finger on it, but something's . . . not quite right. It's like the tickle of a hair caught in her lashes, impossible to see clearly, maybe just a feeling. But everything is dazzling. Everything is new. It's all the sort of thing she dreamed was waiting beyond Gothel's tower, isn't it?

Admittedly, she hadn't factored blisters into the equation.

Her heels were already raw by the time they left the opera house, and when they leave the amphitheater, she can feel a full-blown boil swelling up. Climbing back into the carriage is even worse, as the back of her slipper digs in deeper.

It comes to a head—well, more like a foot—at the tour of the Northeast Secondary Sunmill while the chief engineer explains the main pump mechanism over groaning pipes, creaking timbers, and the rush of water. ". . . and as the sails on the mill spin, that turns . . . well, it turns a bunch of shafts and cogs, but *eventually,* it turns this water screw." From their perch on the catwalk ringing the interior of the sunmill's main tower, she indicates a giant hollow cylinder rising from the ground at an angle, and a spiral-threaded shaft rotating inside, its diameter nearly twice as wide as Rapunzel is tall. A steady stream of water flows from the bottom rim of the cylinder into a great pool. "This water screw reaches all the way down into one of Astera's natural aquifers."

"Amazing," Rapunzel says sincerely, because it's the sort of engineering feat that would bore Eugene to tears but makes her want to throw the people responsible a parade. And if her heel weren't throbbing, she'd probably have about a hundred follow-up questions, but instead at least half her attention is devoted to discreetly taking the weight off her right foot. "And this supplies all the water for the district?"

The engineer looks pleasantly surprised at her interest. "First it passes through our filtration system, and then it feeds out into our distribution system via the transmission mains—"

"I don't think we want to bore our guest with the technical details," King Enver lightly interjects.

"Oh no, please do," Rapunzel lobs back, then corrects herself. "I mean, it's not boring to me at all!"

The chief engineer's eyes flick to the king, and at a dip of his chin, she continues. "At first, residents got water directly from the sunmills, but for the last fifty years, we've operated a system of public fountains. Our next stage of development will be installing pipes in community buildings to provide fresh water on demand. Does Kourenne have something similar?"

The tightness in Cressien's face suggests she should answer carefully, but Rapunzel's not sure why. Or maybe she's imagining it because her left ankle is now getting a bit wobbly from doing double duty.

Either way, they've practiced an excuse to get her out of any dodgy questions: "I'm sorry, my tutors haven't gotten to our water system just yet." Then, because she chafes at playing ignorant, and she *did* read the geology book in Gothel's tower cover to cover over a thousand times (she counted): "Though I don't think we could create anything like these structures in the capital. It's built on a granite deposit, and I assume Astera's springs are volcanic." Oh no. She's starting to lose her balance. Rapunzel overcorrects, only for her blisters to flare up. "*Ow-rrr* is it," she tries to cover, "a, a—karst—syst—"

A firm hand steadies her elbow. "Princess Rapunzel, is everything all right?" rumbles King Enver.

She looks to Cressien, who seems just as wary and disappointed as ever.

She remembers Eugene's warning to stay on her guard.

But . . .

What was the point of leaving the tower, if she's just going to see everyone new as a Gothel waiting to happen?

"I'm so sorry, Your Majesty, I seem to have some blisters," Rapunzel confesses. "I'm still getting used to shoes."

Minister Cressien runs a hand over his mouth.

But to her surprise, Enver just lets her go with a booming laugh. "I never even considered! Of course you'd have no need for them, living indoors all that time. We can pause the tour and go back to the palace. You'll have plenty of time to see the rest."

"Do you usually just go around barefoot?" Verette asks. Rapunzel can't tell if it's with surprise or derision; she's barely spoken the entire tour.

"Oh! Would that be more comfortable for you?" Enver doesn't *sound* bothered, despite Cressien's obvious and increasing mortification. At her sheepish nod, he laughs again. "Well, no need to"—he elbows Verette—"*stand* on ceremony, eh?"

"If you're sure," Rapunzel says, already peeling her slippers off. Cressien's face says this is going into the next report, but she can't bring herself to care. "Now, about the spring systems . . ."

The chief engineer's face lights up, but Princess Verette clears her throat. "The Councilor of the North will answer your questions at this afternoon's social. I'm afraid we must be on our way if we're to return in time."

"That's my Verette, keeping us on schedule," Enver says with a chuckle.

"Understood, Your Highness. Right this way." The chief engineer leads them down the catwalk, footsteps clanging on the hammered iron.

Rapunzel falls in step with Verette, trying not to favor her blistered heel too obviously. The crown princess has mostly let Councilor Teophine and King Enver take the lead on the tour today, and for someone who's about to have her eighteenth birthday, she doesn't seem terribly excited.

Then again, Rapunzel is still working on estimating peoples' ages. For most of her life, she had her own mirror to judge from, and Gothel's fluctuating youth, and that was it. So her best guess is that Verette is about eighteen, like Rapunzel, but . . . she's not entirely confident. There's something younger in the softness of her face, something older in the pinch of her narrow lips, and something steely in her bearing that promises prying will be a waste of time.

But if there's anything Rapunzel can do, it's get people to open up. "So," she says merrily, "your birthday's next week! Do you know what presents you're getting, or is it a surprise?"

Verette tilts her head, twin loops of pale braids swaying at the sides of her face. "Presents?"

"For your birthday?" Rapunzel rubs the back of her neck. "You know, like . . . well, I wanted paint this year, but I got wine. And a carriage."

"Ah," says Verette, tipping from confusion into reluctant obligation. It's an emotion nonetheless, so Rapunzel counts that as progress. "We don't do that here. There's a benediction ceremony, where your family and friends say their hopes for your next year, and the pledging of deeds during the banquet, and finally invitations."

"Invitations to the birthday party?" Now it's Rapunzel's turn to be confused. Cressien coughs pointedly behind her.

"No," Verette says in the sort of tone you use with a small child, "invitations to gatherings, future festivities, and so on. Like what my father sent to you."

FIVE

Rapunzel is trying, *very* hard, not to see Gothel in Verette, too, even if that answer *did* feel a little condescending. As they leave the Northeast Secondary Sunmill, she says, "You know, that actually sounds better than presents. I don't even know what I'm going to do with all the wine I got. So we should probably invite you to our kingdom for your birthday, too, right?"

"We," Cressien interjects swiftly over Rapunzel's shoulder, "can wait for the proper time and place for such an invitation. Your Highness."

Of course. Just because Rapunzel's trying to keep an open mind doesn't mean they know what she'd be inviting into their home. Not yet.

"Right, sorry," Rapunzel says in a rush.

"Her Highness has a generous spirit." Councilor Teophine smooths it over as they descend the steps. The sun-drenched stone feels pleasantly warm under Rapunzel's soles.

The crowd waiting just beyond the wall of their guard escort might be the largest yet. In every gathering, the faces greeting them have been full of excitement and something eerily like . . . hope. And just like the previous crowds, these people are making themselves heard.

"Blessings on the princess!"

"An auspicious year to you, Princess Verette!"

"Hail the queen to come!"

Rapunzel sneaks a glance at Verette and Enver. Verette's mask is as opaque as ever, but—

When she looks at Enver's expression, all she can think of is the moment Mother—*Gothel*—told her, *Don't ever ask to leave this tower again.*

A sudden shout of alarm rings out. A small figure ducks under a guard's arm, running for Verette—

And it's as if the princess tosses her mask aside. Verette throws a hand up to the guards as a little girl comes to a wheezing stop before her, something clenched in her cupped fists. Verette kneels, her face breaking into a warm smile, her voice too low to catch beneath the crowd's murmurs. The little girl nods. Her hands open to reveal a curious little charm: a pale, crude seashell butterfly threaded on a loop of blue ribbon, the ribbon ends weighted with misty sea-glass beads and dangling like twin tails.

"I'm so sorry, Your Highness," a man calls from behind the line of guards, wrought with worry and chagrin. "She just slipped away from me—she was working on it all last week—"

Verette stands, palming the charm as she takes the little girl's hand in her own, then walks her over. "No, don't apologize, this is lovely. Only a week? That's incredible. I worked a whole month on my first one."

"And the moth still came out lopsided," King Enver calls after her. He makes a face at Teophine. "So much for staying on schedule, hm? Might as well get in the carriages so we can move along when she's done."

That feeling is back again, not so much a hair in her lashes now. No, this is like every time she's looked at a sketch, and even though she couldn't see where just yet, she *knew* somehow it was—unbalanced.

Something's not quite right with this picture.

Rapunzel would be lying if she said she didn't actually appreciate that, for a moment, she gets the carriage to herself. Councilor Teophine, Minister Cressien, and King Enver are all in the first coach, and without Verette in hers, Rapunzel can take the chance to just breathe and stop worrying about the eggshells she's walking on. (Or the shoes she was walking in.) As she looks out the window, her eyes are drawn up to the palace high on the hill, where hopefully Eugene is having a much easier time. Especially since she's going to bore him senseless chattering about the sunmills later. There's even one in the palace that she can . . .

Rapunzel's train of thought snags. The palace sunmill's sails are perfectly still.

If that's how the palace gets its water, shouldn't they be moving?

The door rattles and opens to admit Verette. A ghost of a smile still clings to her lips, and the charm still swings in her grasp. With a jolt, Rapunzel realizes the butterfly—no, moth—has a familiar iridescent shimmer to its surface, just like—

"What are those shells?" flies out of her mouth before she can give it the layer of polish it needs.

Caution darts through Verette's expression, though Rapunzel wouldn't have caught it if she hadn't spotted it in

Eugene the past month when he thinks she's not looking. The princess holds up the trinket as the carriage jolts into motion. "It's a charm called a verette. According to an old legend, the moon is really a faraway cocoon woven by moths each month, and when they hatch, they carry blessings down to the earth, and their bodies are left behind as seashells. You make verettes for others so the blessings find them, and since it's my namesake, people like to give them to me around my birthday."

"That's really sweet," Rapunzel says with a touch of envy. Of course she's grateful for the extravagant gifts everyone gave her at the ball, but everyone likes wine, jewelry, expensive things. There's something irreplaceable in a token that's made just for *you*.

There's also a critical part of her question that's gone unanswered.

"So," she tries again, "do those white shells have a name too?"

Verette tilts into mild bewilderment again, bordering on suspicion. "*Verai*, in Old Asteran. Moth-shells. Why?"

"I'd love to find some before I go. They make this fantastic paint that's really hard to find. Nothing else catches the light the same way." Rapunzel sees Verette frowning at the seashell moth and realizes she skipped a step. "They're ground into powder and mixed with a binding medium—"

"You crush them up?" Verette asks, voice verging on strangled.

"Is that wrong?" Rapunzel wrings her skirt in her hands.

For a brief moment, the only sound is the staccato of hoofbeats and the creak of the carriage. Then Verette's expression closes off again. "No. It's fine."

It is *excruciatingly* not fine.

Rapunzel wishes Eugene were here. He does a sort of social alchemy, transmuting awkwardness and blunders into laughter and newly minted inside jokes, and Rapunzel's still trying to pick apart the formulas behind that.

But he's not here, and silence makes an unwieldy third passenger in the carriage for the rest of the ride, the charm still clenched tight in Verette's hand.

Six

Eugene

Eugene doesn't exactly have a large polling sample to draw from, but if he had to rate the Asteran palace, at present, he'd give it a generous seven out of ten.

Is it *technically* bigger than Rapunzel's palace? Sure. Is the view from every single balcony majestic? Unarguably. Is it aesthetically pleasing? Well, there are some interesting architectural motifs, like leaf-shaped archways and columns carved in spirals, and somehow all the stone has what can only be described as an ineffable glow, so, academically speaking, yes.

But they've been here since late yesterday afternoon, and *still* haven't had a formal tour of the palace yet. (Deduction: half a point.)

Six

Minister Cressien's room in the guest quarters is wedged squarely between Eugene's and Rapunzel's. (Deduction: half a point.)

There was that whole bizarre business with King Enver lying to get out of dinner last night. (Deduction: one point.)

Even though it's summer, Eugene is *constantly* cold in here, and he can't shake the feeling that he's being just as constantly watched. There was even a seagull planted outside his window this morning, and all it did was stare at him through the glass and scream. (Deduction: a full point for the seagull, half a point for the resultant shivers. He's not sure if all Asteran seagulls burn with that sort of malice or if, somehow, Gothel *has* returned.)

And most aggravating of all, his record search in the palace library is proving to be a wild goose chase. (Deduction: one point.)

(Coincidentally, math has never been Eugene's strongest suit.)

"I'm sorry, sir," the head librarian tells him, poring over the massive catalog on his desk with a perplexed frown. If Eugene were to guess, he's around forty, and unaccustomed to coming up empty. "You're sure the author's name is Rothar?"

"A. Drew Rothar," Eugene says, keeping a tight hold on *The Tales of Flynnigan Rider.* It's not as if the librarian's about to snatch it out of his hands, but the man's had a rather manic gleam in his eyes since they landed on the royal seal inside the cover. Eugene makes a note to hide it extremely well in his guest room. Or maybe Pascal can camouflage himself as the book, since he's currently napping under Eugene's coverlet. ("How chameleons work, broadly" may be another gap in Eugene's general expertise.)

"I'm afraid we have no record of this book in our archives, or of anything by that author," the librarian says with a sigh. "Frankly, I've never even heard of either."

"Is it possible for a book to have this seal and *not* be from this library?" Eugene asks, tucking the book into his satchel.

The librarian thinks a moment. "Possible, yes, but . . . only just this side of *im*possible. It would have to come from a, er, personal collection. A royal one."

So, the royal family's private shelves. That does sound impossible. "There's some kind of a garden party meet and greet this afternoon. Maybe I can ask around." Then Eugene snaps his fingers. "Hold on, I know exactly who to ask. I just need to track her down here. Do you have access to the municipal records too?"

Five minutes later, the librarian has escorted him to a very dusty corner of a very dusty basement stuffed with a concerningly flammable amount of paper. Eugene is trying not to focus on that as he repeats, for the fifth time, "Vald, V-A-L-D. First name Solena. Vald is her maiden name, though."

The librarian, hunched over a veritable accordion of files in a drawer, grunts, "These are the citizenship enrollment records for when you say she arrived. She would have enrolled under her own name . . . but I'm not finding anything under Vald."

Six

"She left town around April of that year," Eugene insists. "She said she was marrying an alchemist. Do you see anyone with the first name Solena?" The librarian rolls his eyes, and Eugene scowls. "Come on. There can't be *that* many people who want to give up everything and move here forever. At least over the course of one April."

To his credit, the librarian at least does a cursory sweep through the registry before shaking his head. "I apologize, sir. There's no Solena, no Vald, and definitely no Solena Vald in our records for that entire year."

"Not to be rude, but on a scale of one to ten, how would you rate your confidence in your records system?" Eugene asks skeptically. "Because now we're zero for two."

Before the now deeply affronted librarian can respond, there's a shuffle near the entryway. "Excuse me?" a messenger pipes up, poking their head in. "Is the, er, Princess Rapunzel's? Companion? In here?"

"I'm afraid to say yes," Eugene answers.

"Could you come to the stables?" The messenger looks frazzled. "The princess's steed seems to be? A bit unsettled?"

Even if that weren't already four question marks past Eugene's comfort level, the fact that Maximus is causing trouble is a blazing red flag. It was the queen's idea to send him along, as what she politely framed as an "undercover extraction specialist," in case things go very, very awry. At the least, Maximus can get Rapunzel down to their ship in a pinch, and frankly, Eugene wouldn't be shocked if he could also swim her straight back home. After all, eleven hundred pounds of angry horse will extract whatever he bloody wants.

He follows the messenger down to the stables, where he hears the thuds well before they reach the row of stalls. As they approach Maximus's box stall, Eugene spots an older man standing at the half door, an apple in one hand. From his simple uniform, Eugene guesses he's a groom, perhaps the stable master. "Whoa, boy. *Whoa*."

There's an irate whicker. The door shudders on its hinges from another kick.

Max doesn't get antsy for no reason. The hair on the back of Eugene's neck prickles.

He does his best to cover anyway, calling, "Come on, Max, if you wanted a visit you could have just sent an invitation." The only response is a snort.

"I brought the princess's companion," the messenger adds. The older stableman looks their way.

And then—his face drops.

He ducks his head and swiftly mops his tanned brow with a hanky embroidered in blue flowers. "Good—good," he stumbles. "Maybe you can calm him down."

Eugene draws up beside him in front of Maximus's stall, face perfectly neutral as he tries to sneak a look out of the corner of his eye. The stableman is on the shorter side, maybe in his early fifties, his dove-gray hair pulled into a short tidy braid and a neat beard. It could be Eugene's imagination, but he'd swear . . . yep, the man's definitely avoiding eye contact.

SIX

It's like yesterday, the uncanny feeling of being almost—recognized.

Recognized in a land he's never set foot in before.

Recognized by a king, his chamberlain, and now a palace stableman.

Before he can get in a follow-up question, the stableman rattles out, "Well, you've got him under control," pushes past, and all but bolts off.

Eugene looks to the messenger. "What was that about?"

But the messenger only shrugs and bows. "No clue. Good day to you, sir."

"Huh." Eugene waits until the messenger's gone and, as far as he can tell, no one's close enough to eavesdrop, then asks under his breath, "Was that guy bothering you?"

Max shakes his head, though he does blow a puff of air in the direction the stableman went.

"Then what gives? Should we be concerned?"

The stallion just tosses his head again and keeps pawing the ground.

Eugene leans on the door, glancing around. The stableman's long gone. "Yeah, this whole place is weird. That's the second time someone acted like they're hiding something from me." Then he holds up the stableman's embroidered hanky. Generally he's tried to leave picking pockets behind, but desperate times, desperate measures. After all, Maximus has a very particular set of skills, scent tracking among them. "Want to find out what?"

It takes a bit of maneuvering. First Eugene takes Max for "a walk" around the stables just to look for the old man, but when the trail leads out toward the palace gate, Eugene has to shift tactics. He approaches a stable hand mucking out a stall. "Excuse me. Do you know who's in charge of saddling up my friend here? The princess will probably want to go for a ride when she returns."

It's a blatant lie, but it gets Eugene what he wants when the young woman sets aside her shovel and peers around. "Should be Master Sulian, sir, but he said he had to run an errand. I can see to your mount."

The man's name is Sulian, then, and he *is* the stable master. This all comes in handy when Eugene rides Max through the gates and politely declines a guard escort by claiming he's meeting Master Sulian in the city below—he just went on ahead, didn't you see him?

Max's nose takes them down into the city proper, which, from what Eugene can tell, is *also* called Astera, because somehow they thought giving a city and a nation-state the same name wouldn't be confusing at all. Once they're out of sight of the palace walls, Eugene dismounts and lets Max lead him on foot, winding through an imports market with everything from overseas textiles to bushels of rice and dried beans.

It's distinctly bizarre to wander around a place *literally* out of a storybook. *The Tales of Flynnigan Rider* describes how the rooftops are shaped almost like squashed bells, and he can see the flare and curve of the timbers around him; in the book, the districts are laid out like starbursts around central plazas, and as they move through the vendors' stalls, Eugene finds narrow streets branching out from the marketplace.

But the book didn't say anything about the structure in the middle of the plaza. He can't tell if it's just a statue or a long-inactive fountain; a marble figure in robes stands atop a pedestal, its arms outstretched, with dull bronze stars heaped in its open palms. A dry basin rings the pedestal, rimed over in dead leaves and the faint accumulated crud of disuse.

In the book, the streets sparkled. The stone walls shimmered like pearls. The shingles glowed like sea glass in the sun. The palace lives up to that, but down here—well, Eugene knows better than to expect a fairy tale, but he can almost see the ghost of that splendor. As Max takes them away from the market and down a lane, they pass cracked cobblestones, mildew creeping up plaster, missing shingles. More and more storefronts are boarded up; more and more glances are swiftly averted, passersby hurrying along. Even in Eugene's orphanage days, he remembers idly kicking a barrel at the greengrocer's while Solena chitchatted with the clerk. Here, the only place people linger is in the long line for a clinic.

It feels like a hole worn into the tip of a sock, too small to put a toe through but impossible to ignore. Something's gone stale in Astera, and for too long.

Max finally comes to a stop at another abandoned shop in a deserted alleyway, sniffing before he gives a decisive whicker. A signpost sits barren over a barred door, the front window mostly papered over. Frowning, Eugene steps closer to peer at the entrance—and is abruptly yanked back by the collar.

He finds himself, unfortunately not for the first time in his life, inundated with the hot oaty dank of horse breath as Max hauls him around the corner of the building and then across the alley. A month ago this might have inspired more protest; now Eugene obliges, if for no other reason than the payoff from following Max's instincts tends to be worth the slime left on his shirt collar.

A quiet clank and rattle sounds from the derelict shop.

Sure enough, when Eugene ventures a look . . . he sees Master Sulian's silver braid stark against the man's retreating back as he hurries away from the seemingly abandoned shop front.

This is officially moving from the "weird" to "deeply suspicious" column.

Once Sulian's rounded a corner, Eugene steps out—

Only for Max's teeth to clamp down on his collar once more.

"He's gone," Eugene hisses. Max lets out a whuff of dissent and drags him back.

Another figure, cloaked and hooded, enters the alleyway from the other end. Eugene goes very still. There's a familiar rhythm to their gait, a well-worn walking stick gliding along in time with their right leg; he remembers the thump of it on the orphanage floorboards every morning before the smell of porridge flooded the room. Even beneath the hood, he recognizes the glimpse of a pale narrow face and short-cropped steel-gray hair.

SIX

Solena Vald reaches the abandoned storefront, then casts a furtive look around. Eugene and Max flatten themselves to the wall out of sight.

The clank and rattle sounds again. When Eugene dares to peer around the corner . . . Solena's gone.

Max doesn't stop him this time, so Eugene knows the coast is clear as he darts to the window and peers through a gap between papers. There's no sign of Solena inside, or anyone at all besides at least five generations of spiders competing for cobweb real estate. Dust covers every square inch, from empty tabletops and scattered chairs to what appears to be the store's original sign propped against a counter. If he squints, Eugene can just make out letters on it . . . *H*, *E*, *R*, *B* . . .

Herbert & Fitz.

For the second time in the last hour, he goes completely still.

Yesterday, when he met Councilor Teophine on the ship, he thought she was only put off by his lack of title. That it was impossible for her reaction to be recognition instead of distaste.

Now the question isn't whether she knew his name. It's whether "Fitzherbert" is even a real one.

Solena's here, in Astera, despite not being in their records. She's snuck into an abandoned store, the same one that was just exited by the stranger who somehow knew Eugene on sight.

Just like Hughes did.

Just like the king did.

Eugene hopes Rapunzel's tour wraps up within the hour, because if he can't talk with her about this pronto, he's fairly sure his head's going to explode.

Max whickers a warning. Eugene retreats to their hiding spot, and another cloaked figure comes along, this one practicing better hood discipline than Solena and Sulian. Eugene can't make out a face, but he does spot a scar on the person's right hand, a shiny dark sunburst below bony white knuckles.

And this time, he sees the figure wrap that hand around the door's pull handle and *twist*. The iron bar rotates, moving a disk-shaped section of the door's wood with it. The figure pushes the bar so that the disk sinks deeper into the wood.

A section of the wall beside the door swings inward, admitting the visitor, then silently seals shut behind them. By the time Eugene looks back to the handle, it's already returned to its former position, the edge of the disk blending perfectly into the door.

So *that's* how to get in.

Max headbutts Eugene's shoulder. Eugene nods and whispers, "Yeah, we need Pascal." Strolling right into whatever this is would almost certainly end badly, but the chameleon can scout ahead.

The whole ride back to the palace, Eugene's head clamors with a thousand conspiracies and questions. Why isn't Solena in the records when she's clearly in Astera? Was her hair always that silver? What's hiding behind the storefront?

Is his last name even Fitzherbert, or did someone just make

it up? *Solena*? His earliest memories are from the orphanage, and she was always there—

They reach the palace before he knows it. "I'm going to get the frog," he tells Max distractedly, hitching him by the stables.

But when he returns from the guest wing with Pascal in his satchel, Sulian the stable master is unsaddling Max in the yard, a furrow in his brow. Eugene makes some recalculations, then saunters up, nonchalant. "Hey, didn't catch your name earlier—I'm Eugene."

"Master Fitzherbert," Sulian says a bit too quickly, touching fingers to his forehead in greeting. For the most part, he's recovered from earlier, maintaining a bland demeanor; Eugene can't tell if he's slipped in calling him Fitzherbert. His last name could have gotten around the palace by now, but it could have also been exactly what Sulian ran to the storefront to discuss. "Do you require this horse?"

"Actually, I was hoping you could tell me how to get to the kitchens. Acute case of the pre-lunch snackies."

Sulian gives him clipped, terse directions, and leads Max into the stables. On his way to the kitchens, Eugene helps himself to a scullion's work clothes from a storage closet and a bushel basket from the laundry, hiding Pascal and his satchel under a heap of towels. From what he's seen, everyone's hair goes white by their thirties here, so he dusts a fistful of ash from a cold hearth through his hair until it's about the right shade of pewter for an Asteran his age.

After that, he just has to follow other bustling servants to a much more modest palace gate, and look like he's a man on a mission as he trails them down into the city once more.

Eugene would be lying if he claimed he didn't miss this sometimes—the costumes and the sneaking and the gleeful little buzz of danger. Maybe it'll help him adjust when Rapunzel's parents finally give him the boot.

Though . . .

The king, his chamberlain, and at least some palace staff already know him somehow.

His name seems *heavily influenced* by the front for what looks like a secret gathering spot.

He has a book from a private royal collection.

And one of the women who raised him clearly has more of a history with Astera than she ever let on.

Eugene would *also* be lying if he said his imagination wasn't already running wild with what that could mean. When he started calling himself Flynn Rider, it was half because "Eugene Fitzherbert" didn't make for a compelling Wanted poster and half because, well, when he wanted to stop being Flynn, he *could.* Flynn wasn't real, not like Eugene. The name could be dropped like any other disguise.

It never occurred to him that "Eugene Fitzherbert" might be a mask he didn't choose.

If there's more to his story than just being a thief and an orphan—if his family is *anything* to speak of—maybe Rapunzel's parents will tolerate him for more than a month or two.

Six

It takes a bit of wandering to find the dry fountain again, then the abandoned storefront of Herbert & Fitz. Eugene ducks behind the same corner as before and kneels to lower Pascal to the ground. The noon sun overhead has warmed the cobblestones enough to be tolerable for a chameleon, even if it also means Eugene's time is running short.

"You can hide by the doorway," he says, "and wait until the secret entrance opens. Rapunzel and I have some kind of garden party later, so we have an hour at most. Just go in, scope out what's going on, and come back as fast as you can, okay?"

Pascal *brrrs* and scurries across the alleyway, blending in to the plaster and stone. Eugene can barely see his outline at the boarded-up door. One minute goes by, then five more, then another ten, as the previously busy door stays annoyingly shut. He's just getting antsy when a peddler cuts down through the lane, metal pans swaying and clanking from their hooks on his cart. Eugene pretends to dig in his satchel as the man passes, trying to look at least a little less suspicious.

He glances up just in time to see the peddler's gaze narrow on him—and then shift to something over his shoulder.

Eugene has one crystal clear moment of realization: his own conspicuousness was, in fact, not the thing he needed to worry about here.

Then rough, heavy cloth drops over his head, and everything goes black.

Seven

Rapunzel

"This," Minister Cressien whispers tightly in the shade of a pergola practically sagging with wisteria, "is becoming a problem."

Rapunzel catches herself once again picking at her sleeves and hides her hands behind her back. "Eugene's probably just running late," she insists for the umpteenth time.

"I *told* him to stay in the palace today." Cressien squeezes out a smile and nod as the Councilor of the North and Master of Scholars, a stiff-spined woman whose professional distance disintegrated into glee the moment Rapunzel dropped the word *aquifer*, lopes past en route to the refreshments. Once she's out of earshot, Cressien adds under his breath, "If Master

Fitzherbert was not prepared to treat this visit with the seriousness it requires . . ."

Rapunzel's been keeping her stare on the nearby flower bed so Cressien can't see her frustration. He's not wrong. This social is to introduce them to Astera's nobility and allow them to mingle with the higher-ranking government officials. She's well aware of how it looks to have the princess's companion skipping the first official social event: almost as bad as going barefoot. (She's compromised with a pair of sandals that don't cross over her blisters.) But . . . Eugene knows better. Doesn't he?

A wiggle of silver in the dark soil suddenly catches her eye. Rapunzel blinks. It looks like a tiny, almost threadlike worm, something she's never even heard of—

"Are you even listening, Your Highness?" Cressien asks incredulously.

Before she can answer, that same low horn that bellowed in the ocean mists sounds again, this time at the far end of the garden. King Enver strolls in, Hughes and Verette at his heels, though Verette splits off toward Councilor Teophine as her father makes a beeline for Rapunzel.

Rapunzel curtsies when King Enver halts a few feet away. "Good afternoon, Your Majesty! These gardens are absolutely incredible. I've already found five species that weren't anywhere in my botany book."

"We do take pride in our roots, in more ways than one," King Enver laughs, brown eyes twinkling. Rapunzel can't help laughing too, especially because it's the sort of pun Eugene would make.

Then Enver looks around, puzzled. "I recall you brought another companion, Princess? I do hope you know he was welcome to attend this."

Rapunzel's belly wrings. "Oh, of course! I mean—I told him—I mean—he knew—" She can feel herself stumbling and giggles nervously, trying to twirl a too-short lock of hair around her finger. All the veneer of poise flakes away. "He's just like a house cat, that Eugene! Comes and goes on his own schedule."

"There were some errands," Cressien glosses, "that the princess's companion wished to attend to."

Hughes, the chamberlain, speaks up, deploying a degree of stoicism that makes Verette seem high-strung by comparison. "I believe, sire," he says with an almost mournful chew of each syllable, "that the young gentleman went for his own tour of the city in the company of palace guards."

King Enver beams. "An adventurer! I admire that in a fellow. I wish we'd had time to speak last night. I'm afraid I didn't catch his title, and I'd hate to address him incorrectly. . . . May I ask what rank the Herbert family is?"

"I believe Fitzherbert was raised in an orphanage," Cressien interjects, smoothly slotting in the name correction.

Rapunzel recognizes that tactic. Gothel would do something like tell Rapunzel to hang the dishes up to dry, and Rapunzel would ask if she meant the laundry, and Gothel would scold

You know I meant the laundry, don't be difficult, until Rapunzel learned to respond instead that yes, she'd get to the laundry right away.

She always thought that was, well, life with Gothel. But maybe there's a diplomatic use for all the little tricks and strategies she taught herself in the tower.

King Enver is shaking his head in amazement. "An orphanage! Remarkable. So his background, his parentage, it's a complete mystery. However did you become acquainted?"

Cressien shifts his weight uneasily, but Rapunzel thinks she knows how to handle that. "It's a bit of a long story, but he helped me escape the witch who held me prisoner."

"The one who stole you for your hair," Enver says with a somber nod.

Cressien's chin lifts. "I wasn't aware His Majesty had heard of that."

"Two Kourenne ships landed at Merchant's Crescent, oh, eighteen years ago?" Enver runs a finger along his jaw. "The first was searching for the sundrop flower to save the queen. Then a few months later, they were searching for the kidnapped infant princess. According to Councilor Persevault, they mentioned you already had nearly a foot of hair like sunlight."

Rapunzel catches her hand sneaking toward the blunt ends of her hair again and turns it into an ungainly flutter. "It went back to brown when it was cut."

"But the sundrop flower's magic remained." Something

like wonder flickers in King Enver's stare. For a moment, she remembers the soft wood-grain ridges of the tower's windowsill under her fingers on her birthdays, the simmer of anticipation in the dark before the lantern light bloomed.

She swallows hard. "No, that's gone too."

Is it sympathy sending a shadow through the king's face, or disappointment?

"Are you certain?" he presses. "A power like that—I imagine it would change you forever. There's truly nothing you can do?"

"I, uh." Rapunzel's stomach twists. "I can . . . draw your portrait?"

King Enver's smile is cramped. "That's . . . quite a talent as well."

He doesn't have to say it—she can read it in the drop of his shoulders, the averted gaze. This is a letdown.

Without her hair, *she* is a letdown.

King Enver changes the subject. "So, what was your favorite part of the tour today?"

That she can't fall short on. "All of it," she says in a rush. "The sunmills are incredible, and I've never seen anything like the solstice pavilions—oh, and Princess Verette told me the story behind her name! I love that legend!"

"I was worried it might be a bit trite, but her mother insisted," Enver says warmly. "Her health wasn't the best at the time, and she believed Verette was truly a blessing."

"I've seen the white moth shells before, but in paint pigment, not as charms." The second Rapunzel says it, she realizes she's put her foot in it.

Sure enough, Cressien clears his throat, picking up the signal she didn't mean to send. "Oh, yes, Her Highness has been on the lookout for those white seashells. Perhaps we can go inquire with one of the councilors—"

"Oh—no—" Rapunzel jumps in. "I mean, uh, different white shells! Not the ones we discussed yesterday!"

Cressien looks like he's internally composing several new scripts for her to stick to, along with another paragraph for his next report. All he says is "I see."

"The shells we use for verettes *are* white, though," Enver says, pleasant but perplexed.

"They definitely are, and I think they're really neat," Rapunzel babbles.

Enver steps back with a forced laugh. "It's a quaint tradition. My people do love their old stories, no matter how trite. I should go say hello to my councilors before they try to oust me. Hopefully young Herbert can join us soon."

His departure leaves a mortified silence between Rapunzel and Minister Cressien, one she forces herself to break after an excruciating delay. "It could have gone worse?"

"Academically speaking," Cressien says through teeth gritted tight as a treasury vault, "that is correct, Your Highness." He heaves a sigh. "We should return to the guest wing to strategize for future . . . interactions."

"Do we need to?" Rapunzel's trying to keep a whine out of

her voice, but they already spent so much time at sea in etiquette lessons and strategy sessions. "I think I'm getting better at this."

"Engagement with a monarch demands perfection," the minister says coolly. "Even small talk, as you now know. What if he tries to negotiate aspects of trade agreements outside official channels? Or asks about our military strength? Or—what will you say when Fitzherbert misses the *next* gathering?"

It's one thing for Cressien to grill *her*, but she draws the line there. "Eugene has *never* let me down," Rapunzel says, a little heated. "I'm sure there's a good reason he's not here, and if he misses anything else, I'm sure it'll also be for a good reason, and I'll be happy to tell King Enver that if need be."

All Cressien says is "I see," which Rapunzel now understands to mean *I don't believe you.*

"I'm going to walk around the gardens first," she tells him, and doesn't wait for his permission. There's no point if she's already getting another lecture as it is.

Rapunzel scans the garden as she strides away. The only other people she's really spoken to are Councilor Teophine and the Councilor of the North, Katou Laroux, who are both engrossed in conversation already. Verette is nowhere in sight, and Rapunzel has the squirming feeling the other princess doesn't want to talk to her anyway.

Instead she heads for the less crowded end of the gardens, slips around a corner, and keeps going until the party's noise is muffled to a dull murmur and all the attendees are far behind her. Then she slips off her sandals with a hiss of relief and leans against a low stone wall, trying to work through the knot in her throat.

If she still had her hair, she could have fixed her father's foot with a song.

If she still had her hair, she wouldn't have disappointed King Enver.

How is she ever going to prove she's enough without it?

Even now, she can imagine exactly what's going into Cressien's next report: *Sloppy. Gullible. Naïve.* And he wouldn't even be wrong. So far she's managed to upset both Enver and Verette in the space of a few hours.

But that information is going straight to her mother, when she promised herself she would make her mother proud.

A flick of silver in a flower bed catches her eye.

Another threadlike worm coils in the dirt a few feet away.

Rapunzel isn't sure princesses are supposed to be this interested in worms. But at this rate, her list of Princess Conduct Infractions seems to be growing out of control, so what's one more?

Rapunzel checks to make sure no one's watching, then crouches for a better look. It twitches back, and only then does she see how *long* it is—and it's not alone, either. Another pale flash stitches through the soil nearby. Then she spots another in a different bed . . . and the curious thing is they're all oriented in the same general direction, like a tiny broken road scattered over the garden.

She straightens up and slowly walks along the lawn, following the crude trail. It winds through the flower beds and around another wall, and when she turns the corner, she finds an old, unassuming iron door set into the palace's stone wall, half obscured by an enormous lacy fern. A faint track has been worn into the dirt leading to it.

What an odd little puzzle. The door isn't *hidden* per se, but it isn't exactly a garden feature—yet the dirt track says it's getting regular use. And a heavy-duty door like that can't be for something like a tool closet.

Something about this—the dirt, the wear, the flaws—finally cracks the unease that plagued Rapunzel for the whole tour.

Everything she's been allowed to see is polished. Rehearsed. Curated. Any time she slowed to look closer, any time she dug for more detail, she was carefully, deliberately redirected.

Maybe it's just the same sort of defensive diplomatic lacquer Minister Cressien's trying to get her to perfect.

Or maybe something's under that veneer.

Distant shouts break through her thoughts from somewhere below the gardens. There's a faraway scuffle, then more cries spike from the party. Rapunzel whirls around to look back the way she came—

Only to find Maximus charging toward her, an ash-smudged, groggy Pascal plastered between his ears. An older stableman is giving chase. "So sorry, Your Highness," he gasps between heaving breaths. "He just broke out—we'll have him back and safe in a trice—"

Max skids to a stop in front of Rapunzel, hooves shaving dark gashes into the manicured lawn.

"I've got him," she says, grabbing his bridle and trying not to panic about what Minister Cressien is going to make of *this* new fiasco.

Then Pascal lets out a long trill, and everything else promptly gets shoved off her mental desk.

Rapunzel plucks him off Max's head, eyes wide, pulse rising. "What do you mean, *kidnapped*?"

EIGHT

EUGENE

As far as abductions go, Eugene has to give this one a grudging eight.

Not on the experience, of course; that's a solid zero out of ten, would not repeat. But there's undeniable competence here that reveals a certain degree of expertise, and he has to at least recognize the work of a professional. The trick with the peddler was a nice little misdirect; knocking him out without physical force is always appreciated; and for the second time in just over a month, he's waking up tied to a chair. Unfortunately, they've also thought to blindfold him.

So far, he's just had to deduct two points. The first: Blindfold or no, he still woke up to the muffled rush of water and groaning timbers somewhere beyond the walls. Between that and the limited distance you can reasonably smuggle an unconscious adult man, it probably won't be too difficult to track this place down when he gets out.

And the second point is why he's so confident that's a *when*, not an *if*: Whoever bound his hands behind his back got lazy with a clove hitch.

They're going to lose another point if they take much longer to notice he's awake. He's heard murmurs, and multiple distinct footstep patterns have moved in and out of the room; he's clearly being monitored.

Then the soft scrape of a wooden walking stick punctuates incoming footfalls. Eugene holds his breath, refraining from leaping to conclusions—

". . . telling you," comes Solena's quiet, raspy whisper. "Eugene would never work for a man like that."

"Eugene would like to not be blindfolded," Eugene announces, already bored with pretending to be asleep. "Solena, long time no see. Hypothetically. You know, because of the blindfold."

A choked silence grips the room.

Eugene rolls his head. He's found it helps to play melodramatic in times like this. "Come on now, do you really think I wouldn't recognize those dulcet tones? Funny story, I was actually going to visit you the more-normal-less-kidnapping way, but it turns out there's no official record of you arriving in Astera. I had some questions about the book you gave me.

The one that apparently came from a *private royal collection*." That too is met with silence. "Really, anytime now, feel free to just jump in and start telling me what the devil's going on."

A strange voice, a sawtooth contralto, picks up much too close to Eugene. "Our questions come first."

"Sorry," Eugene snivels, "Solena taught me not to talk to strangers."

There's an irate pause. "You may call me Torch. Now—"

"It's not fair you get a mysterious code name and I don't," Eugene protests, internally calibrating his approach. Whoever this is, they want information from him, and with Solena also in the mix, Eugene doubts he's in any real danger. Annoyance makes people slip up and show their hand, and if there's anything he has an honorary degree in, it's petty antagonism.

"Who sent you to spy on us?" Torch asks.

That much Eugene can be honest about. More or less. "No one. I'm new in town, and I was sightseeing."

"You expect us to believe that?"

"Oh, I am very much new here," Eugene says, fully aware that's not what Torch meant. "I'm actually a brunet—I just put ash in my hair to blend in. You can give it a good ruffle if you don't believe me. Go on, fluff around and find out."

"You left the alley and came back," Torch growls. "Why?"

Eugene fires back, "I don't know, maybe it has something to do with why people keep acting like they recognize me. Any chance we want to dive into *that*?" When he's answered with only shuffles and crackling silence, he scoffs. "Tell you what. No one seems to be getting much out of this conversation, so why don't you let me go and I'll write this off as an embarrassing misunderstanding, because *I* very much have a prior engagement I need to scoot along to."

"Your itinerary should be the last of your worries right now." Fabric rustles near Torch, almost like the sound of a rough gesture—then Solena's walking stick clacks out of the room. "I'll ask one more time. *Who sent you?*"

Eugene's measure of assurance ebbs a few notches with Solena gone. "No one sent me. Frankly, if you hadn't made this a whole thing, I would have just assumed you were a very selective book club."

A new voice, deep and polished, mutters some distance away: "My stars, but the resemblance is uncanny."

Torch makes a disgruntled *hssst* sound. There's a commotion off to Eugene's left, a flurry of words and footsteps striding closer. Another voice echoes from what sounds like a hallway, oddly warped: ". . . as soon as I could. I'll take it from here."

"But Torch and I are friends now," Eugene objects. "You can't just break us up like this. We have rapport."

The new voice takes that in stride. "I'm sure you do. You two, watch his back. Everyone else, out. Fitzherbert, you can call me Moon Eye."

"This is just getting rude," Eugene grouses. "Moon Eye? That's such a good code name. Everyone else has one and I'm starting to feel left out."

"You're right." Brusque hands yank off his blindfold. "You can be Yappy."

As Eugene's eyes adjust, he can see where Moon Eye's name

comes from. The person in front of him is cloaked and hooded in plain gray wadmal; their only defining feature is a heavy pale mask carved in the shape of a moon eye moth. Or at least, it matches the drawings of them in *Flynnigan Rider.* A strange disk, likely what's distorting their voice, covers the place where Moon Eye's mouth ought to be.

Eugene takes quick stock of the surroundings: stone floors, stone walls, wooden door, no furniture apart from his chair. No sign of the source of the water noises or the creaking. Maybe he can aggravate Moon Eye into a hint about where they are.

"Appreciate the attempt, but 'Yappy' is a hard nope for me," Eugene says. "And just to get you caught up, no one sent me, I wasn't spying—"

"Why did King Enver bring you here?" Moon Eye interrupts.

That's a new line of questioning. Eugene doesn't have much to hide there. "He invited Rapunzel to some party for his daughter, and I'm her plus-one."

"Why? What's going to happen that's worth breaking centuries of isolation?"

Eugene can't help an annoyed huff. "Genuinely: You tell me! I've never set foot in Astera before, so whatever goes down at your birthday celebrations is well outside my area of expertise. The invitation just said something about her coming of age. If that means anything in particular to you, *phenomenal.*"

"Enver didn't tell you anything else?"

"No. But he *did* look like he saw a ghost when he met me.

And he just about ran off screaming when I said my name. I'm assuming he's not just coincidentally allergic to handsome scoundrels."

Moon Eye rocks back on their heels. Then they ask, "Who did you see entering the shop? And *don't* pretend you didn't."

Eugene himself takes a beat to think. If these people were going to kill him, they wouldn't bother hiding their faces. And they're not the only ones who need answers; maybe he can barter. "I saw three people go in. Here's a freebie: Solena was one. I'll give you the other two *after* we get through some of my questions."

Moon Eye folds their arms, wordless.

After a moment, Eugene decides to lay one more card on the table, since this is looking increasingly conspiratorial: "I saw the Herbert & Fitz sign inside the shop. Is 'Fitzherbert' even a real name, or did someone make it up?"

Moon Eye steps back, the mask tilting as they consider. "I'm afraid you've misjudged your negotiating position, Yappy. Here's my counteroffer. No, it's not coincidence you're being recognized in Astera. Yes, the reason involves your birth parents. And we'll tell you why . . . *if* you keep us informed on the princess's movements."

Behind him, someone sucks in a breath.

"Verette?" Eugene asks in disbelief. "What is this, some kind of secret insurrection club?"

"The *other* princess. Rapunzel."

He barks a harsh laugh. "You must be joking. You want me

to spy on the brilliant and incredible girl who's the sole reason I'm not dead or in a dungeon . . . just so you'll toss me some scraps about the people who abandoned me? Again, hard nope."

This time the person behind him makes an uncomfortable noise in their throat.

Moon Eye sighs. "Then I think we're done for today. The offer's open, but if you tell anyone . . . well, we know where to find you. And when you change your mind, you know how to find us. Torch, bag him."

Eugene ducks his head just enough to make Torch's hands slip as the hood comes down. He doesn't see much, just leathery suntanned skin—and at the base of Torch's thumb, a tiny black tattoo of a dagger. Not the easiest identifying mark, but better than nothing.

He waits until after the hood's on, then slips his hands out of the long-loosened rope. Just to make it abundantly clear he's stuck around this long of his own volition, he wiggles his fingers in a flourish. "Now I *know* Solena didn't do these knots."

To his surprise, Solena herself hisses behind him, "What did I *tell* you about the clove hitch?"

They faked her exit to try to intimidate him more. Out of professional courtesy alone, Eugene adds another half point to his abduction rating.

Eugene's arms are twisted behind his back and shackled this time, and then he's hauled to his feet. "Walk," orders Torch, pushing him toward the door as it rattles open.

"I don't even get to say goodbye?" Eugene pouts.

Moon Eye says grimly, "You'll be back soon enough."

But on the way out Eugene gets one terrible little crumb of something like an answer:

"Your parents didn't abandon you, Eugene," Solena calls after him.

Didn't—

Then how did he end up in an orphanage?

Before he can ask, he hears the door slam shut at his back.

His mind is spinning even as he tries to keep his cool, even though he knows flustered people slip up. And he almost slips up, too; it's not until he's guided around a corner that he realizes he should be counting the steps and turns. He knows in his gut it can only help Future Eugene if he memorizes the way out. *Twenty paces. Right. Five. Right again. Thirty paces, stairs, left.* The air has a damp, earthy quality that comes and goes with the sound of rushing water. Maybe he's in a cistern of some sort? The smell isn't anywhere near as foul as a sewer.

It's still a relief when they exit into the open, even if the hood remains. Torch walks him around a few blocks to try to confuse him more, and when they finally stop and the hood comes off, Eugene finds he's facing a stone wall.

"Keep still or the bag goes back on and we go for another walk," Torch warns. "I'm taking the shackles off. Count to fifty, then you can leave this alley. Understood?"

"Sure thing," Eugene lies. The moment the shackles unclasp, he throws himself back—

And stumbles into the opposite wall.

Torch is nowhere to be seen.

In fact, the only other living creature in sight is a seagull perched on a nearby barrel, its beady yellow eye fixed on Eugene. It holds his stare a long moment, then opens its beak and screams.

"Gah." Eugene flinches back and elects to leave through the *other* end of the alleyway. His stomach lets out a ferocious grumble, which is his first cue that something's wrong, not counting the seagull. He shouldn't be *that* hungry; he got captured around noon. . . .

Then, as he wanders into a completely new marketplace, he sees the length of the shadows. The social started well over an hour ago.

"Oh no," he groans, eliciting a sidelong look from a nearby merchant. Sure, light kidnapping is a decent excuse to be late, but Rapunzel's going to think he flaked on her. And until he figures out how to get back to the palace—preferably without the help of guards, since he's still disguised as a servant—she's going to keep thinking that.

His stomach rumbles again as he tries in vain to get his bearings. There's another one of those statues? Fountains? *Something* at the center of this market, which feels even more run-down than the one he passed through earlier. When he makes his way to the statue's base, he can see the tops of the sunmills peeking over the roofs. Eugene squints. From here, the fans all look alike, but the tallest ought to be the one on the palace, right? No matter what, it's going to be a long walk.

And to make matters worse, the nearby vendors will only accept Asteran currency, which Eugene discovers when he tries to buy himself a belated lunch. He winds up successfully begging a day-old loaf off a baker, then gets a few mouthfuls of musty water from a public well before he sets off in the approximate direction of the highest sunmill.

He makes it five blocks and a quarter of the way through the loaf before admitting he's lost. The walls of the narrow lane rise too high for him to see the sunmills anymore, and every passerby avoids eye contact and scurries away before he can ask for directions.

Then a familiar, dreadful toot sounds from above.

Eugene halts in place. Looks up.

A—*the?*—seagull is perched on a balcony, head tilted, yellow stare pinned. Not on Eugene.

On the loaf.

"No," Eugene says instantly, "don't you dare—"

The gull spreads its wings, lets loose a war shriek, and dives.

Eugene bolts down the lane, cursing and trying to shield himself from the beating wings. A sharp beak pecks at his arms, snapping after the loaf as he switches it from hand to hand. "Get *off*—leave me alone—I didn't even get lunch today! Where's a frying pan when you need one—"

The gull's beak closes on the bitten end of the bread. It flaps and squawks and, worst of all, maintains perfect eye contact with Eugene.

For a moment, he has the horrible thought that for all his joking before, this actually *could* be Gothel's escape plan gone awry.

"Eugene!"

Hoofbeats clatter over the paving stones toward them. The gull, clearly not expecting Eugene to have reinforcements, rips free a dry strip of bread and takes off.

Rapunzel slows Maximus to a halt in front of Eugene. Guilt zings through his belly; she's even in a silk party gown. As she swings down from the saddle, he launches into the apology he's been cobbling together: "I'm so sorry, I didn't forget about you or the thing this afternoon, I was—"

"Kidnapped," Rapunzel finishes for him, grabbing his arms. "Pascal filled me in. What happened? Are you all right?"

The back of Eugene's neck prickles. *We know where to find you,* Moon Eye had said. Whoever these people are, they're competent enough to snatch him off the streets unseen; they could still be watching him.

"It's not safe to talk here," he says under his breath, then adds loudly, "Just a misunderstanding! I look like some guy who didn't pay his tab. Come on, let's get going."

Rapunzel nods with a tight smile, and mounts up again. "Max, you know how to get back?"

He whickers an assent. Eugene ditches the servant uniform's distinct coat—the shirt and breeches are generic enough to not raise red flags—and pulls himself up behind her. "Cressien must be pulling his hair out right now. How did you get out of the palace on your own?"

"Maximus didn't give the guards much of a choice." Rapunzel pats Max's neck. "I think some tried to follow me. We'll let them 'find us' and escort us back, and if anyone asks . . ."

"I was mistaken for someone else." Eugene runs a hand through his hair, shaking out the ash, then winds his arm around Rapunzel's waist to hold on as Max sets off. It's nice, riding like this with her.

And—even though it's utter folly, even though he doesn't have anywhere near enough information to be sure—maybe this doesn't have to be the last time.

His parents didn't abandon him. And his parents were—are?—Asteran. Or known in Astera. If Solena's telling the truth . . .

There has to be a good reason he's lived his whole life elsewhere.

A *big* reason.

Maybe big enough to have a real future with Rapunzel after all.

It doesn't take long to attract the notice of the guards, who hustle them back up to the royal palace expeditiously. Both Minister Cressien and King Enver are waiting at the front steps, two separate variants of thunderstorms brewing in their faces.

Enver strikes first, striding toward them as Eugene dismounts. "By the skies, what happened? Princess Rapunzel said you were abducted. We didn't even know you were gone—how did you escape?"

Eugene has roughly one split second to figure out how to thread this needle.

On the one hand, if he betrays his captors to Enver, he might lose his one shot at learning the truth about his parents.

On the other . . . how did a book that belonged to Asteran royalty make it all the way to his orphanage across the sea?

How does Solena know his parents didn't abandon him?

Why is there something deeper than garden-variety concern lurking in Enver's eyes? Something almost like . . . dread?

Eugene decides to try a cousin of the truth. "I think it was a misunderstanding, because they just let me go. I must look a lot like someone they know."

"You were supposed to remain in the palace," Cressien says icily.

"I had some free time and thought I'd go see if anyone's selling those white shells Rapunzel was looking for." Eugene doesn't so much stress "white shells" as give the words a light bother. Cressien's brows rise for a moment, but he doesn't push further.

Enver's expression, however, only darkens. "Where were you captured? Where did they take you?"

"I'm not sure," Eugene fibs, since he's made his way to the exact spot twice now. "It was near the import market, I think? I woke up in some kind of hideout, but they kept me blindfolded."

"Are you *certain* they didn't recognize you?" the king presses urgently as Princess Verette arrives at his elbow, her round face drawn, brown eyes wide.

Brown eyes just like Eugene's.

King Enver's voice snaps him back. "How many of them were there?"

Solena, Torch, Moon Eye, the fourth speaker . . . Eugene hedges again. "A couple, maybe?"

"Do you remember *anything* at all that could help us find them?" King Enver steps closer. "I cannot allow a threat like this to go unmet."

Verette places her hand on Enver's elbow. "Father, perhaps our guests might appreciate a moment to collect themselves? This sounds like quite the shock."

King Enver pulls back, eyes closing. "Forgive me. Of course. For now, I will assign additional guards to the guest wing, in case this is . . . more than a simple case of mistaken identity." He swallows. "I would also like you all to join Verette and me for dinner this evening. There is an important matter we must discuss."

His gaze catches Eugene's for a moment before he flinches, turns, and marches up the steps before anyone can get in another word.

Eugene's heartbeat picks up.

This is—

Too much to be coincidence.

Too much to hope for.

Too much.

He knows how Flynn Rider would handle this: scheme, try to play both sides, try to have it all. No risk, no reward.

But the last time he operated that way, he wound up hand

delivering Rapunzel back to Gothel and getting himself express shipped to the gallows. And he could have stopped it if he'd just trusted Rapunzel with the truth.

Guards usher them back to the guest wing in relative silence and double the numbers, which feels like an excessive security measure. (Unless . . . ?) Cressien's lips are pressed so tight together that Eugene knows he's bottling up either a very long lecture or a lengthy cross-examination. When they reach their parlor and relative privacy, Eugene sees the minister's mouth open—

Eugene doesn't hesitate, just links his arms through Cressien's and Rapunzel's and drags them both into Cressien's room as the minister sputters a protest. Then Eugene swings the door shut behind them, checks the doorjamb for the shadows of eavesdroppers, and finally turns to face the other two.

Flynn Rider might try to keep secrets, but Eugene—Eugene knows when he's in over his head.

"I," he begins, "have had an *incredibly* strange day."

Part Two

Moon Eye

NINE

RAPUNZEL

Rapunzel first saw the floating lanterns on her fifth birthday.

In retrospect, if Gothel had known about the lanterns, Rapunzel has no doubt she would have lied and claimed Rapunzel's birthday was a week earlier, or locked all the windows before bedtime, or slipped something into her dinner so she'd sleep through the night. But Rapunzel had already been sneaking around to look at the stars for months at that point, and so the distant lights were one last birthday surprise.

When she saw them on her sixth birthday, she thought they might be meant for her.

By her tenth, she knew they were.

She couldn't explain it—what they were, why she was so certain, how she knew in her bones that everything would change if only she could reach the lights. How she believed they would lead her to where she really belonged.

It was easier to be certain from the window of a tower she never thought she'd leave. And it was easier to stay with Mother—*no*, Gothel—telling her she'd only ever be wanted for her hair.

The problem wasn't believing that those lights were meant for her.

The problem is that she followed them to where she should belong, and now, as a princess, with a home she can leave and parents who love her . . . there are no clear answers in her windows. She feels like she keeps looking for what she's meant to do but finding nothing in reach, only distant, scattered stars.

Like now, with Eugene telling her he has to choose between the truth about his past . . . and her.

"I didn't agree to anything," Eugene is saying as he paces at the foot of Cressien's bed. "In fact, I told them to get stuffed, more or less. They seemed very convinced I would change my mind."

Minister Cressien looks like he's thinking fondly of Duke Louis's five barrels of rosé, perched stiff as a board on the edge of the mattress. Rapunzel can't tell if he's more distraught by the invasion of his personal space or the burgeoning political crisis. To her surprise, though, when he speaks, it's not nearly as prickly as she was bracing for. “Master Fitzherbert, I would not typically pry, but . . . do you recall *anything* from your childhood that might be related? Any time spent on a ship? Any unusual visitors?”

“Nothing,” Eugene answers bluntly, rearranging decorative knickknacks on one of the guest room’s shelves. Rapunzel’s clocked by now that his anxiety tends to be stored in his hands. “All my earliest memories are in the orphanage. And *please* call me Eugene. ‘Master Fitzherbert’ sounds like a mean teacher in a kiddie book.”

Cressien ignores that. “What about this Solena?”

“Part of the orphanage staff. She never said anything about knowing my parents or having a connection with Astera, and when she left, she said it was because she was settling here. But she’s not in the Asteran immigration records.”

“Maybe her real name isn’t Solena,” Rapunzel suggests from her post in the desk chair. “Or she snuck into Astera. Or both.”

Cressien pinches the bridge of his nose. “Master Fitzherbert’s profile has certainly become more prominent in the last month. . . . It is possible that this invitation was issued with the intention to bring him here.”

“Mm,” Rapunzel hedges. Cressien looks up at her in a way that implies a gaze over nonexistent spectacles. “Well, Verette said her father invited me, and she doesn’t seem happy we’re here. But if King Enver expected me to bring Eugene, he wouldn’t have been so shocked when he saw him, right?”

Cressien’s brows rise. “Fair point.”

"I do think this is something, well, big," she says, fumbling for the right words. "This organization wants Eugene to spy on me and Enver, they have at least one operative here as the stable master, and . . . I felt like they were acting strange on the tour."

"How so?" Cressien asks.

"It was like they didn't want me looking too closely at anything. I—I wasn't trying to pry or be rude—" Rapunzel catches herself fiddling with a sleeve. There's no reason to be nervous. She knows what she's talking about. "They kept changing the subject or moving us along. And a *lot* of the stonework in the palace has been repaired. You can tell because the patch material has a different luster. The damage it's covering would have been huge. I think the palace was attacked at one point."

"Perhaps natural causes . . ." Cressien starts, then shakes his head. "No, I concur, we were being handled on the tour, but we would have noticed repairs to other major structures. An attack on the palace suggests Astera may not be as united as it seems."

"Moon Eye was asking about Verette's coming of age ceremony, like they suspect something might happen," Eugene pitches in, moving from the shelf to fuss with the dried flowers in a decorative urn. "I said I didn't know about the plans."

"I don't think any of us do," Cressien says slowly. "She seems to be popular among the citizens of Astera, and they referred to her as the 'queen to come,' but when I asked Councilor

Teophine if Verette would be ascending the throne at this ceremony, she just said, 'We'll see.' Traditionally, many more royal families would be invited to attend such a coronation."

Rapunzel rubs the back of her neck. "Does . . . does anyone know how old Verette actually is? I'm not really good at guessing."

Eugene and Cressien trade looks. "Beats me," Eugene says, and drifts over to stand near her at the desk.

Cressien's gaze narrows. "So to summarize: There are signs of previous violence within the palace. Master Fitzherbert has connections to Astera that were concealed from him with, it seems, great effort. It seems increasingly likely that the princess's coming of age is a smoke screen, though we're not certain to what end. And an underground organization is attempting to extort Master Fitzherbert into spying on the king and Princess Rapunzel in exchange for information they hypothetically have about his parents."

"Aaaand you've been holding out on us," Eugene says with a sudden jolt of delight, gawking at the contents of a desk drawer he'd idly pulled open. Rapunzel glances down, bewildered. Inside is a skein of coral yarn, a crochet hook, and . . .

"Is that a crab?" Rapunzel asks.

Cressien lunges faster than she knew he could move, swooping on the contents of the drawer like a hawk and slamming it shut. "It's an octopus, if you must know, and it's purely for meditation." He stuffs the whole business under his pillow, scowling, and adds resentfully, "And it's incomplete."

"Color me impressed," Eugene says, and when Cressien gives him a suspicious frown, he holds up his hands. "Truly! If I had an octopus like that as a kid I'd take him everywhere. I'd probably call him Mister Fitzherbert, even, and he'd have a job as a mean teacher."

Rapunzel can't help a smile at the image of a baby Eugene sleeping with a crocheted octopus. Then her smile wavers. He grew up with so little; it's not fair to deny him more.

She catches his sleeve. "I trust you," she says, "and I don't want to cost you your one chance at learning more about your family. If spying on me helps you with that . . ."

Eugene covers her hand with his, then drops to a crouch by her chair, all bravado suspended for the moment. "Look, Freckles. Even if I was willing to put you in danger—and I'm not—you're also a little too good at putting everyone else's needs first."

"Isn't that my job as a princess?" she pushes back. "To help everyone?"

"To a point." Cressien, to her surprise, is staring at the far side of the bed. After a moment she realizes he's not wringing his hands, just rubbing the knuckle of his bare ring finger. "Selflessness is an easy default when you feel lost, Your Highness. But ultimately, if you overextend yourself, you hurt the people relying on you."

Rapunzel swallows. "What if we gave them bad information? Or a mix of information that's true but useless, and fake information, and then we see who acts on it? Say I like cherry tarts, for example. Then if the Councilor of the North tries to bribe me with them, we know she's involved."

"That could work," Cressien allows, "if we're all very, very careful. But if Astera is indeed having some sort of internal dispute, it's best we stay out of it as much as possible. All we have to do is make it through this week without further disaster. Now, about this serious matter the king wants to discuss—"

There's a knock, not at Cressien's door, but the guest parlor's. They find Hughes standing just outside. "His Majesty wishes to let you know you will be escorted to dinner with him in an hour."

"Thank you for the notice," Cressien says. He shuts the door again as Hughes bows and leaves, then eyeballs Eugene's severe dishevelment. "There's no use speculating what this dinner is about with as little information as we have currently, so I would suggest using our time to . . . freshen up. Unless either of you has anything else to add?"

Eugene's eyes flicker, but he just brushes a stray breadcrumb from his sleeve. "Nope. All set to dress to impress."

Rapunzel doesn't need the full hour to get ready, but it does take her a couple tries to get her cosmetics right. Years of delicate brushwork and pigment blending make some parts of it easier, but they don't steady the shake in her hand.

It'll be fine, she tells herself. She can handle this, no matter what. Maybe King Enver will admit why he really invited them. Maybe he wants to talk about the coming of age ceremony. Maybe there's a problem, one only she can solve.

Whatever it is . . . she can handle it. With or without her hair.

(And then Minister Cressien can put *that* in his report.)

As polished as Rapunzel thinks she looks when she steps out of her room, Eugene still casually makes her stomach jolt as he paces in the parlor in a burgundy tailcoat that sets off his eyes, rearranging the porcelain cat figurines lining the fireplace mantel. She matches his embarrassingly goofy grin with her own as she tugs at the cuffs of her long sleeves. "How do I look?"

"Perfect" leaps out so fast she knows he didn't practice it. He takes her hand. "Can I make a suggestion?"

"Sure?"

He carefully folds her sleeve up and back so the cuff falls just below her elbow, then does the same to the other arm. "You want to know a secret? I used to fidget with my sleeves all the time when I was nervous. That's why I started rolling mine up."

"I can't imagine you ever getting nervous," Rapunzel says wryly.

His grin tilts at that. "Really? Because that's how I feel basically all the time around you."

A tactical cleared throat unfortunately cuts in.

Princess Verette is standing in the open parlor doorway. "Good evening. I'm to escort you all to dinner."

Rapunzel jumps. "Oh! Er." She fumbles for solid ground. "I think we're just waiting on Minister—"

"I am ready, Your Highness," Cressien says behind her.

Nine

Rapunzel jumps again. She didn't even hear his door open. "Great! Then let's be off!"

"Let's," Verette says blandly.

As they set off down the hall, Rapunzel tries to scrape together small talk—only for Eugene to pick up the conversation for her.

"So, Your Highness," he starts, "I apologize, but we know very little about Astera or your traditions. You saw for yourself yesterday, the best we've got comes from an old storybook. Is it all right if we ask what probably seem like very basic questions?"

Verette eyes him with mild caution, but says, "You may."

"The invitation mentioned you and your father. Do you have any siblings? Cousins? Embarrassing uncles I should watch out for?"

"No, it's just us." Verette gazes stonily ahead. For a moment, that seems like the end of that—then, surprisingly, she counters. "And you? Are you an only child?"

"I—Well, I helped with other kids in the orphanage," Eugene stumbles.

The brief lift of Verette's eyebrows seems to betray surprise. That's strange; Rapunzel would have expected King Enver to loop his daughter in by now.

But Verette seems to have different concerns, glancing from Eugene to Rapunzel and back.

"An orphanage? Do you know anything about your parents, then? Or where you come from?"

Even Eugene can't hide that that hit a nerve. His answer is a short "No."

"What a shame." There's a stiff pause. Verette lifts an eyebrow at Rapunzel. "Your parents must be very . . . understanding."

Eugene flinches.

"We are fortunate that Their Majesties value a person's deeds more than their lineage," Minister Cressien finesses, to Rapunzel's surprise.

Rapunzel reaches for another tactic for managing Gothel's moods: changing the subject to Gothel. Or in this case, Verette. "So the ball is the day after tomorrow, and then your coming of age ceremony is a few days after that? Are you excited?"

"That is the current schedule," Verette says, retreating back to toneless brevity. "And I will be honored by the celebration next week."

"I can't wait." Rapunzel pauses, but when Verette doesn't elaborate, she ventures another prompt: "What's your favorite part of the ceremony?"

"I enjoy it all equally."

All right, maybe Verette doesn't like to talk about herself as much as Gothel did. Rapunzel switches gears, scanning the view from a passing window until inspiration strikes in the form of a glittering sunmill sail far below. "Oh, I wanted to ask—I know what the other sunmills are for, but what about the one in the tower here? It doesn't look like it's active."

At that, something like concern ghosts briefly through

Verette's face before it closes off again. "It's no longer of use to Astera."

"But it was before?" Eugene prompts.

No dice. Verette only snips out, "Yes."

Another strained pause stretches taut as they pass through a stone arch and into what Rapunzel assumes is the royal family's quarters, given the large portrait of Enver and Verette that watches them go by. It looks recent, capturing Enver's knowing smile and Verette's, well, reticence.

Rapunzel makes one more attempt at chitchat. "Thank you for bringing us here. I know it must be annoying answering all our questions, and I haven't even seen much of my own kingdom yet, but there's so much in Astera I've never even *heard* of before." She laughs. "Even the bugs—I saw these silver worms in the garden today, and I didn't—"

"Silver?" Verette's frowning. "I've never seen anything like that."

"You don't strike me as the gardening type," Eugene drawls.

Her dark eyes flick to him. It's almost like someone shook the real Verette awake, her stare suddenly focused. "You'd be surprised. What did they look like, exactly?"

"Long, and really thin," Rapunzel says quickly. At the edge of her sight, she can see Cressien trying to hide both bewilderment and dismay, doubtless because decades of refined etiquette have been superseded by a mutual enthusiasm for worms. "It almost looked like a—a herd of them. They were all moving in the same direction."

"And this was in the gardens?" Verette leads them through a door flanked by guards into a dining room smaller than Rapunzel expected. The view is still spectacular, through one wall made entirely of glass in star-shaped panes that overlooks a harbor drenched in the tawny golds of early-summer sunset.

King Enver waits for them at the head of the table, gripping the back of his chair with both hands. His face hardens as they walk in.

"Good," he says tersely. "You're here. I'll get right to the point."

Only then does Rapunzel realize the dining table . . . is completely empty. Not even a butter knife is sitting on the plain white tablecloth.

This isn't a dinner.

"Guards," Enver calls. The two soldiers file in. Before Rapunzel can even open her mouth to demand an explanation, they each seize one of Eugene's arms.

"Hey—" Eugene's protest turns to anger as manacles lock around his wrists. *"Hey!"*

"Your Majesty, what is the meaning of this?" Cressien's voice rises.

Verette looks from Eugene to Enver. "Father?"

"Take him to the dungeon," Enver orders coldly.

Rapunzel doesn't think, just darts to the doorway and throws out her arms to block the way, fire crackling between her ears. *"No."*

Enver jerks back as if she's just slapped him. Verette is outright gawking at her.

Nine

"I don't know what you think Eugene's done, but there has to be a mistake," she insists.

Cressien's voice is like iron. "Surely the king does not intend to cause insult by imprisoning the princess's companion without cause."

"I have cause." Enver's jaw tightens. "I'd heard the boy was some sort of troubled youth, but I made allowances for Princess Rapunzel's judgment. Now I'm certain he's here under false pretenses."

"What?" Eugene sputters.

Anger swells in Rapunzel's belly. She decides she can apologize to Cressien for her lack of tact later. "You don't even know Eugene," she says hotly. "You've barely spoken to him since we arrived, and you already decided he's guilty?"

"People have been treating me strangely all day," Eugene adds behind her with a mordant shrug. He may be playing it casual, but Rapunzel doesn't miss the tension in his shoulders. "Frankly, it's getting a little old. If His Majesty would like to share what's going on, I am *all ears*."

"Don't lie to me," Enver barks. The setting sun blazes through the windows, dyeing the room searing peach. "I *knew* Marietta got away. She's been planning this for years, hasn't she? Where are they? Where's the rest of the People's Dagger?"

"The who now?" Eugene looks utterly bewildered.

But Enver's not convinced. "He's lying to you, Princess. This man is an operative from a dangerous, cowardly clutch of traitors who have been working to depose me for decades. Your courtship is a ruse to get to me and Verette."

If Rapunzel had a frying pan on hand, she would probably be halfway to an act of war. Fortunately (or not), she has to use her words. "You don't know what you're talking about. Eugene *died* for me before we even knew you existed."

"Andreas Herbert and Marietta Fitz were my wife's dearest friends," Enver says, stony. "And on the worst night of my life, they betrayed us both. Verette grew up without a mother because of them." He points a shaking finger at Eugene. "And *you* look just like your parents."

Eugene almost goes slack, like the wind's been knocked out of him, turning deathly pale. After a beat, the shock frosts over into something brittle. The words come out like each one's chipped from ice. "I grew up in an orphanage across the sea. I never met my parents, or even knew their names." His eyes turn steely. "I come from nothing. So whoever you think I am, you have the wrong man."

Enver's nostrils flare.

"Forgive me, Your Majesty, but . . ." Cressien shifts his weight, subtly angling to stand by Rapunzel. "Do you believe Fitzherbert has actually committed a crime, or is your suspicion based on resemblance alone?"

"He snuck out of the palace and disappeared for hours with people he *conveniently* couldn't describe, to a location he couldn't identify, and these supposed captors just let him go out of the goodness of their hearts?" Enver says derisively.

"They just arrived yesterday, Father." Verette's voice tightens with discomfort, her gaze darting from the king to

Rapunzel and back. "And they came straight here from the harbor. Of course Fitzherbert didn't know where he was. And if he had seen his kidnappers' faces, they never would have let him go."

Enver barely seems to hear her.

"You already increased the guard at the guest wing," Verette continues. "Perhaps instead of jailing Fitzherbert, we could have them escort him within the palace grounds, and appoint someone trustworthy to serve as an additional chaperone if we venture out."

Enver runs a hand over his short beard, brow furrowed, stare narrowed on the floor. Finally he blows a hissing breath out his nose and scowls. "Very well. I'll have Hughes do it. I don't trust anyone else." He nods to the guards. "You may release him. For now."

Rapunzel doesn't know what's worse—the look on Eugene's face as the shackles are unlocked, or the fact that he won't meet her eyes. She slides her hand into his as Enver sweeps out.

"I'll . . . go talk to him," Verette says stiltedly, and follows him through the door.

"It'll be okay," Rapunzel whispers.

"Yeah," Eugene mumbles.

But he still looks utterly lost.

It's like the lanterns, Rapunzel realizes. When she was watching from her tower, it was safe to believe whatever she wanted of them; she'd never been so scared as the moment in the boat, before she saw them for herself.

What if it's not everything I dreamed it would be? she'd asked.

And Eugene's answer was just *It will be.*

Eugene's parents were always lights in the sky, too far out of reach for their possibility to be limited. But if Enver is right . . . then that truth has fallen terribly, terribly short.

Ten

Eugene

The first and last time Eugene got caught picking pockets was when he committed the cardinal sin of trying to rob an old lady. Old ladies were universally understood to be off-limits, but like many teens, he simply assumed that meant people were missing out. They didn't want the outrage robbing someone's angel-faced nana would evoke.

So Eugene picked a mean-faced old crone instead.

He learned two very important lessons that day. Unfortunately for him, neither was "Don't judge a book by its cover."

His first lesson was that mean old crones made it to a mean old age by having a firm command of every trick in the book. Including a few he thought he'd invented.

The second was one she imparted when she was done hitting him with her purse. "Give up thieving while you can, boy," the woman scolded. "For one thing, you're no good at it. But even if you get good, then you'll start thinking you can swindle anything and anyone. And it'll be too late when you realize you went and robbed yourself."

Like most practical, heartfelt advice, Eugene proceeded to ignore it until the consequences didn't so much catch up to him as land a sucker punch.

And that's the worst part, really. He should have known better. He knows how a con works: You sell someone a fantasy. (A family that could make him good enough.) You tell them they can have what they're missing. (A future with the princess he loves.)

And when they think they have it all . . . you leave them holding the bag.

That's the problem with dreams. They end when you wake up.

Eugene now knows two things about his immediate future:

First, he is going to make the most of every minute he has left with Rapunzel, because "pardoned ex-con" was already bad enough before tacking on "son of traitors."

And second: No one is going to get the drop on him again. Not even himself.

Morning finds him reverse-alphabetizing a bookshelf in the guest wing parlor, trying to ignore the red ripples left on his wrists by the brief chafe of manacles last night. He, Rapunzel, and Cressien are supposed to have breakfast in their own dining room, but Cressien's mysteriously absent, so Eugene's industriously fidgeting while Rapunzel works on fashioning what looks like a miniature coat for Pascal.

He must not be doing *that* great of a job spackling over his dented mood, because Rapunzel finally says over her stitching, "Do you want to talk about it?"

"I . . . I wish I didn't have to?" Eugene runs a hand through his hair and turns to face her. "I thought . . ." Maybe now isn't the time to throw out *I hoped I might be secret royalty, because otherwise I think we'll have to break up.* As if Rapunzel's stress crafting wasn't enough of a tip-off, she's got pigment under her nails, a sure sign she was up late stress drawing. "I thought I'd never find out about my parents," he haltingly shares. "And now I almost wish that were true."

"I don't think the manacles helped either," Rapunzel suggests carefully.

Only then does Eugene realize he's been rubbing the red marks on his wrists.

Trust Rapunzel to spot a tell like that. He admits, "The last time I was shackled was . . . before the execution."

He leaves out that last night, every dream started with him walking down the aisle of what should have been their wedding, only to find himself standing at the gallows.

Maybe that left a deeper dent than he thought.

Eugene feels like he's hitting his cap for personal disclosure. And he's not the only one still rattled. "How are *you* doing?"

Maybe he should have asked about the weather, because Rapunzel's needle punches through the fabric with excessive force. "Fine," she grumbles, then caves. "No, not fine. Did you know Minister Cressien is sending reports back to my mother? I already feel like I can't do any of this right, and it's even worse now that I know he's *telling* her every time I mess up."

"But you're doing great," Eugene objects. "You even got Verette to open up! You bonded over weird worms!"

Rapunzel's nose wrinkles. "They're not *weird*, they're a vital part of the cycle of—"

She stops as voices seep through the parlor door. An unsurprising knock follows, but the door swings open to admit Cressien before Eugene can reach for the doorknob.

Then . . . King Enver enters after Cressien, somber.

Eugene and Rapunzel both still.

Enver's hands knot together, regret sinking his shoulders. He draws a deep breath. "Princess Rapunzel. Lord Fitzherbert. I wish to apologize for my outburst last night."

Outburst? Eugene thinks but doesn't say. When *he* has an outburst, it doesn't usually involve having someone thrown in a dungeon and then trying to fix it by adding a title to their name.

King Enver's not quite done. "My actions came from a place of fear, anger, and grief, and they were unfair to you. After speaking further with my daughter and Minister Cressien, I have decided that at the very least, I owe you the truth." His head bows a moment, and Eugene isn't certain who the words are meant for when he sighs, "Especially because it can't be used against us anymore. Will you please come with me?"

Enver sounds remorseful. Resigned. Sincere. All in the precise quantities he ought to display.

And maybe, before last night, Eugene would have bought it. Now . . .

He catches himself once again rubbing at the red bands on his wrists.

Something else Eugene learned as he got better and better at stealing: Desperation reveals who you really are.

And the man who nearly threw him in prison for the crime of a family resemblance—that was pure desperation. A man who's lost so much, he'll do whatever it takes to keep what's left.

Eugene needs to know exactly what kind of loss that is before Enver uses it against him again.

"Lead the way," Eugene says.

The king ushers them through the palace, this time away from the royal wing. Now that Rapunzel's pointed it out, Eugene can't stop seeing the scars in the architecture, and Eugene's got a hunch that they're related to that "worst night of his life" Enver was ranting about.

"Princess Rapunzel." Enver's voice rolls back to them as they step into a broad courtyard, headed for the base of an enormous tower at the far end. No—not a tower. It's the silent, still palace sunmill. "Legend says that a drop of sunlight fell to earth and became the flower that saved your mother, and granted you—well, your hair—healing powers."

Rapunzel glances to Cressien, who nods near imperceptibly. "Yes," she says, hesitant, "but I told the truth yesterday. I don't have that power anymore."

They reach the tower doors. Something creaks above them. Eugene looks up at the glittering crystal sails, eerily motionless.

Enver pushes the doors open. "Ours," he says tightly, "was a drop of starlight, not sun."

Eugene sees Cressien's head tilt from the corner of his eye. He himself is somewhat perplexed; "I guess they're just handing them out" earns him a mild elbow in the side from Rapunzel.

"Like yours, it fell centuries ago. But the drop of starlight fell into a spring." King Enver waits for a guard to touch a lit torch to a groove in the wall. A pale gold flame races around the circumference of the sunmill's interior, catching unseen fuses, and then dozens of lamps within ignite at once. They shed more than enough light to reveal a strange, shallow stone basin that covers nearly the entire floor.

In the basin's center stands a familiar statue: a robed figure holding a cluster of dull bronze stars. Just like the ones Eugene saw in the city plazas, albeit twice their size.

"This is—was—the Great Starlight Fountain," Enver says heavily. He begins to pace around the edge of the basin. "Below us is the Starlight Spring itself. Our ancestors found that anyone who drank directly from the spring would be cured of most ailments and injuries, and as time passed, our sailors would return from other lands and swear Asterans lived longer, our food tasted better, everything was just a bit more *alive*. It was as if the whole island were touched by starlight." Enver slows to a halt. His voice shifts. "And a gift like that had to be protected."

Rapunzel's hand tightens on Eugene's. She says slowly, "That's what my . . . That's what someone said about me."

"They were very wise," King Enver says, eyes on the dry stone. "Many generations ago, the royal family realized the Starlight Spring's many visitors were draining it faster than it could replenish itself. They built this fountain and connected it to others all over Astera. Once a year, during the Fountain Festival, this sunmill would activate, and the fountains would flow for a day, free for everyone to take what they needed, while leaving enough in reserve for the starlight to still spread naturally through the land. We knew outsiders would want that power for themselves, so we guarded the secret dearly." He laughs bitterly. "And yet our downfall came from within."

Eugene's voice comes out just as bitter. "I assume this is where you think my parents come in."

"I don't think. I know." Enver resumes walking around the perimeter of the fountain. "A group of insurgents formed a few decades ago, calling themselves the People's Dagger. They believed the royalty were restricting the fountains solely to give ourselves power and control over the rest of Astera. Marietta and Herbert were indoctrinated into their ranks, even though they were close friends of the queen. They asked us to give the People's Dagger an audience so they could plead their case. We granted it, but . . . they came armed." Enver absently flattens a hand to his stomach, as if the memory aches. "It's known now as the Night of the Poisoned Dagger. I believe the insurgents intended to force us to permanently activate the fountains. When it became clear they were outnumbered, they went on a rampage, killing the queen and poisoning the spring so no one could have it."

"The Dagger's leaders could have lied to them." Eugene didn't plan to interrupt, but it flies out of his mouth nonetheless. "If—if these people even are my parents, maybe they didn't know—"

"I saw Marietta Fitz standing over my wife's body." Enver points to the base of the statue. "I watched Andreas Herbert bleed out right there, on that stone. The poison may have come from his own hand." After a moment he adds, "I'm sorry, boy."

Rapunzel's wrapped her arm around Eugene's, and it may be the only thing keeping him from running into the sea right now. She asks, "Have you tested the spring water?"

"Every day," Enver says. "It's been over twenty years. The spring is gradually purging the poison on its own, but it's taken its toll. You may have noticed everything seems . . . stretched thin. Asterans have been a little sicker, our crops a little less abundant—even the shells you like so much, Princess, they're not quite as lustrous now."

"Is that why you decided to allow foreign citizens on the mainland now?" Cressien breaks his thoughtful silence.

Enver shrugs dejectedly. "Indeed. The damage has already

been done. It seems if Astera is to make a true recovery . . . we may need help from beyond our shores."

And if these people really are—*were*—his parents, it's all their fault.

"You're sure they were my parents?" Eugene can't help asking.

Enver's stony expression erodes a fraction. "I didn't know they had a son. Still, you are almost *exactly* like Andreas. He's in your eyes, your voice, even the"—he waves a hand—"motions. But . . . I daresay you have your mother's nose."

Eugene feels it, then, as decisive as the gallows: The dream is over, and he can't deny reality anymore.

He thinks he might throw up.

When he ventures a look at Rapunzel, she's frowning—but not in the shocked or dismayed way he expected. There's a telltale tip of her head, the one she gets when she steps back to assess a painting's composition.

"Thank you for your trust," she says carefully. "I know how important a secret like this is, and you can count on us to protect it."

"Including Fitzherbert." Those are perhaps the last words Eugene expected from Minister Cressien, but he says them nonetheless. "Whatever his parentage may be, it has no bearing on his upbringing."

"'Whatever' isn't the ideal word choice there, is it?" Eugene grumbles.

Cressien gives him a *So help me, I will turn this defense of you around* look and continues, "Is the guards' surveillance truly necessary?"

Enver rubs his brow. "I suppose . . . not within the palace. If the boy wishes to go outside, Hughes will still supervise. We didn't stamp out the entirety of the People's Dagger, and if they recognize him as Andreas's son, they may attempt to make contact."

They'd have to get in line, Eugene thinks grimly.

Then—he remembers the brief glimpse of Torch's hand as they wrestled with the bag.

The tiny tattoo at the base of their thumb: a dagger.

Your parents didn't abandon you, Eugene.

My stars, but the resemblance is uncanny.

The People's Dagger doesn't have to get in line. Not when they were the first in the door.

"His Majesty's compassion is without peer," Cressien says. Then he gives Eugene another sharp look.

Eugene gets the message loud and clear. The words still stick in his throat. "Thank you, Your Majesty."

Enver just nods, curt. He leads them toward the door. "Verette goes into the city with Councilor Savary once a week to provide aid to Asterans still suffering the long-term impacts of the Night of the Poisoned Dagger. If you wish, I can ask for you to join them so you can see for yourself."

"Whatever you need," Rapunzel says immediately, because that's just who she is. Eugene hides a wince. It's not a bad thing that she never hesitates to throw herself into fixing someone else's problems. And he knows it's an instinct she learned in Gothel's tower.

He just hopes that someday soon, she sees that people love her for more than what she can do for them.

"Eugene, do you want to come with?" Rapunzel asks.

He starts to think of an excuse not to go—then it occurs to him that, if he can shake Hughes, this could be an opportunity to return to the storefront.

There has to be more to the Night of the Poisoned Dagger. Maybe . . . they can clear his parents' names. It's a foolhardy idea, but Eugene knows exactly who he is when he's desperate: a relentless, single-minded fool.

"You know what," he says slowly, "I would love to."

Eleven

Rapunzel

The atmosphere in the carriage feels decidedly different this time around.

For one thing, it's not just a princesses-only club; Eugene is sitting next to Rapunzel, and because Eugene is there, Hughes is planted beside Verette. That alone has shifted the energy from awkward silence to something like tentative, muddled confusion. Verette did seem to be expecting them when they met her and Hughes at the palace steps, so Rapunzel's best guess is that the chamberlain has brought her up to speed, at least. Hughes's countenance remains as dismal as ever, but Verette has progressed from staring out the window to sneakily eyeing both Rapunzel and Eugene as they jostle down the hill into the city.

Finally Eugene breaks the ice: "Sorry about . . . er, my parents. And your mother."

Verette swallows. A curious sort of relief seeps into her face. "I'm sorry as well. This can't be easy for you. For what it's worth . . . my mother was very ill at that point. The only thing keeping her alive was the Starlight Spring, and only a miracle could have saved her. I'm not even sure . . ." Her voice trails off, and she shakes her head. "I don't think we should be judged by our parents' choices, just the choices we make in the aftermath. But I appreciate your sympathy."

"And we will appreciate your discretion," Hughes adds with a bit more steel.

Rapunzel catches herself tugging the ends of her hair again. "Believe me, I understand. The power to heal, to prolong your life . . . I was locked in a tower for eighteen years so someone could keep that kind of power to themselves." She pushes her long sleeves back to her elbows. It's been a lot to absorb, the tragedy and the history, but her mind has been racing almost all morning. "If it's okay, I have some questions."

"Go ahead." Verette's almost jarringly cordial. Perhaps with Astera's secrets laid out, she doesn't feel she has as much to hide.

"Do you know how big the spring is?"

"No, I've never seen it in person," Verette answers. "Every route into the spring's cavern was sealed off except for one, and only the current monarch has the key to it."

"What if he loses it?" Eugene asks. When Hughes gives him a dubious look, he shrugs. "I'm just saying, I have dropped my keys into some vile places before."

Hughes is unamused. "How fortunate for us all that the king has more grace."

"Do you know what kind of poison it was?" Rapunzel asks. "Or how much?" Verette shakes her head to both, lips thinning. "Did anyone ever look into the source of the spring?"

"Councilor Laroux may have more thorough knowledge," Hughes politely suggests.

"I wish I knew," Verette admits. "But why do you ask?"

Now it's Rapunzel's turn to hunt for an answer. Sadly, the problem isn't that she doesn't have one; it's that it's embarrassing.

Despite the heartache, this is the best she's felt in weeks. The last month as a princess has been completely uncharted territory—no routines to follow yet, no goalposts to reach. No way to show her parents she could do anything they asked, that she was ready not just to be a princess, but their daughter.

The invitation to Astera was her first opening, but it was also open-ended. It called for mastery of tact, intrigue, and etiquette, and her people skills are . . . limited.

This? A tangible problem she can tackle? That's finally solid ground.

"I'm here to help," Rapunzel says. "Any way I can."

She doesn't miss the looks Verette and Hughes trade.

"Can someone explain the whole councilor thing to me?" Eugene asks. "Back on the ship, Councilor Teophine said she was the south, or something? It's been a couple days."

Hughes draws himself up with a hint of drama, as if

bureaucratic minutiae might be the highlight of his day. "The Cardinal Council comprises five advisors, each of whom runs a separate wing of the administrative hall, which their role is named for. The north wing covers education and research—hence Councilor Laroux of the North may have more knowledge of the Starlight Spring. You've met Councilor Teophine Trahan of the South. Councilor Brevala Savary of the East deals with labor and public welfare, Councilor Persevault of the West oversees the harbor and the navy, and Councilor Matelin of the Center is in charge of records and general administration."

"The council used to be chosen by the people of Astera," Verette adds. "If a monarch passed away or was incapacitated before their heir was of age, the council governed in the interim, and they also had the ability to overrule a monarch's decision by unanimous vote."

"What an interesting use of past tense," Eugene observes as the carriage slows.

It halts before Rapunzel can squeeze in a follow-up. As they exit, though, Verette says, "I'll try to get you a meeting with Councilor Laroux this afternoon."

"Thank you." Rapunzel tries to hide her surprise.

Minister Cressien and Councilor Savary climb out of the carriage behind theirs. Councilor Savary is a short, stout woman near Cressien's age, with laugh lines in her deep gold face and a grandmother's watchful eye. She sweeps an arm at the two mismatched stories of the building before them as a rangy, almost birdlike doctor bows by the door. "Welcome to

Third Street Hospital, Your Highnesses. My wife is the director, and she'll be guiding you through the visit," Councilor Savary says.

"So sentimental," the doctor laughs, planting a kiss on Savary's cheek. Then, peering at the group, she wrinkles her nose. "Seven people might be a bit crowded. Why don't the gentlemen head through the children's ward first, and we'll take the adult wing, then switch?"

"Very prudent, Dr. Savary," Hughes says, to which she swats him lightly on the arm and motions them all in.

"I've told you a thousand times to call me Gwenna, you fuddy-duddy. Now go, and *no* lecturing the kids on civic duty this time." She shoos them down a cramped hall to the right, then leads Rapunzel, Verette, and Councilor Savary to the left.

Inside, it's just as close quarters as Gwenna had warned. Rapunzel can see the lines of what used to be a small clinic, voids where walls were knocked down, divots in the floor from when beds were spaced farther apart. A ramp leads upstairs, its wood a younger, paler hue than the floorboards. Everything spells the prioritizing of hasty expansion over aesthetics, and she can see why; there's a waiting room full of unhappy-looking patients, but nearly every bed is full.

"After the Night of the Poisoned Dagger," Rapunzel starts, only to pause when Dr. and Councilor Savary both look at her, alarmed.

"Father told them," Verette says quickly. "Please, continue."

"Was there a surge in illness?" Rapunzel asks. "The symptoms might help identify the poison." At Gwenna's bafflement, she adds, "I grew up with three books total, and one of them was on botany. I read the section on poisonous plants a *lot*."

Gwenna's mouth twists. "It's actually been the inverse. We took our health for granted, and when the Starlight Spring was cut off, it took a few years for the long-term effects to start showing. People were developing chronic conditions, seasonal illnesses hit them harder—all things we didn't realize the spring water was keeping at bay." She touches her own tight white rows of braided hair. "It used to be that the starlight turned everyone's hair white by eighteen. That was how you knew someone had come of age. But now it takes nearly twice as long."

Rapunzel looks around the room and finds shades of pewter, sterling, slate; only people past their mid-thirties have true snowy hair. Something about that itches in the back of her mind, but she can't put her finger on it.

The area upstairs seems intended for longer recuperation. Some patients are carefully walking around with a nurse's help, others sitting up and reading or bickering with their neighbors. Little personal touches mark the walls by each bed; Rapunzel spies the pale shell moths of verette charms dangling from bedposts or pins in the walls or even worn as necklaces, crafted with everything from crude hemp and clay beads to silk ribbons and crystal.

"It's been too long, Princess!" croaks an older man, grinning broadly, from a bed.

"It's been one week," Verette retorts with a grin of her own, "same as last time. How have you been?"

"We're feeling it everywhere," Councilor Savary says under her breath as Verette goes to speak with the old man. "The fountains haven't run with starlight for over twenty years. Oh, the sight of it was . . . almost as beautiful as Gwenna."

Her wife pushes her shoulder with an embarrassed smile. "You old sap." The smile fades a bit. "But you're right. The cost keeps growing. People aren't recovering the way they should."

"Fewer fish in the coves, smaller crops, even the hens don't lay as many eggs," the councilor says grimly. "We're making do with less and less, but we can't stretch much more."

Rapunzel twists a lock of hair around a finger, thinking. Something like a theory is snowballing in her head; she just knows it needs another push or two. "And the sunmills, they're tapping normal underground springs?"

"I would presume so?" Gwenna shrugs. As Verette rejoins them, she asks brightly, "So, Your Highness, do you think this year's coming of age ceremony will be the one?"

Verette's shoulders stiffen, just for a moment, as her gaze flicks to Councilor Savary. She laughs in a way that reminds Rapunzel of how she'd laugh at Gothel's "teasing." "Well, we'll see in a few days, won't we? But my father knows best."

"You'd think the king would give you more of a heads-up," Gwenna says.

Verette's empty smile doesn't crack. "You would think."

They continue through the rest of the second floor, pausing

to let Verette and the councilor check in with patients and staff. Rapunzel can't help overhearing more questions about the coming of age ceremony, if the throne will pass to Verette, what the first thing she'll do as queen is. She deflects them all with refrains of "We'll see" and "I trust my father" and "If he thinks it's time."

Rapunzel also can't help noticing more verette charms on the nurses and doctors, pinned to collars or swinging from belts. Unlike the variety of the patients' verettes, though, all of theirs seem to be crafted with the same midnight-blue cord and golden beads. Like they carry more meaning than a blessing.

They've just reached the top of another ramp leading back downstairs when a kerfuffle erupts below. Voices rise, Eugene's among them.

Rapunzel hurries down the ramp and finds him attempting to keep *The Tales of Flynnigan Rider* out of the grasp of a flailing elderly nurse. "*You* asked me to read a nap-time story to them," he grunts, trying to back up while avoiding the dozen or so children strewn about the room on heaps of pillows, cushions, and blankets.

"Not from *that* book!" The nurse makes another swipe for it. "The king banned it twenty years ago! We could get shut down just for having it on the premises, you foolish—"

"It's fine," Verette interrupts from behind Rapunzel. "It's all right—"

"I wanna hear about Flynnigan Rider!" shouts a girl of about seven, clutching a stuffed toy sea turtle to her chest.

"Yeah! Let him read!" another boy yells. Three children, all in the vague stage Rapunzel thinks is between ages three and five, take the opportunity to start wailing at the top of their lungs, setting off a chain reaction of hysterics through the children's ward.

The nurse also looks ready to cry as she scowls at Eugene. There's real trepidation in her eyes, like he's brought a wolf into the nursery. "Now look what you've done!"

"I didn't—it's just a *book*!" Eugene protests.

Hughes clears his throat from the doorway, steadfastly ignoring the toddler hammering his shins with a toy horse that, for reasons beyond Rapunzel, squeaks with each blow. "Minister Cressien stepped outside for some fresh air. Perhaps the young gentleman and I might join him."

The toddler loses interest in Hughes and shifts targets to Eugene, who neatly sidesteps him with a bewildered shrug. "Fine! Fine. I'm going."

Rapunzel squeezes his shoulder as he passes. "You didn't do anything wrong," she tells him.

Eugene briefly folds his fingers over hers. Then a shadow slips through his face, and he lets go. "It's not worth worrying over."

It's the same tone from the ball a week ago, when he said *Me? They're never going to like me.*

Rapunzel is starting to see the outline of an entirely different quandary. But before she can pull on that dangling thread, he's already left with Hughes.

"I WANNA HEAR ABOUT FLYNNIGAN RIDER!" howls the girl with the sea turtle.

"I'm sorry, Your Highness," babbles the nurse. "I didn't know, he just said it was a book from when he was a boy."

"I've never even heard of it," Verette says . . . a little too smoothly for Rapunzel to believe. She claps her hands and projects her voice over the clamor. "Do you want to hear a special song?"

It works. The older children feign disinterest, flopping back onto pillows, but the littler ones bounce with excitement. Gwenna leans in closer to Rapunzel, voice low. "These ones are either patients' children, or healthy enough to play under observation. Sometimes, they get a little . . . wound up."

"The princess has a knack with them," Rapunzel notes.

Gwenna nods. "We'll be very lucky to have her as queen."

That itch returns to Rapunzel's thoughts, just like with the tour yesterday. Something in this room isn't quite sitting right.

Verette crouches as the last of the children settles. "I learned this lullaby from my mother, Queen Gaelle, and she learned it from her mother, and from her mother's mother, all the way back to when the stardrop fell to Astera."

"That's *old*," murmurs a child from under a stack of pillows.

That's when Rapunzel sees it. Every child's hair has a delicate gradient; the ends, the oldest part of the hair, are the closest to the locks she assumes they were born with, from black to blond and every shade in between. But their roots are paler, less vibrant, starting to fade to white. If Eugene had grown up in Astera, she'd guess his hair would be a dusty taupe now.

Gwenna said the starlight used to turn their hair white by eighteen. That it takes nearly twice as long now.

Why does something about that feel *wrong*?

The answer's almost in reach, Rapunzel can feel it—

The first notes of Verette's lullaby float through the room.

And to Rapunzel's shock—she knows them.

"Starlight, gleam and glow," Verette sings. Goose bumps sweep over Rapunzel's arms. *"Moon, lend us your eyes."*

The words are different, but the melody—identical. Frightening, even, to hear someone else singing it for the first time in years. Once Gothel decided Rapunzel was old enough to do it herself, she never sang a note.

Whenever Rapunzel called on the power of the sundrop flower, she could swear she felt sunlight itself welling up in each vein and spilling down her hair. She hasn't felt it in over a month, except in her dreams.

But now—it's not the same, not blazing sun but a flicker of dawn—and yet the song calls to her. Her blood remembers. Her bones remember.

The room goes still, like they're all frozen in glass, until the last notes fade. Every child is asleep. Even the adults look calmer, steadier.

In the quiet and the clarity, Rapunzel's thoughts compose themselves into one corner of the picture:

Somehow, starlight *has* to still be in the water supply. The children's hair wouldn't be turning white without it, even if it's taking longer, like Gwenna said.

But the only source is the poisoned spring. And no one here is sick from poison.

And *that* means Rapunzel has a theory to chase.

She casually sidles to the nearby window, hoping to spot Eugene. This calls for skills outside of her wheelhouse, but firmly in his.

The garden outside is sadly devoid of Eugene. Still, a faint glint draws Rapunzel's eye to the windowsill.

Strange silver threads are climbing the glass outside, pressed to the panes.

Fascinating.

She leans closer. They look almost like the worms she saw yesterday—

Not worms, Rapunzel realizes. They stretch all the way down to the flower bed below the window and taper at the closest ends to a hair-fine point.

They're roots. Silver roots.

Rapunzel jerks back with a gasp, drawing Verette's notice. She turns to Rapunzel, and Rapunzel silently points to the windowsill.

Verette's eyes widen. She tiptoes around the sleeping children to stand by Rapunzel, and whispers, "Is that what—"

The roots shiver and whip back, shrinking into the soil until no trace of them remains.

". . . you saw," Verette finishes, blinking.

"In the royal gardens," Rapunzel confirms with barely muffled intrigue. Her botany book described plants that trap insects, and plants that roll up their leaves at a single touch, but those are simple, functional reactions. This seems different. Not a reaction, but an *answer.*

Either the same plant species grows both on the palace grounds *and* somewhere near the hospital, or . . .

Something has roots that run from the palace all the way here.

And the last time she saw them . . . they were stretching away from that iron door in the gardens.

That settles it.

It doesn't matter if she has to find a new path into the Starlight Spring, or break into the king's way with Eugene's help. Rapunzel is going to see the spring for herself.

Tonight.

TWELVE

EUGENE

"You know, if we keep meeting like this, I'm just going to assume you have a thing for me," Eugene declares as he once again finds himself blindfolded and bound to a chair in what he's now assuming to be the hideout of the People's Dagger. Or what's left of them.

This time, though, there's a bit of a complication.

It's not that he's been abducted again. In fact, he was gunning for that specifically. Third Street Hospital happens to sit near the same plaza as Herbert & Fitz. He let Hughes boot him and his book out because it gave Eugene an opening to go for a convenient walk "to clear his head" and provoke the People's Dagger into making a move.

The complication is that Cressien was supposed to keep Hughes occupied. And instead, somehow, Cressien is *also* bound and blindfolded in this room with Eugene. (He's presuming Cressien also gets a chair, but he's not sure. There was only the one last time.)

"Don't antagonize them," Cressien hisses.

"Too late for that," Torch says brusquely. They sound very self-assured for someone who spent the last five minutes berating their lackeys for grabbing Cressien along with Eugene. "Apologies for dragging you into this, Minister. And apologies again for taking you out."

There's a noise of startled protest from Cressien, then a guttural mumble and light snore. Eugene makes a mental note to figure out what they're using for knockout powder, because the only thing he's found to be as swiftly effective is a skillet with a potential side effect of brain damage.

"You can speak freely, Yappy," Torch continues. "He's out like a light. So you're accepting our offer?"

"I want to know more about my parents," Eugene says, dodging.

"Then let's start with your dinner with the king last night. What happened?"

If they know about that, then they have to have someone embedded even deeper in the palace than the stable master. Eugene decides to keep his cards close to his chest for now. "The king had to cancel. Something came up."

"That's all? What about the princess? Rapunzel?"

"We just returned to the guest wing." Eugene isn't lying; he's just leaving out the part where Enver arrested him for looking like a dead man.

"And then what?"

Eugene bristles. "And then you told me about my parents."

"I'll tell you more when you say something worth knowing," Torch growls.

"Not much of a deal, then, is it?" Eugene barbs. "What's to stop you from deciding nothing I say is good enough?"

"He does have a point," rumbles a voice—the same deep, smooth one that mentioned his resemblance yesterday. "Perhaps we might set some tangible benchmarks."

Torch snorts. "I don't need your help—"

Eugene makes an executive decision to cut to the chase. "So is this really the People's Dagger?"

The room goes quiet.

Finally, Torch asks, deadly calm, "How do you know that name?"

"I'll tell you," Eugene says at peak smarm, "when you say something worth knowing."

"Just give the boy something already," the unnamed voice snips.

There's a scrape and rustle that sounds like pacing. Torch sighs. After a long beat, they speak. "Your parents, Marietta and Andreas, owned and ran the printshop you saw."

"Herbert & Fitz." Eugene's pulse rises. He remembers Enver snarling, *I knew Marietta got away.*

So that much is true. Andreas and Marietta. Their names feel odd, distant, as personal as a street sign.

Torch continues, "They wrote *The Tales of Flynnigan Rider* under a pen name, A. Drew Rothar, and printed the book themselves."

"Which is apparently banned?" Eugene asks.

"Which Enver banned after the Night—" Torch's voice catches and stops.

". . . of the Poisoned Dagger," Eugene finishes, numb.

It's all real, then.

His parents really were part of a rebellion. They betrayed the king and queen. They may be the reason Third Street Hospital is overflowing even now.

His parents were traitors to the throne.

And how far can one apple land from the tree?

Forget sticking around after they return home. Eugene's not even sure he'll be let back on the ship.

"What did they tell you?" Torch asks.

Eugene flatly repeats everything Enver told them this morning. There should be no harm in that; it sounds like every Asteran knows the story, after all. But he can hear Torch pacing again, their footfalls scraping harder against the floor with Eugene's every word.

"He's lying," they bark when Eugene's done. "He's been lying for years."

"Where's the lie?" Eugene asks.

But Torch just says, "I need to talk to the others and figure out what to do with you."

TWELVE

"We're not releasing them?" queries the mysterious other voice.

"I don't know that we can anymore." There's a rattle of hinges, then quiet.

Eugene sucks in a breath. He—he can't think about his parents right now. This was just supposed to be a visit to fish for info, but now Cressien *and* indefinite captivity are in the mix.

And almost as unsettling as everything else . . . this feels *right*.

Another man might be sensibly distressed by the situation—and he is, at least a little—but this is what he used to live for: risk, danger, intrigue. His head feels clearer, sharper than it has in *weeks*.

And that might just be why, as Torch leaves, Eugene notes he only heard one set of footsteps.

He waits for a few moments, then says into the empty air, "You knew my parents."

The deep-voiced stranger, whom Eugene has mentally dubbed Stranger, shifts with a creak of a stool as if surprised to be addressed. They clear their throat. "I did."

"Anything you can tell me that *isn't* top secret?"

"I really ought not to," Stranger starts.

"Not even public knowledge stuff?" Eugene wheedles. "Things I should know, since I was born here?"

"You weren't," Stranger corrects him, then seems to realize their mistake and emits a resigned *ugh*. "I suppose, if we're not letting you go yet, I might as well . . . The last I saw Marietta, she was barely showing. She was involved with one of the Councilor of the East's subcommittees, and she and Andreas had become the queen and king's primary printers for royal records years before. They wound up getting close with the queen. Even gave her the first copy of *Flynnigan Rider.* And Enver was . . . different, then. Closer to the man he was as a duke."

"I heard the, uh, Directions Council can't overrule him anymore," Eugene prompts.

"Cardinal Council, and correct. Following what *he* dubbed the Night of the Poisoned Dagger, he enacted a series of 'emergency' measures that became permanent—taking the throne himself, appointing his own council, stripping us of the power to oppose him." Stranger shifts in their seat again. Eugene resists the urge to pick at that very intriguing *us* while Stranger's on a disclosure roll. "He claims he's only waiting to transition power until Verette's old enough to take the throne. And he let her grow into a leader the people love and hope for . . . so much so that that hope alone is enough to placate most who would resist. That's the game, you see. Because year after year, he says Astera's not stable enough to let her take over yet, and promises the next will be the one."

"But we were invited to Verette's coming of age ceremony," Eugene says, with no small degree of confusion.

Stranger lets out a bitter chuckle. "Dear boy . . . Verette has come of age at least four times. Perhaps six? I've lost count."

Before Eugene can ask what on earth *that's* supposed to mean, the door creaks. "We need you," Torch rasps.

Eugene hears Stranger's chair legs scrape. "Are you certain we can leave them—"

"Yes," Torch interrupts. "One's unconscious and they're both tied up."

"Say hi to Solena for me," Eugene hollers as the door closes.

Then he yanks his hands free of the shoddy bindings—the People's Dagger *really* needs to stop relying on a clove hitch—and pulls his blindfold off.

He turns to Cressien. The minister is already sitting upright. Eugene whips *his* blindfold off and finds him wide awake. Cressien drawls, "That was certainly illuminating."

"But they drugged you," Eugene says, utterly confounded.

"They held a kerchief over my nose and mouth," Cressien replies with a scathing lip curl. "I held my breath and went limp so they would think it worked. Now are you going to do something about these ropes or not?"

Another complication manifests once Eugene unties Cressien: The minister attempts to stand, and immediately topples into Eugene's side with a vexed *oof*.

"Excuse *you*," Eugene says blithely, propping Cressien up again.

Minister Cressien mutters, "Don't test me," then tries to take a step and collapses face-first into the ground.

"I thought you didn't inhale." Eugene helps him back to his feet.

"May have underestimated," Cressien wheezes, "the potency."

Eugene studies the room again. It looks practically the same as before: drab stone everything, with a stool in the far corner, the chairs they were tied to, and the rope. Not much to use, no idea when Stranger or Torch will return. He stuffs the rope into his satchel. "Can you walk?"

"Of course I can," Cressien says indignantly, only to lurch to starboard.

Eugene catches him by the elbow, then slings the minister's arm over his shoulders, keeping his voice low. "I didn't hear the door lock. If we wait, you might recover in time to help surprise them when they come back, but I think we're better off trying to sneak out while we have the chance."

"Agreed." Cressien doesn't sound thrilled—when does he ever?—but at least he stays ambulatory as Eugene maneuvers them to the door.

Eugene frees a hand to ease the door open and peers through the crack. The light fixtures in the empty hall ring a chord in his memory, but he doesn't spend time trying to place them, instead hunting for signs of life. Very, *very* faint voices are murmuring behind a closed door halfway down the passage.

"I think we can make it," Eugene whispers. "We just have to keep quiet."

"You know where you're going?" Cressien asks.

"Counted the steps last time. Ready?" At Cressien's nod, Eugene steps out, the minister staggering beside him. Eugene pulls the door shut and then sets off down the long, long hall, trying not to wince at every scuff and shuffle. The voices behind the door don't waver as they pass; Eugene can even pick out Solena's words.

"... barely seen my brother. Or half of his fleet. That *can't* be coincidence."

"But why go to the effort of bringing the princess *here?*" That's Stranger. "It makes no sense. And do we think it's coincidence he brought Andreas and Marietta's son?"

"Yes," Solena says firmly. "Ruvon, I left you behind for years to be sure that boy was out of Enver's reach."

"Apparently he became a common thief, so perhaps you ought to have stayed longer," Torch sneers.

Cressien makes an odd noise in his throat as they wobble out of earshot. Eugene just shakes his head. He's sure there's a well-intentioned *You have a fresh start; if you work hard enough you too can be a productive member of society* consolation speech in the minister's arsenal, but it can wait.

They've just reached the first right turn when he hears the clack of a sliding bolt. Voices and footfalls spill into the hall behind them. Eugene hurries them around the corner and hisses, "Get ready to run."

"Er," Cressien says.

Eugene hauls him along at an expedited hobble, counting each step. *Nineteen. Twenty.* There's the corridor opening he was waiting for on the right.

Shouts rise at their backs. They've found the empty room.

He shoves Cressien into the corridor and orders, "First right, then head straight for the stairs!"

Cressien stumbles onward. Eugene looks around for anything he can use to slow the People's Dagger and finds odd, low little pipes running on either side of the walkway. He grabs the rope from his satchel and ties a quick trip line, then follows Cressien. The minister's made it halfway to the stairs, steadying himself against the wall as he wobbles along as fast as he can.

Eugene hooks his arm through Cressien's and hurries on. "We'll go left at the top of the steps."

"You really—memorized the—whole way out?" Cressien puffs between breaths.

"What kind of amateur do you take me for?" Eugene stumbles to the landing. "No—don't answer that."

Behind them, there's a thud and a flurry of swearing. On the plus side, the trip line worked. On the downside:

"They went this way!"

Cressien's finally able to jog on his own. He follows Eugene through the last few turns, but they're not fast enough. Footsteps pound closer as they hurtle through a door and into the open air. Eugene finds a cramped little alleyway with no one in sight but him and Cressien. He runs for the nearest end before their pursuers can join them.

Light, prismed and honeycombed, shifts and warps over the cobblestones ahead, sweeping closer. Eugene looks up, confused—

And finds the crystal-lattice sail of a sunmill rotating overhead, refracting the daylight.

That's why he recognized the light fixtures—they were just like the palace sunmill's.

Eugene stores that fact for later dissection as he and Cressien careen into another alleyway, similarly narrow and inconveniently devoid of possible kidnapping-deterring witnesses. Two masked figures race into view after them, and Cressien says a very rude word Eugene didn't expect him to know.

Luckily, this time there's a rubbish bin at the end of the lane. Eugene flings it at the knees of the two lackeys on their trail, who jump back to avoid a spray of garbage and mysterious green-brown juice.

"We need to lose them somewhere," Cressien ekes out, breathing hard.

Instead of answering, Eugene racks his brains. The lane opens up to a plaza beyond this block—if they can reach that, they might lose their pursuers in the crowd, but they *have* to break the line of sight somehow—

A piercing, familiar wail yawps overhead.

And inspiration strikes.

"Come on," he grits out, and bolts for the plaza. He only pauses to knock over every rubbish bin he sees. Each time, he's rewarded with more mewling shrieks.

They reach the plaza and its shops and stalls. Another fun fact Eugene stows for later: It's the same plaza he saw yesterday, the one near Herbert & Fitz.

A bakery looms to his left. Eugene finds its rubbish bin, tears off the lid, and heaves its contents directly at their two pursuers.

Unsellable bread rains down around them in a shower of burnt loaves, stale breadsticks, and mold-spotted rolls.

And the flock of seagulls he's been accumulating descends in a screeching chorus.

"HA," belts someone nearby—no, not just someone, *Cressien*—as the People's Dagger lackeys are engulfed in a veritable hurricane of wings and open, snapping beaks.

Eugene pulls him around a stall, then down a street, and finally bears back toward Third Street Hospital. Once he sees the edge of a carriage at the corner, he flops against the wall out of sight. "Better catch our breath first."

"Agreed." Cressien mops his damp brow. Astera's still cooler than they're used to, but Eugene doubts the life of a high-level bureaucrat involves a lot of running. After a moment, Cressien asks, "Why didn't you try to find guards?"

"Not typically my gut instinct," Eugene points out. "But also . . . they answer to Enver. And if we had to explain why we were being chased, it'd lead them right to the People's Dagger. I don't trust the Dagger, but I'm not getting a great feeling about the king right now either."

"What makes you say that?"

Eugene's stomach twists . . . but whether or not Cressien agrees with his reasoning, he's still the son of rebels, so there's precious little approval to lose anyway. "Even if we don't buy what the Dagger said about him, he nearly put me in a dungeon last night just for looking like my parents. He took away the council's ability to refuse him. He banned a book that—that—" Eugene's voice hitches, and he flushes, but pushes on. "Whether or not my parents really wrote it, I read *Tales of Flynnigan Rider* a thousand times, sometimes for the other kids and sometimes for myself. And it's just about a man who goes on adventures, falls in love, sees the world—everything a kid could dream of. I don't know why he thinks that's dangerous."

Eugene half expects Cressien to scoff. Instead, the minister nods, sober as a judge. "Astera was always reclusive, but they still let their people visit other nations until about fifty years ago. Perhaps the danger was in letting children dream of leaving." Cressien rubs the bridge of his nose. "There's something else . . . but I believe we should continue this conversation with Princess Rapunzel."

"Good idea." Eugene peers down to the carriage. It looks like it's the only one still there, so he's guessing Rapunzel and Verette already returned to the palace. "If anyone asks, we got lost."

A minute later, Hughes is regarding the two of them with unbridled doubt. "You got . . . lost," the chamberlain repeats. "And nothing else occurred?"

"Nope," Eugene lies cheerfully. "Terrible sense of direction, that's all."

Before Hughes can figure out another way to cast aspersions on them, Cressien cuts in. "Is there a hazard His Majesty would wish us to be mindful of?"

Hughes looks annoyed. "Nothing His Majesty has not already disclosed to your party."

"After the unfortunate incident last night, I would hope we are operating in an environment of mutual trust," Cressien says with a smile narrow and thin enough to cut through glass.

"Indeed," Hughes returns with his own iron-tinged smile,

"one would hope that given Master Fitzherbert's connections, all possible caution is being exercised."

"Even were concerns regarding his connections *not* utterly baseless, I'm certain we have given no reason to believe caution is not being exercised."

"Yeah!" Eugene chimes in. The other two men look at him like he's just set a drink down on their chessboard. He embraces it. "Caution's being so exercised it's got a mean set of abs. Shall we be skedaddling?"

Hughes reaches for the carriage door. "As the young master wishes. Her Highness Princess Rapunzel wished to speak with you in the palace."

Eugene climbs into the carriage after Cressien and settles on a bench, crossing his legs. "Probably wants to ask what's so bad in *Flynnigan Rider* that it—got me . . . kicked out."

He falters.

Hughes has dropped into the bench across from them and is pulling the carriage door shut. For the first time, Eugene sees the back of his hand without the cover of a glove.

A familiar dark starburst scar splays over its ridges and veins.

He saw that scar yesterday. He saw *Hughes* yesterday, even if he didn't know it.

Because he was the first person Eugene saw operating the door of the People's Dagger's hideout.

Thirteen

Rapunzel

"And according to Councilor Laroux, even though Astera is a volcanic island, it contains limestone deposits, and the majority of the basalt is also relatively porous," Rapunzel whispers to Eugene, who is busily picking the lock on the iron door as she keeps a lookout for guards on their night patrols in the royal gardens. It was already hard enough to ditch the personal guards assigned to each of them the moment they set foot back in the palace. Even Minister Cressien couldn't shake his "additional security," despite his increasingly direct hints that he wanted a private word with her and Eugene.

(Part of Rapunzel can't ignore that King Enver promised *not* to assign more guards. The rest of her is insisting that there has to be a good reason. That she *can't* keep looking for Gothel in every shadow.)

Not that any of that could stop Rapunzel and Eugene from sneaking out. When Councilor Laroux confirmed earlier that the unremarkable iron door Rapunzel had discovered does in fact open to the king's path into the Starlight Spring, she probably assumed the regular guard patrols were enough of a deterrent, and the lock would do the rest.

Councilor Laroux probably needs to spend more time with Rapunzel before making that sort of assumption.

Rapunzel scours the darkened lawns for the torchlight of an approaching patrol and continues. "The groundwater's mostly in highly permeable karst aquifers, so when the rainy season increases the watershed's intake, any contaminants ought to be diffused throughout the whole system. Do you see?"

Eugene, who graciously did not ask too many questions when Rapunzel knocked on the glass of his bedroom window earlier tonight and asked him to help her break into the Starlight Spring, says under his breath, "Not even a little, Freckles."

"The Starlight Spring is connected to all the other water sources on the mainland. Starlight is in the whole water supply, even in small amounts—it's why even the children are still going gray. But if the starlight's in the water . . ."

". . . ah. The poison should have spread too." There's a faint click. Eugene eases his lockpicks from the keyhole and stands, then opens the door with a bow. "After you, my lady."

THIRTEEN

"*Thank* you, kind sir." Rapunzel curtsies, grabs the lantern she "borrowed" from a low-lying garden lamppost, and heads inside. "And yes, exactly. Something—"

She pauses as Eugene's fingertips brush her lips. He yanks the door shut, then holds his index finger to his own mouth. The orange glow of torchlight and muffled footsteps swell at the doorjamb behind them, then fade.

"You were saying?" Eugene asks once the patrol passes.

Rapunzel tucks her hair behind an ear, hands tingling. "Something must be giving King Enver a false positive. I want to get a sample to test ourselves."

She heads off down the dim stone tunnel, partially just to keep from getting too distracted. Even before guards were shadowing their every step, they hadn't had any true alone time since setting foot in Astera, and it doesn't seem like Enver's about to willingly let them off the leash anytime soon.

It's a familiar, unsettling kind of surveillance. Rapunzel remembers bargaining with Gothel for *years* for the "privilege" of hanging curtains over her bedroom doorway; a month of having real privacy was enough that Rapunzel doesn't ever want to give it up again.

"Do you think someone's messing with the tests?" Eugene asks.

"Councilor Laroux said the king does them himself every morning." Rapunzel swings the lantern around, studying the rock walls. Strange, shiny veins play through the rough-cut pillow basalt—maybe some kind of mineral? If they had more time, and she had her sketchbook . . . "It *does* sound like conditions in Astera are worsening, but I don't think it's due to contamination. I think something's been draining the Starlight Spring so less of it seeps into the other water sources. We know plants can absorb the magic, like the sundrop flower did, so my best guess is it's something like that."

"Because of the roots you saw?"

"Right. They seemed like they were reacting to the song like my hair used to."

The lantern light jumps abruptly around a corner. They've reached a fork in the tunnel.

"I thought they said every route but one was sealed off," Eugene says behind her.

"Maybe they just meant the entrances." Rapunzel lifts the lantern to study both options.

Eugene points to the ground on the left. "Look, there's moss growing on the path." Then he gestures to the barren stone on the right. "This one gets more use. If Enver's down here every day, that's gotta be it, yeah?"

"Good—" Rapunzel stops short as the hinges of the iron door creak.

Eugene steadies her elbow as they duck down the mossy path. Rapunzel finds the lantern's shutters and yanks them down, then plasters herself to the wall.

Footsteps thud closer. Rapunzel risks leaning out for a better look—and even though she can't quite make out the stout figure as it briefly passes, headed for the other branch of the path, she can tell that's not Enver's silhouette against the swaying torchlight.

Isn't the king supposed to have the only key into this passage?

Rapunzel doesn't even have to say a word. Once the coast is clear, Eugene whispers, "So we're following, right?"

"Right."

She tweaks the lantern shutters to let only the thinnest hint of light out, then heads after the newcomer. The path doesn't branch out again, but there's no telling how close they are to catching up. Neither she nor Eugene makes a sound—until Rapunzel stops in her tracks, and Eugene bumps into her with a quiet *oof.* It's her turn to hold a finger up.

For a long breath, she's half convinced she imagined it. Then she hears it again: a rumble of voices.

"I'm starting to get the feeling they did not in fact seal off every entrance," Eugene says under his breath. "Want to go back?"

Rapunzel grips the lantern tighter. "No. We'll just be careful."

They keep moving, taking extra care to hold the light low and avoid stepping on any noisy loose gravel. The voices continue to echo back to them, indistinct but growing louder. Finally they turn a corner and find firelight spilling out from an entrance cut into the passage wall—firelight and the dull roar of faraway water.

Rapunzel sets the lantern down a few paces back, close

enough to light the last few feet, far enough that it won't draw notice. Then she and Eugene creep closer.

When she carefully peers around the timber bracing the entrance, she finds it's the top of a ramp leading down into the biggest cave she's ever seen—almost an underground harbor. At least a dozen ships are bobbing at a long torchlit dock below while crews move crates and barrels into cargo holds. A stocky man is pacing over the planks, shouting orders—the man they followed here.

She recognizes him now from when they arrived and she was introduced to the king's council. "That's the Master of Seas, Councilor of the West, Erwan Persevault."

Eugene's breath hitches audibly. "I heard Solena say something about her brother's fleet." He squints. "She used 'Vald' for her last name back home—maybe that was short for Persevault. But why on earth are they hiding ships down here?"

Rapunzel scours the dock but doesn't see anything obvious. She waits until they've retreated to the lantern to answer, still keeping her voice hushed. "Maybe it's just so people underestimate the size of their navy?"

"There *has* to be an easier way to do that." Eugene looks past the entryway in the wall; the corridor carries on into the dark. "Onward, or back to the fork . . . wait. If what we're looking for is growing from the spring, could you follow the roots?"

The lantern light catches ridges in the stone wall, and Rapunzel frowns, running her fingertips along a streak worming through the basalt. It's not limestone, not any kind of rock she recognizes—and she memorized her geology book's table of rock varieties when she was eight, so she knows her schist.

She draws a breath, then, as quiet as she can, hums the opening stanza of the lullaby.

Light sparks beneath her hand, shimmering along the streak. It spreads up, branches through the walls, and slows to a pulsing halt no more than a few paces away. After a moment, it fades.

But not before she sees the fraying pattern of roots in the glow. And they look like their source is back the way they came.

"Come on," she whispers.

Once they return to the fork in the path, she hums the lullaby again and doesn't stop this time. She doesn't even have to touch the walls for the roots to ignite, glimmering with a silvery iridescence that reminds her of the white shells, and shining brightest around her. Even the moss clustered on the unused path pulses with a faint green-gold glow.

For a moment, she feels almost upsettingly . . . at home.

Not the way her parents' palace feels like home, but the bitter way cold flagstones under her soles sometimes remind her of the tower's tiles in winter—how she'd huddle by the fireplace until the floor's chill didn't bite. Or how petrichor reminds her of watering the window planters in summer, and that she's not sure how to ask her parents if she can go get them, if the petunias are even still alive.

That's the problem with truly seeing where you grew up from the outside. You have to figure out how to explain that when something feels like home, that's not always a good thing.

"How are you doing this?" Eugene sounds almost awed. He *dah-dah-daahs* a few notes under his breath, with no reaction from the roots. "It's not just the song—it's responding to *you*."

Rapunzel pushes the treacherous nostalgia away and starts methodically picking her way around the clumps of moss. "I think it, er, translates? From the sundrop flower? It doesn't feel the same, just . . . familiar."

She hums another line to light the way and can almost picture her hair, not these roots, lining the walls. It's a faint echo of when the magic used to *sing* through her, nowhere near enough to heal people the way she once could. But . . .

King Enver said a power like the sundrop would forever change her. Maybe he was right.

It's an idea that feels like home. And not in the good way.

Rapunzel decides she needs to think about something else. "So where did you sneak off to while we were at the hospital?"

"Well, I learned something new today, and that is that Hughes definitely can't be trusted." Eugene fills her in on the rest of his and Cressien's escapade as he follows her up the path and concludes with "So I don't think we can trust Enver, either." For some reason, her heart twists. Eugene doesn't miss it. "What's the matter?"

Rapunzel's been walking her fingers over the walls, observing how light ripples from them whenever she touches a root. The farther they've gone, the thicker they've gotten, until there's less exposed stone than root. She swallows. It's not the easiest thing to explain, even to Eugene; she's not quite sure she understands it herself. “I want to—to fix this,” she stumbles. “I miss being able to fix things. And when Enver told us about the spring this morning, he sounded so . . . hurt.”

Eugene catches her shoulder. When she looks back, he cups her cheek in a hand. “Even if you still had your hair, you know this wouldn’t be easy to fix. And it wouldn’t be your job, either.”

He has a point, and she wishes he didn’t. “I just don’t know what to do.”

“Let’s start by getting your spring water sample,” he says, planting a kiss on her forehead, “and leaving the creepy caves. Then we’ll figure it out from there.”

She laughs at that and makes herself keep going up the coiling pathway. “Fine. So . . . Hughes. You said the leader wasn’t there this time. What if it’s him?”

“Could be,” Eugene says uncertainly. “They wore a mask with a voice changer and big bulky robes. But they didn’t talk like him, if that makes sense.”

“Moonface could be trying to throw us off.” Rapunzel hums more of the lullaby. Even more of the tunnel lights up this time, the roots like frozen lightning striking all around them.

“Moon Eye,” Eugene corrects. “The mask is shaped like a moon eye moth. Big crescent marks on the wings.” He winces as an enormous root by his head swells with light almost too bright to see. “Freckles—how do you feel about that nickname, by the way?”

Rapunzel considers. “Better than Punzie?”

"Oof. We can do better. Anyway, how *big* do you think these plants are?" He ducks under another huge root, this one nearly as wide as his torso.

"Maybe the starlight's making them grow bigger than they should," Rapunzel speculates.

Then the next turn of the passage gapes into an opening, and she finds she's half right.

They climb over another set of roots and into another cave, not as immense as the underground harbor but still yawning broad and high, nearly four stories by Rapunzel's estimate. A path has been cut into the wall ringing the hollow, with stairs descending to an expanse of bare wet stone at the bottom. A glittering gradient marks the history of a retreating waterline, the highest levels just a faint dusting, the lowest stripe of residue sparkling like diamonds along the floor. More roots of every size, some even bigger than Maximus, shape a drunken lattice over every surface.

And at the heart of that lattice, on the far side of the cavern, shines a single massive tree.

Clearly it was never meant to be here, in what should be a lively subterranean spring. It's growing around what looks like the remains of one of the giant water screws Rapunzel saw on her sunmill tour, the enclosing barrel reduced to rusting peels of iron, the screw shaft's spiraling ribs strangled by a gnarled, bulbous pewter trunk. There's something squat and stunted about the proportions of its branches, even though they're jammed tight up against the cave's stalactites as if trying to push the lid off a pot. The dark leaves, all vibrant indigos, violets, even inky blacks, grow in billowing clusters of small round blots. Like its roots, the tree marbles with pearly light, and when Rapunzel whispers *"Starlight, gleam and glow,"* luminous ripples race over every twig.

Then, just as she spots a series of divots in the ground, the ripples converge on a single point. Crystalline light bursts from a tiny dangling shape on the lowest branch, blindingly bright.

"Gah!" Rapunzel throws a hand up to block the blaze. By the time she can see again, Eugene's moved past her, headed for the stairs. "Eugene, wait!"

"I'm just going to check out what that thing was," he calls back to her.

Rapunzel rushes after him and catches his elbow just as he reaches the bottom step. "Stop! Look—" She points to the ground.

It's not stone, but slick mud.

And there's already one trail of shallow footprints leading to the tree and back.

Someone's already been down here.

"Hooo, good catch." Eugene steps backward up the stairs. "But that means someone already *knows* about the tree. And if they aren't bothering to cover their tracks, they don't expect to get caught."

"I think . . . this is what's left of the spring." Rapunzel's stomach flops. "This tree is absorbing almost all the water and starlight before it reaches the rest of the island. And . . ." She peers across the mud, to the tiny ball still shining in the tree. "I think that's an *apple*."

"Either Enver's been lying about testing the spring," Eugene says grimly, "or he's been lying about the poison."

"It—it could be a way to filter out the poison. Plants can absorb toxins." Rapunzel doesn't know why she keeps looking for a way out for the king. Maybe it's because she's tried so hard not to see Gothel in him, to leave the tower behind. Maybe it's because she wants to find a wound she can still heal, even without the magic of the sundrop.

Maybe that's why he showed her a wound as big as a kingdom.

"Maybe." Eugene, to his credit, keeps nearly all the skepticism from his voice. "So we've got secret creepy caves, secret creepy giant apple tree, and—well, I guess the boats aren't creepy, just secret. If we poke around much more without looping in Cressien, he's going to strangle us with his crochet yarn."

Eugene is rarely cautious on principle, so Rapunzel takes that as a good indicator they've pushed their luck enough for the night. "Okay. We have to rest up for the reception ball tomorrow anyway."

Eugene catches her hand with a grin and starts leading her back up the stairs. "Please. I'm a professional liar—you'll have to try harder than that. I don't believe you're going to sleep a wink."

Rapunzel, in fact, does not.

She stays up nearly to sunrise filling her sketchbook with the images crowding her head like overgrown roots: the ships, the tree, the caves. The sunmills with their crystal sails. The verette charms at the hospital. Her feet are dirty, her hands are smudged with color and graphite, and Pascal is napping on the bedspread; she feels almost like her old self again, just without the weight of her hair.

But after she makes herself finally put the sketchbook down and wash up for bed (a few hours' sleep is better than none), one more root of a thought keeps digging persistently around her skull.

A month ago, she gained a loving family, a new home she can *leave*, the freedom of moving without seventy feet of potential tangles.

She hasn't really let herself look at what she . . . lost.

No more easy fixes for scrapes and burns. No more quiet mornings knowing it was just her and Pascal and a chore list and then—whatever she felt like. No more little life in a little tower in a little valley.

Rapunzel wouldn't trade what she has now for anything, but sometimes she misses parts of that little life.

When she falls asleep, she dreams of Gothel again, but not the withered, vicious witch in her last moments. Not even the Gothel who called her clumsy and underdressed, who told her she couldn't survive in the real world. She dreams instead of the Gothel who brought her pigment made from white shells, and let her paint flowers and flourishes on every inch of the tower, and tucked her in to bed every night for years.

The one who made Rapunzel feel like a beloved daughter whenever she wanted to use her.

It may have been a lie, selfish beyond measure. But for eighteen years, it felt true.

✧ ✧ ✧

"We don't have much time," Cressien hisses, hours later.

He's huddled with Rapunzel and Eugene in the empty vestibule outside the palace ballroom. King Enver and Princess Verette just swept out the door to go formally begin the official reception ball honoring Rapunzel's delegation, and Eugene and Rapunzel will follow for an opening dance.

They have only a few moments before guards come to fetch them. And it's the first time the three of them have been unmonitored all day.

"We have a *lot* to catch up on," Eugene starts, but Cressien cuts him off.

"It's Enver," the minister says. "The man at the hideout yesterday said Enver used to be a duke. And the last our kingdom heard from Astera before this was the announcement of the marriage of Queen Gaelle and *Duke* Enver, remember?"

Rapunzel remembers Verette's saying *I learned this lullaby from my mother, Queen Gaelle.* But—"Wasn't the announcement sent a long time ago?"

Cressien nods with an air of *now you're catching on.* "Over fifty years ago. Before your parents were even born."

"And the same guy said Verette's come of age at least four times," Eugene chips in, rubbing a thumb along the line between his brows. "She remembers a lullaby from her mother, but didn't the queen die twenty years ago?"

"Dr. Savary said Asterans usually come of age at eighteen, when their hair's completely white." Rapunzel feels like the picture's in her head, but the sketch isn't coming out right. "Verette's hair isn't exactly white, though. It's more multicolor, like—"

Rapunzel catches herself.

Like the roots.

Like the shells.

"Like starlight," she whispers.

The door swings open. A guard calls from the hall, "It's time."

Eugene wraps his hand around hers and says quietly, "If you want to make a run for the ship, we can probably make it."

And then what? Return home a failure, after she pushed to go? Her parents will never let her out of the castle again.

Rapunzel shakes her head. "We can do this. It's just a few more days."

"Let's go, Your Highness," the guard urges.

The walk to the ballroom is short, and then they're ushered through velvet drapes and into a grand hall. Painted stars and their paths dance across the vaulted indigo ceiling in silver and gold, snowy alabaster columns glow by candlelight, and intricate spirals of pale polished stone inlays lace the floor. A glittering crowd wreathes the room, a few now-familiar faces of councilors among them.

In the middle of the dance floor wait King Enver and Princess Verette.

It's just like the ball that started this entire mess. This time, she has to do better than just "have fun." Rapunzel's palms start to sweat. Every step of the waltz has fallen out of her head. Everyone is staring at her. Her violet satin gown feels like it's clinging to her legs, the tiara on her head too heavy, too tight. Even the slippers she's finally broken in feel too smooth to get a grip on the glossy floor.

She remembers her father just last week, telling her, *Sometimes people stare because they like what they see.*

Maybe it's like the birthday ball—but she *did* make it through the opening waltz just fine. She's practiced her steps. She knows what she's doing.

King Enver bows. Her curtsy is impeccable. And when the orchestra begins to play, Rapunzel steps into the dance just the way she remembers.

"I hope you've enjoyed your time in Astera thus far, Your Highness." There's a faintly wooden edge to Enver's voice.

Rapunzel tries to study his features without being obvious. She's heard of infants being betrothed, but even if that were the case with Gaelle and Enver, he doesn't look like he's fifty. White hair aside, he doesn't even look a day over forty. "I've already learned so much," she says, hedging.

"Yes, I imagine it may get overwhelming." His words have a

familiar clip, one she can't quite place. "Shut away for eighteen years. The real world must be a bit much to take, sometimes."

Rapunzel's neck prickles. She tells herself it's just the cold. "Sometimes."

"You know," Enver says, swinging her into a turn, "something occurred to me, and I wonder if you or your parents have considered it. Your magic came from the sundrop flower, correct?"

Eugene and Verette are waltzing nearby. Rapunzel feels Verette's stare.

"Yes, but it's gone now." *Like I said yesterday,* Rapunzel silently adds.

"How did that happen?"

Rapunzel turns a wince into an uncomfortable shrug. "It went away when my hair was cut—"

"No," Enver interrupts. "I mean the flower. It was also destroyed?"

Rapunzel swallows. "I—I'm not sure—I think so—"

"Did you ever return to where the magic flower was found?" Enver pushes. "Perhaps another grew in its place. You might be able to reclaim your power."

It's the same hint of impatience that Gothel used to have. Rapunzel hears it now. She'd climb in the tower window and rush through the perfunctory small talk, not really listening, then shove the hairbrush into Rapunzel's hand.

Verette's voice suddenly cuts in. "I believe it's time for us to trade partners."

She and Eugene have moved closer. Eugene catches Rapunzel's eye with an *everything good?* look; Verette's expression has regained that manufactured calm.

Enver's calm, however, seems to be wearing thinner. "Not for a few more turns, sweetheart."

"The song's halfway through—"

"Now, Verette, really. In a few days, you'll have a whole hall full of people giving you blessings and invitations and pledging their deeds in your name." A trace of reproach steals through Enver's face. "If you can't let someone else be the center of attention for one night, perhaps you're not as ready for the crown as I thought."

Verette goes pale.

Rapunzel may have tried her best not to see Gothel in Enver's actions. But she hears Gothel in his every word.

She doesn't have a frying pan handy, so she deploys the next best thing and steps with all her weight on Enver's boot toe.

"Oh, I am *so* sorry," she lies as he stumbles and lets go of her. "I'm still learning how to dance! Madame Frangeline would kill me if she knew!"

Eugene turns his face away, transparently trying not to laugh. Verette gawks at Rapunzel like she's grown a unicorn horn, the white shell moths on her hair ornaments twinkling under the chandeliers.

Something falls into place, then, the missing piece of the greater picture. It's so enormous, Rapunzel both resents that it took so long to see it and understands precisely why it did.

She looks from Enver to Verette, and makes a decision Cressien may yet strangle her for.

Maybe she doesn't have the political savvy just yet; maybe she doesn't have the magic she used to. But she still wants to help. She *can* still help.

Even though it went unspoken, Rapunzel swore a week ago she'd make her mother proud; that after eighteen years, she'd be everything they've dreamed of. And she never, *ever* breaks her promises.

"I'd like to make a pledge early," Rapunzel announces, raising her voice so it carries through the entire room. The orchestra falls silent. Eugene looks at her like she might have actually smuggled in a frying pan.

And to be fair, diplomatically speaking, this is pretty much the same thing.

She takes a deep breath, knowing her words will reach everyone in the ballroom, and declares: "In honor of the future queen's birthday, I, Princess Rapunzel, vow to restore the Starlight Spring."

FOURTEEN

EUGENE

"The sheer *audacity*."

Eugene tries not to smirk into an outrageously tiny sandwich. The reception ball has kicked off in earnest now, and Rapunzel has no shortage of intrigued partners on the dance floor—and no shortage of skeptics on its edges, such as the gossips clustered around the refreshments. Most of them take one look at him and lower their speculations to snide whispers, but others clearly want to make themselves heard.

Such as: Councilor Persevault, snarling into his champagne, "What would an outsider know about our island? Absurd!"

Councilor Laroux, the recipient of his tirade, shrugs. "The

princess has a respectable command of the related fields of study. Perhaps she sees something we don't."

Eugene decides to be an unmitigated stinker and saunters up to Persevault. The man bristles, glowering. Even though he sees the physical similarity to Solena, the councilor's all puff and no spinach, hand giving an underbaked twitch toward a saber hilt too polished to have seen much, if any, use.

Eugene holds his glare. Then, with utmost schmooze, he says, "Pardon my reach," and leans over to snag a canapé from the platter behind Persevault.

"You are pardoned," Persevault returns icily.

As Eugene stuffs the canapé into his mouth and turns on a heel, he sees Cressien deep in conversation with Councilor Teophine. Cressien's face is showing the ironfisted neutrality of a man who's dying inside. Eugene can't blame him, considering they didn't make it to the "By the way, there's a giant mutant apple tree guzzling all the water from the Starlight Spring" segment of their brief pre-ball conference. He decides to have mercy on the minister and at least let him know Rapunzel's vow is actually feasible.

On the way over, however, he gets distracted, first by the allure of a cheese fountain, and then—the quiet orders being given to two of the guards lining the wall behind him.

". . . when Princess Rapunzel leaves, she's to be intercepted at the guest wing and brought directly to the king for questioning. No harm is to come to her. Understood?"

"Yes, sir."

Eugene's chest tightens. He makes himself linger casually by the cheese fountain—not *that* big of an ask, really—but watches out of the corner of his eye. A guard with a captain's sash walks past, heading for another pair of guards, no doubt with the same orders.

Eugene finds Enver in the crowd. He looks pale, drawn, one hand fussing with the buttons of his waistcoat while he babbles away to Hughes.

Enver's been lying for years. Decades. And now that Rapunzel's calling his bluff, that raw edge is back in the king's eyes: desperation.

Cressien can wait. Eugene needs to get Rapunzel out of here, *fast*.

Can he feign sick? No, Dr. Savary is here; she'll catch him faking. Is there a terrace they can slip away to? No, the ballroom only has one far wall of windows overlooking Astera—no way out but the handful of guarded exits.

His eyes land on the dark spikes of champagne bottles in ice buckets at the far end of the refreshment spread. An idea sprouts. It's risky, and if he gets caught—

Well. There's no one to impress here. Even the rebels think he's nothing more than a common thief.

Eugene swipes a final wedge of bread through the cheese fountain and mutters, "I'm so sorry. You were too good for this world."

Two minutes of discreet tampering and light larceny later, Eugene has helped himself to a champagne bottle and

Persevault's ornamental saber, and destabilized the cheese fountain's supportive base. He takes up position near the pyramid of champagne flutes and waits until he sees the cheese fountain start teetering.

Just as it begins to tip over, Eugene runs the saber up the bottle seam just the way an old friend taught him—

And the bottle mouth shears off with a crack, firing the cork and broken glass tip into the pyramid of glasses.

The champagne flutes descend in a terrible shattering cascade. It's immediately followed by the cheese fountain explosively toppling to the floor, dragging a corner of the tablecloth with it. More platters and chafing dishes fly into the air with metallic clangs as screams break out. For a final touch, Eugene ducks behind a flower arrangement, pitches his voice into a falsetto, and yells, *"THE PEOPLE'S DAGGER!"* before shoving the arrangement into another table.

And that turns it from a mishap to a stampede.

Most of the attendees are on the dance floor and too far away to notice anything but the crashing and screams. Cries of *"The People's Dagger!"* strike a match through the ballroom. Every guard converges on the king, searching the pandemonium for enemies that aren't there. King Enver himself has gone from pale to bone white, eyes wide, expression terrible, almost—resigned. Not the scrambling panic Eugene expected.

But what matters is finding Rapunzel. He searches the crowd for her sparkling tiara and finds it—slipping through a far door, Verette all but dragging her out.

A hand locks around Eugene's upper arm. "What in the name of every blessed corner of the continent do you *think* you're doing?" Cressien hisses.

"Getting us out of here." When Cressien gives him a non-plussed look, Eugene snaps, "To look for *white shells*, I guess? Why else?"

"We are so far beyond white shells I'm going to die happy if I never hear of them again. Where is the princess?"

"With Verette. I'll get her and meet you in the guest wing." Eugene takes off before Cressien can protest and weaves through the chaos after them as fast as he can. He makes it into the hall just in time to see Rapunzel's purple skirts fluttering around a distant corner. The palace is flooded with frantic guests rushing away from the ballroom and guards trying to push through toward it, so by the time Eugene reaches that corner, Verette and Rapunzel are even farther ahead, hurrying under a grand archway Eugene recognizes from two nights ago—the entrance to the royal wing.

Even though he runs as fast as he can, they're already out of sight when he enters the wing. Luckily, the guards also seem to have been summoned from their posts, so no one's there to question him as he trots down one corridor, then another. The furnishings are getting more lavish, so he's close to the royal living quarters, but there's no sign of either princess.

He's perilously close to shouting *Cerulean and cobalt are the same blue* so he can find Rapunzel by her outraged yelling—and then footsteps echo down the hall. Not the skip-shuffle of slippers, but the heavy slap of boots, moving fast and getting close. Eugene swiftly ducks through the nearest door and shuts it behind him.

When he looks up, he sees moonlight streaming through a wall of windows . . . and landing on a desk inlaid with the royal seal in gold.

Eugene holds his breath as the footsteps pass, and takes a better look at the room. It's hard to make out much by the full moon, but he can see the furniture is ornate, richly made, worthy of a king. A portrait of Enver hangs on the far wall, directly across from the desk, near bookcases stuffed with excruciatingly boring-looking books on topics like Asteran law and political theory. The desk itself sports only an ink and quill stand and an unlit candle that looks like it's got one last late night left.

This has to be the king's personal study.

And that means Eugene has a chance he almost certainly will not have again.

Rapunzel's with Verette, and the guards are too distracted to bring her in for questioning. A few minutes should be fine.

Eugene has been in many wealthy peoples' homes, usually for illegal reasons, and almost always in pursuit of things they tried to keep locked down. If Enver is hiding something, and there's any kind of paperwork to that effect, it'll be somewhere out of the way of a servant casually cleaning the study, and inaccessible to someone casually snooping.

But a paranoid man like Enver? He'll keep his secrets close.

Eugene eyeballs the bookshelves; too open, too easy. A compartment behind Enver's portrait would be too much of a pain to get to. The desk, however . . .

The golden inlay flashes in the moonlight as Eugene closes in. The desk has drawers on either side of the chair well, and he's not surprised to see keyholes on the top two, nor to find those drawers locked. The thing is, he's *certain* those aren't worth his time, because no one becomes as powerful as Enver by keeping their secrets somewhere so obvious.

Instead Eugene yanks open the other drawers, prodding for panels at the back or bottom. No dice. There *is* a noticeable heft to the desktop itself, just thick enough to raise Eugene's suspicion. He quietly knocks on the underside of the panel, tapping in circles until there's a hollow thud.

There's a compartment. Now to get to it.

The release mechanism can't be too conspicuous, *or* too inconvenient. Eugene studies the desktop, checks under the inkpot and candle . . . then sees a faint gleam on the inlay. The western star has been worn a little more than the others, polished by regular contact.

Eugene jabs a finger into it. He hears a click, then a *clunk*. A panel in the desktop sinks and slides back to reveal a velvet-lined box containing four pieces of parchment, each of their wax seals broken.

Three are addressed to Rapunzel's parents and bear Cressien's insignia as the minister of diplomatic affairs. Enver has been intercepting Cressien's reports, every single one.

The last letter is addressed to Rapunzel. And the remains of the seal belong to her mother.

Eugene stuffs the messages into his doublet and starts to return the panel, then pauses. At this point he's fairly confident tonight ends with them being smuggled onto the royal galleon to make a swift getaway, but on the slim chance he's wrong, they need a scapegoat for when Enver discovers the messages missing.

The first idea to come to mind feels . . . oddly appropriate.

Eugene pulls a scrap of blank parchment from one of the other drawers, then uses the quill and ink to scribble a tiny, crude dagger.

The parchment goes in the compartment, the panel goes back into its place in the desktop, and Eugene goes straight for the door, waiting only to listen for voices or footsteps before heading back into the corridor.

But this time, when he rounds a corner into a long hallway, he finds Councilor Erwan Persevault pacing toward him from the opposite end. Persevault's face turns stormy. He breaks into a run, shouting, "*You!* Andreas's boy! I saw you!"

Eugene backs up, hands raised. Escaping by sea will be a *lot* harder if he can't get the master of Astera's armada off his case. "What? I'm just looking for Rapunzel—"

"Don't lie to me," the councilor snarls. "I saw your little stunt with the champagne! You started this whole mess!"

"Are we sure?" Eugene falters. "It might not have been champagne. It doesn't count if it's not from the region—"

"It was a misunderstanding." Hughes's voice cuts down the hall as he strides up behind Eugene and clamps one bony hand around his shoulder. "Her Highness asked young Fitzherbert here to show her how to saber a bottle of champagne, and the boy was confused. You know how hard it is to hear in a ballroom. Now please excuse us—the princesses are very eager to make sure he's unhurt."

Before Erwan or Eugene can object, Hughes pushes him onward. Eugene does wait until Erwan is out of earshot to mutter, "I appreciate the save, but if you're taking me to Moon Eye, I'd rather just take my chances jumping out the window, thanks."

"Of course I'm taking you to Moon Eye, you fool," Hughes drones, and to his credit, he doesn't even sound surprised to be called out as a member of the People's Dagger. He steers Eugene into a parlor that's almost insultingly larger than the guest wing's, one that's leaned really hard into butterfly motifs.

"I'm not leaving Rapunzel on her own." Eugene digs his heels in. "Enver wanted to question her, and I'm not going *anywhere* until—"

"She's safe."

The familiar distorted voice comes from *behind* him.

He turns and finds Moon Eye, mask, hooded cloak, and all, standing with their hands on their hips in the yawning void of a hidden passage, one that grows only wider as the bookcase that was obscuring it continues to grind aside.

Eugene sorts his new avalanche of questions in descending

order of priority; Rapunzel takes precedence over Secret Tunnel in the Parlor at the moment. "How do you know that? The last I saw her, she was with Verette."

Moon Eye hesitates and looks over their shoulder.

"If you think I'm leaving this palace without her—"

Rapunzel herself steps out of the passage, wearing the same kind of gray cloak as Moon Eye, a torch in one hand.

"I'm fine, Eugene," she says. Moon Eye pushes their hood back and lets a long, pale, iridescent braid spill over a shoulder. Then, as his head reels and the mask falls, Rapunzel adds, "Because *this* is Verette."

FIFTEEN

RAPUNZEL

Rapunzel points to the moth charms still in Princess Verette's hair. They didn't have time to change when Eugene threw the ball into chaos; she just hissed, *"I know you're Moon Eye,"* to Verette, at which point the princess hauled her over to the royal wing. Or, more accurately, a hidden passage in the royal wing, one that connects to the guest wing, among other places. They spared a moment to collect a drowsy Pascal and Rapunzel's sketchbook from her room—if their quarters are searched, Rapunzel doesn't want them finding her drawings of the tree—and then bolted back for cloaks and Verette's mask. "These charms are called verettes. And this kind of moth—"

FIFTEEN

"Is a moon eye moth. Well, don't I feel sheepish." Eugene looks from Hughes to Verette, connecting the dots, as Rapunzel passes Verette the torch. It seems like decorum has largely flown out the window with the introduction of a masked vigilante princess, so Rapunzel might as well ditch her shoes.

Verette's already rattling off orders to Hughes. "Tell Father that to make up for the disaster of the ball, I'm taking them out on my pleasure barge for the evening. If you can find Minister Cressien, send him down to the palace docks too. Master Sulian's already gone to get Leona. We just need to buy time for Father to cool off."

"*Will* he cool off?" Rapunzel asks.

"He ordered the guards not to hurt you, only take you to him for questioning," Eugene points out.

"Oh, Eugene. *That's* why you made a scene?" Rapunzel stands on her tiptoes to kiss his cheek. "My hero."

"I told Councilor Persevault you asked Fitzherbert to saber the champagne and he misunderstood, if it comes up," Hughes drawls. "Any further instructions, Your Highness?"

Verette shakes her head. "Just—be safe. You know how he gets."

Hughes's mouth pulls tight. "I do. Safe travels to you as well."

He leaves, shutting the parlor door behind him, as Verette motions to the empty tunnel. "Follow me. While we're walking, you need to remain completely silent, and move as quietly as you can. Any questions?" Eugene opens his mouth and she says quickly, "No, it's not because of giant rats. Those were just made up for *Tales of Flynnigan Rider*."

"You've read it!" Eugene says delightedly.

Verette rolls her eyes and passes the torch back to Rapunzel long enough to pull her moth mask back on. "Only like a hundred times. Now no more talking until I give the all clear."

It's a long, taut walk in the narrow tunnel, and all Rapunzel is certain of is that they're headed downhill. The passage connects to a wider stone tube, and at first she assumes it's a pipe, then rules that out because it's bone dry, then reassesses when she sees the same glittering residue on the walls as the fading waterline of the Starlight Spring.

They're traversing the pipes that feed the fountains. The ones that haven't run for two decades. No wonder they're all parched.

It isn't until they reach a junction and switch to a different set of pipes that Rapunzel understands why Verette wants them to keep quiet. As she pads beside a thin trickle of entirely mundane water, sprinklings of dust and dirt periodically rain down from above them. *Something* is moving in the earth overhead. And Rapunzel has a pretty good idea what.

Finally they reach a metal ladder that stretches to an iron grate. Verette climbs up, pushes it aside, and waits for Rapunzel and Eugene to follow. They've emerged into a dark, close alleyway; the briny mist, creak of timbers, and slop of waves betray how close they are to the shore.

FIFTEEN

Verette moves the grate back into place, then leads them out onto the long arm of a lonely dock, and sighs, "We're in the clear. Sorry for the quiet, we can't risk alerting—"

"The roots?" Rapunzel blurts out.

". . . my father," Verette finishes slowly. "What do you mean, the roots?"

"The silver roots from the tree. They're picking up vibrations." Rapunzel doesn't see any comprehension in Verette's eyes. "They run at least as far as Third Street Hospital."

Verette runs a hand down her face. "Of course, *that's* why it's safe to talk on the water—right. Okay. We have a *lot* to catch up on." She points to lights glimmering through the fog, drawing closer. "My pleasure barge is about to pass us. We'll jump on from here."

The vessel drifts into sight almost unnervingly close to the dock's end, blazing with brass lanterns cut like the sun, moon, and stars and festooned with banners bearing the royal Asteran seal. Verette taps Rapunzel's shoulder. "You go first."

Rapunzel backs down the dock, then takes a running leap and lands on the deck with a stumble. Deckhands politely but firmly help her out of the way. Rapunzel spots neat little verette charms swinging from their belts, with indigo ribbon, brass beads, and the white shell moth.

Just like at Third Street Hospital.

The captain, the helmsman, every crew member she sees, they all wear the same verette.

Eugene and Verette each land with a thud as Rapunzel

checks on Pascal in her satchel. He's still curled into a ball in the little coat she made him, sound asleep from the chill.

"Your Highness, what on *earth* is going on?" Cressien is gripping the barge's railing with both hands nearby, looking distinctly green around the gills. He attempts to step toward them, then reconsiders when the deck gently rolls beneath their feet.

"My father was about to have Princess Rapunzel detained," Verette says.

Eugene wobbles over to Rapunzel's side. "And he's been intercepting our messages. I found your reports in his study with the seals broken."

"What?" Rapunzel gasps.

Verette's face tightens. "My father is . . . especially rash where the People's Dagger are involved. We're going to put distance between you before he does something we'll all regret. Please, Princess Rapunzel, follow me."

"Just Rapunzel is fine," Rapunzel says as she follows Verette down a narrow, steep set of stairs into a salon below deck.

The other princess is already rummaging in a closet nearby. She emerges with a spare plain blue crewmate uniform in roughly Rapunzel's size, and passes it over. "Here. Go change in my cabin and leave your gown inside, then stay down here. We'll have a crew woman pose as you above deck in case we're being watched."

Rapunzel ducks into the cabin. She's just belting on the sturdy breeches when the barge tilts and a narrow door nearby creaks ajar, revealing a cramped little closet.

Verette charms—yarn and clay beads, silk ribbon and crystal, lopsided and expertly crafted—crowd every hook, shelf, and bin inside it. Foremost on one hook is the charm the little girl gave Verette just a couple of days ago.

Verette said people liked to give them to her; Rapunzel just didn't realize how many she actually meant.

When Rapunzel leaves the cabin in uniform, a sailor is already waiting outside to change into the violet silk gown left on the bed, a heavy velvet cloak draped over an arm. Rapunzel returns the sailor's bow and paces around the salon, only stepping aside to let the crew woman pass above deck, the hood of the cloak now drawn up to hide her hair.

It's funny; one of the many, *many* lines on Rapunzel's itinerary was a trip around the bay on a royal pleasure barge, but considering that was supposed to happen on the coming Tuesday, they're well ahead of schedule. Though she imagines Councilor Teophine had different circumstances in mind.

Verette's voice trails down the open stairwell:

". . . we'll take the dinghy to Merchant's Crescent in fifteen minutes. While I'm gone, take the barge two full circuits around the bay, and make sure the doubles keep their hoods up. We'll row the dinghy back out to meet you close to midnight."

"Understood, Your Majesty."

Verette pauses at *majesty*, but all she says is "Fitzherbert, you should go change."

"Don't threaten me with a good time." Eugene all but bounces down the steps, a crewman following, and swipes a shirt, jacket, and breeches from a nearby closet with an air of utmost mischief, despite being directed specifically to do so. After a moment he emerges from the cabin in disguise and tosses his fancy suit to the crewman, then flops into one of the salon's chairs and drops a handful of parchments onto the table. "Cressien's hugging the railing right now. I think they won't switch him out until the last minute."

"Are those the messages Enver intercepted?" Rapunzel makes herself stop pacing and sit next to him at the small round table. He nods as she picks one up and finds one of Cressien's reports, dated for Friday, their first full day here.

She shouldn't. She knows she shouldn't read it, that it's only going to get in her head.

She can't stop herself from smoothing the parchment out anyway. Eugene makes a noise, but doesn't stop her.

The report starts off relatively neutral, detailing King Enver's peculiar reactions, observations of the Asteran economy and rituals, notes on the governmental structure. Then she finds the note she was dreading:

> . . . Princess Rapunzel's general well-being remains satisfactory. However, she has largely disregarded my instruction on etiquette and decorum. I continue to believe that this is beyond her current diplomatic capabilities, and that her lack of preparation and experience will ultimately jeopardize the mission.

The next report contains similarly blunt remarks.

FIFTEEN

. . . The princess does not appear to grasp the seriousness of engaging with foreign nobility. Her natural curiosity has unfortunately led to her asking invasive questions of both King Enver and Princess Verette, and her ~~eccentricity~~ ~~caprice~~ free spirit has just now led her to hare off, on horseback, from a gathering with Asteran dignitaries, supposedly in pursuit of Fitzherbert. . . .

Her throat hurts as she picks up the last report. It's slightly tempered but . . . not what she hoped.

. . . and Princess Rapunzel has handled these mounting challenges to the best of her ability, which does her credit. However, for all her good intentions, I fear she simply does not have the instincts for foreign affairs. I cannot recommend sending her abroad again for a very, very long time.

The parchment rattles against the tabletop as she sets it down, eyes burning.

Eugene's arm wraps around her shoulders. "Who cares what a fussy old geezer thinks," he murmurs into the top of her head.

"I do," she sniffles, "because he's not *wrong*. I wanted Enver to be . . . someone I could help. And now look at the mess we're in."

Eugene's breath stirs her hair. "You see the best in everyone. Some people rise to it, some people run from it, and, well, some people will try to take advantage of it. You know that better than anyone. But that choice . . . it's theirs. If they choose wrong, it's on them, not you." He nudges another parchment toward her. "There's a letter from your mother, too."

Somehow that scares her more than Cressien's reports. Yet the broken purple wax seal gleams under the swaying lanterns in the salon, and the idea that Enver read this before she could makes her angry enough to pick it up.

My dearest Rapunzel,

You've barely been gone a day, but I couldn't help writing already. By the time this letter finds you, I hope you're in the heart of a wonderful adventure. I can scarcely believe you're my daughter, because you're so tremendously brave to head into the unknown for our kingdom's sake . . . and when I watched your ship set sail yesterday morning, I felt like such a coward for wanting to bring you back before it could even clear the horizon. But there's so much of the world waiting for you, and I am so, so proud of you, dearest, for having the courage to leave this castle and chase it. I'm counting the days until you can tell me everything you've seen.

Love always,

Your mother

Rapunzel's vision blurs with tears.

Not because of what her mother wrote—but what she didn't.

There's no *I hope you're representing us well.* No *How are discussions going?* No *Remember what we told you.*

Nothing to justify. Nothing to prove. No expectations, just joy, just pride.

She was waiting for scrutiny, for needling, for doubt, because every shortcoming was an excuse for Gothel to say Rapunzel wasn't yet ready to leave. But that was never about Rapunzel, or anything she did wrong; she was never going to prove she could leave the tower, because Gothel never intended to let her go.

And the mother who loves her—well, she doesn't need Rapunzel to prove anything.

It didn't matter that her lost magic was a disappointment to King Enver. It doesn't matter if she's falling short of Minister Cressien's standards. She's already the person she wanted her mother to see.

And maybe—maybe it's because seeing the best in people is a family trait.

Eugene carefully dabs at her face with a sleeve. "Better?"

"Better," she confirms shakily, tucking the letter into her pocket.

Footsteps thud unevenly down the stairs. Minister Cressien staggers into the salon, a crew member steadying his elbow. "I believe we'll be departing shortly," he croaks. "To protect the crew, should they be questioned, Princess Verette has asked to wait until we're off the barge to discuss specifics . . . of the . . ." He trails off as his eyes land on her tearstained face, then fall to the reports scattered on the table.

For a tortured moment, only the dull slosh of waves and the groans of the hull fill the salon.

"Your—Your Highness," Cressien starts.

Rapunzel shakes her head. "Later."

Before Cressien can argue, Verette clomps down to the salon. "The dinghy's almost here. Get ready to move."

If Minister Cressien was having a bad time on the barge, he has an even worse time on the cramped dinghy being buffeted by the waves, with Eugene and Verette rowing toward the lantern-dotted shore of Merchant's Crescent. Once there's enough distance between them and the barge, Verette grits out between oar strokes, "We're getting you to a safe house tonight. Then we'll stage a diversion so your galleon can pick you up from here and take you home."

"Wait," Rapunzel says. "You want us to leave?"

Verette ducks her head. "While you still can. I don't think it's safe anymore, not with Father acting this way. I was supposed to become queen upon coming of age, except . . ."

"It's happened four times now," Eugene finishes. "And he's still held on to the throne."

"I was hoping—" Verette's voice catches. "I thought maybe him inviting Princess Rapunzel meant it was real this time. But everything he's doing points to something worse."

Suddenly, all Rapunzel can hear is Enver, not even two hours ago, saying, *Perhaps you're not as ready for the crown as I thought.*

How many times has he held that promise over her?

How long has she been trying to prove herself?

And that's when Rapunzel realizes Verette doesn't need a savvy aristocrat. She doesn't need the magic of the sundrop.

What she needs is someone who knows how to leave the tower.

She reaches out and grabs Verette's oar. Verette and Eugene both still.

Rapunzel says, "No. I'm staying."

"You don't owe us any help," Verette insists.

"I made you a promise." Rapunzel doesn't let go. "Maybe your father doesn't keep them. But I do."

Verette looks to Eugene for backup. He just shrugs. "We're a package deal. I go where she goes."

"Minister Cressien." Verette turns to him next. "*Please* make them see reason."

Cressien clears his throat and says queasily, "I do not command Her Highness. Yet even if I did . . . I would not advise a different course of action."

Verette searches the three of them, scowling. Then she gives her oar a shake. "Fine. But we'll bring you up to speed at the safe house. My father can't hear what you need to know."

SIXTEEN

EUGENE

Eugene didn't know it was possible to miss a place you've never been to, but somehow, he's missed Merchant's Crescent.

Or maybe he's missed places *like* it. The way the fog dulls the lanterns in the night. The tang of salt on the breeze, old seaweed, tar-laced dock timbers bristling with barnacles by the changing waterline. The grit of sand in the mud beneath his boots, and the way guards don't even spare them a second glance, because for the first time since their arrival, brown hair on an adult doesn't raise an eyebrow.

Eugene's not completely sold on whatever Verette's deal is just yet, but Rapunzel is all in, and that means he is too. So when Verette leads them into a shipping clerk's office, he's not asking too many questions.

Amazingly, the clerk is still at the counter. Eugene spots little blue verette charms dangling from her earrings as she bows her head to Verette and says, "They're upstairs."

"Thank you," Verette says softly.

A door off to the side leads to a narrow staircase, and every step squeals as they pass, so when they reach a wide space that looks to be a meeting room of sorts, the other occupants do not look remotely surprised to see them.

"Welcome to the safe house." Councilor Teophine's voice glides from a rickety chair to the right, where she's sitting in her ball regalia with a steaming cup of tea, looking distinctly out of place amid the worn-down furnishings. There's a broad table with a motley of chairs and stools angled around it, maps and charts on the faded brick walls, ramshackle shelves full of scrolls and logbooks. A round window at the far end of the room reveals the bay and main island. "Tea?"

"Please," Cressien all but wheezes.

"Yes, of course. Please, make yourselves at home." Verette hangs her mask on a wall hook and heads for a kettle on a squat iron stove. "I apologize for the secrecy, and how standoffish I've been, and how bizarre this all must be."

"Not for kidnapping me?" Eugene grouses.

"No," Verette says smoothly, "that was hilarious. Peppermint tea?"

"I saved you some of the little pickles from the refreshments," Councilor Teophine calls from her chair.

Verette's face lights up as she turns back toward Rapunzel, Cressien, and Eugene, all still clustered by the door. She waves a handful of mismatched mugs. "Raise your hands for tea? Two? Great. So, for starters, my father has found almost every other base we've had in the last four years, but not this one or the one we took Fitzherbert to."

"He seems to have ears everywhere these days."

The voice echoes from behind them. Eugene jumps as Rapunzel flattens herself to the wall. Master Sulian stands outside the door. Behind him is another man, a few inches taller but much wider, with tight white curls cropped short and a pair of golden spectacles gleaming against a face darker even than Cressien's, the black eyes behind them twinkling.

"Not everywhere," the bespectacled man corrects in a deep baritone, shuffling forward. Eugene recognizes that voice as the one he dubbed Stranger, the one who once slipped and referred to the Cardinal Council as *us*. "Don't mind us, now, I heard there was tea. But yes, Enver's always seemed to sniff out our retreats, and the closest pattern we can identify is it's always after a busy meeting or when people chatter on the way in."

"Only place he's never found us on the mainland is under the sunmills," Sulian adds as he settles himself in a chair by Teophine. "We had to relocate to this safe house after you two"—he gestures to Eugene and Cressien—"escaped our headquarters. Couldn't risk you leading Enver to us."

"I think he's finding you with the roots." Rapunzel walks

fully inside and sets her satchel down on the table. Pascal groggily climbs out, then scales her arm and curls up on her shoulder.

"Is that a tiny coat?" Verette asks wonderingly at the same time Councilor Teophine says, "Roots?"

"We snuck into the Starlight Spring last night," Eugene says as he comes to stand beside Rapunzel. "The water's all gone, and it looks like it's feeding a huge tree growing down there."

Everyone else seems to take in a breath almost as one, their faces spanning the spectrum from comprehension to confusion, all with an undertone of dismay. Verette's brow furrows, a hand over her mouth as she thinks.

Stranger leans forward, adjusting his spectacles. "What manner of tree?"

"Like an apple tree, but it only had one apple." Rapunzel pulls out her sketchbook and starts flipping pages. "Its roots run at least as far as Third Street Hospital, maybe farther. Roots are really sensitive to vibrations, so someone with the power of starlight may be able to use them to eavesdrop." She finds her drawing of the tree in the cave and holds it up. "Here. It looked like this."

"That's a cloud apple tree," Stranger says with a frown. "But the leaves should be green, not . . . that. And it's the largest I've ever seen. Typically, they produce a single apple after three years, then die."

"Feeding from the Starlight Spring could have changed it." Rapunzel accepts a mug of tea from Verette. Then she also frowns, setting the sketchbook back down. "Wait. Your Highness—"

"Verette is fine." Verette has found the plate of tiny pickles and is eating them with what Eugene can only describe as relish.

"Did your father ever give you a strange apple to eat?" Rapunzel gestures to her own short hair. "When I had the magic of the sundrop flower, my hair was, er, unusual, too."

Verette swallows, expression stiffening. "No, not exactly."

Eugene's trying to follow. "Right, we think your father is using the roots—no, hold on, that doesn't make sense either . . ."

"Unless *he* . . ." Sulian begins.

Stranger almost spills his tea. "Of course—the reduced aging, and this root surveillance—that would explain everything!"

"*Would* it?" Eugene says dryly.

"We did promise to share what we know," Teophine reminds Verette. "And gentlemen, introductions . . . ?"

The shorter man nods to Eugene. "He already knows me. Sulian, palace stable master."

"Councilor Ruvon du Val of the North," rumbles the other man between delicate sips of tea. He correctly reads Eugene's confusion and adds with a touch of ire, "Formerly. Katou Laroux holds the position at present, despite her *egregious* disregard for the field of anthropological—"

"Let's start from the beginning," Teophine interjects,

looking like she's ready to wrest control of the presentation away from the rest of the group.

"The Night of the Poisoned Dagger?" Eugene asks as he and a reluctant Cressien settle into chairs.

Verette shakes her head. "Earlier."

"And we're not the People's Dagger." Sulian leans back. "Not for a long time. I think it started . . . oh, fifty years ago or so, when the king moved all the international trading off the mainland, over to Merchant's Crescent."

"Earlier, even—Queen Gaelle's health started declining a few years into their marriage," Ruvon says. "Enver banned outsiders from the mainland so word of it wouldn't leave Astera. Especially because the only thing that seemed to help her was drinking from the Starlight Spring every day. We all understood that was why the queen's aging slowed. But years later we realized . . . the king wasn't aging either. We couldn't confirm anything, but we suspected he was helping himself to the spring as well."

Verette has planted herself by the kettle on the stove, clearly fixating on the tea as a distraction. "They kept my mother's pregnancy a secret, and my father took over as acting monarch, claiming she had fallen ill again." She twists a lock of hair around her finger. "From what I can guess, Father kept giving her starlight water daily all through her pregnancy, and I came out with white hair. I'm told childbirth nearly killed us both, so . . . he kept us alive on starlight. And then he never stopped. Every day at breakfast, I had to finish a glass of water before he would let me leave. The water looks almost normal in the daylight, so I didn't know what I was drinking for—years."

"Queen Gaelle never fully recovered," Councilor Teophine adds. "And Enver never announced Verette's birth—word only reached the public when she was a toddler. At that point, he'd skipped the Fountain Festival two years in a row, claiming it weakened the Starlight Spring and the queen needed its full potency."

Ruvon scowls, setting his mug down rather forcefully. "And he was *wrong*. I drafted the report myself! My team determined the fountains could run once a *month* without depleting the spring, and the starlight only fades with time and distance—" He cuts himself off with a bitter laugh before Teophine has to. "All of us on Gaelle's council were concerned. Gaelle tried to resume her full duties, but the strain only weakened her more. When it was clear she didn't have much longer, the other councilors and I planned to invoke the Consort Regency, which would limit Enver's powers to those of a councilor until Verette was old enough to rule. And then Leona's snake of a brother . . ."

"Leona Persevault, former Councilor of the West and Master of Seas," Teophine fills in. "You know her as Solena Vald, Master Fitzherbert."

Ruvon huffs, "*And* my enchanting wife! Her brother wanted her job for himself. He betrayed us to Enver, and . . . well, Enver decided to kill two birds with one stone. He granted a council audience to a political organization known for a more radical agenda, such as ending Astera's isolation entirely, expanding the number of elected councilors . . . and letting the fountains run once a month."

"The People's Dagger," Cressien guesses.

Sulian leans in, nodding. "Torch—none of us knows her real name—was our leader, and I was a lieutenant. I was ordered to stay behind in case things went sideways, to take care of our people. She went to the meeting with a third of our members, including Marietta Fitz and Andreas Herbert." His voice turns hoarse. "Torch and Marietta were the only survivors from our ranks."

Eugene's gut clenches. It's one thing to know his mother had to have survived. It's another to hear how she lost everything.

Verette is staring hard into her tea, silent.

"Enver claimed he was purging the palace of traitors," Sulian continues. "Torch swears his attack was all planned. That she got him in the belly. He must have had spring water ready to heal himself."

"Your mother, young Fitzherbert, saved our lives." All of Ruvon's bluster has fallen away as he holds Eugene's gaze with his own. "Mine and Leona's. Leona was just supposed to take her abroad and get her set up in a new life, but your mother passed a few months after giving birth to you, and Leona wanted to be certain you were cared for."

"The rest you know," Verette finally says. "Mostly. My father lied about a poison in the spring, blamed the People's Dagger, granted himself emergency powers, appointed a new council with no power to override him, and keeps delaying the transfer of power to me." She grips her tea mug. "The surviving councilors and members of the Dagger formed this alliance. We're now the People's Council. We've built a coalition of supporters at every level of Asteran society who believe it's time for Father to end his reign, and are ready to side with me if—if Father defers again."

"How did you recruit *Hughes*?" Eugene asks incredulously. "Most of you I get, but that's Enver's right-hand man."

Teophine sighs. "Hughes has served the king nearly thirty years. The massacre was horrifying enough for him to turn informant for us almost immediately, and then . . . he fell for his contact in our ranks. Marietta's brother Eugene—your namesake, I believe."

"I have an uncle?" Eugene feels sucker punched.

Another blow lands: "I'm sorry," Ruvon says, "but he passed. He and Hughes were engaged to be married, but tragically, Eugene Fitz was caught trying to infiltrate the Starlight Spring and executed."

Eugene Fitz. The name sounds too familiar. Cut short.

How bitterly apt.

"Hughes himself brought me into the People's Council a month later." Verette drains the last of her tea and rises. "So that's where things stand. I'm sorry you've all been dragged into this mess, and we'll do our best to get you out safely. We just weren't sure if we could trust you, since it was Father's choice to break isolation and bring you here."

Sixteen

Teophine says, "I'm sure you have some questions, Your Highness."

Rapunzel looks to Eugene, but he's still processing, staring at the table planks. She gets to her feet. "You can call me Rapunzel. And the most important question I have is, how do I help?"

The words fall into a room abruptly stifled by the mere idea.

"Help," repeats Ruvon, as if decoding an ancient rune.

"We don't know why Enver invited me either, but I'm here now," Rapunzel elaborates. "So what can I do?"

Verette shifts uncomfortably. "Nothing? At least, not right now. If none of us know what Father wants with you, we could be playing into his hands. *Or*, as I've told the People's Council"—iron reinforces words that sound like they hearken to a well-trodden debate—"Father may have invited you because he actually means to transition power at my coming of age ceremony this time, and he wants to leave me with new allies. If that's it, all we have to do is wait."

"And be ready if he doesn't," chimes in a new voice, gravelly and hard. A rangy woman in her late forties lopes into the room and hangs up yet another nondescript gray cloak. (Eugene's starting to wonder how many of these they have on hand.) A long pink scar runs down the left side of her light brown face, and more dance over her bare forearms. Her white hair is cropped just as short as Eugene's.

"Yes, Torch, I know," Verette says a bit testily. "I just want to give him one more chance."

"You really made it into the Starlight Spring last night?" Sulian is staring at the drawing of the tree. "No one's ever been able to get close."

Eugene gives him a dubious look. "No one in Astera knows how to pick a lock?"

"They always get caught, Yappy," Torch says harshly. "No operative has ever come back from that job. We stopped sending them."

"Roots line the whole passage to the spring." Rapunzel picks up her sketchbook again. "When I sang the queen's lullaby, the roots lit up, and they might for Verette too. We saw them at Third Street Hospital." She thinks a moment. "Enver probably hears anyone trying to get to the spring through the roots. But maybe since *I* was using the roots to light the way, I was controlling the ones around us, and they *couldn't* alert him."

"We saw Councilor Persevault using the passage too," Eugene points out. "He led us right to the missing fleet Solena—sorry, Leona?—was talking about yesterday, before you so rudely chased me and Minister Cressien out of your hideout. Turns out there's a big old sea cave under the palace with something like a dozen boats inside, and I bet Enver's not paying attention to foot traffic as long as they stay away from the path to the spring."

"Enver must know about the tree in the spring. . . . How did it even get there? Is it possible someone else planted it?" Teophine asks.

Torch frowns. "What tree?"

One concise explanation later, Sulian is shaking his head.

"Enver took the only key into the spring from Queen Gaelle."

"He also originated the claim that the spring was poisoned," Ruvon adds. "We assumed he did it to turn public opinion against the People's Dagger and exert greater control over the spring, but perhaps it was to keep anyone from finding the tree."

"He looked me in the eye and said that poisoning the spring might have been my father's last act." Eugene doesn't intend the words to sound as strangled as they come out. "He lied to our faces that he was testing the water every day. Whether or not he planted the tree, he's hiding it now."

Ruvon reaches for the sketchbook. "May I?" Rapunzel pushes it to him. He turns the pages back to the cloud apple tree, lips pursing. "There's another paradox, one you spotted yourself, young lady. Verette's unusual hair suggests she's been more deeply affected by the starlight, yet . . . she continues to age, albeit at a reduced rate, whereas Enver seems to have almost entirely stopped. And he seemingly has a level of control over this tree that Verette does not. Is it possible he's not merely availing himself of the starlight-imbued water . . . he's been consuming a star-touched apple every three years?"

Cressien leans in, rubbing his chin. "When our queen fell ill eighteen years ago, the flower itself was distilled to a tisane strong enough to heal her, and its magic passed on to Princess Rapunzel. But the witch Gothel had to regularly reverse her aging with the power of the sundrop flower. Its effects were never permanent."

"We've been very secretive about Astera's stardrop, but

our scholars did theorize about the sundrop in Kourenne," Teophine chimes in. "The starlight water isn't strong enough, for example, to save someone mortally wounded, or terminally ill, unlike the sundrop flower. One theory is that the magic is in the Kourenne soil itself, and the flower drew the sunlight into a more powerful concentration in its blossom."

Eugene's chair creaks as he folds his arms. "You said Enver stopped the Fountain Festival a few years *before* the massacre. Maybe he planted the tree then, hoping the apples would be stronger than just the water, and was trying to buy time for it to bear fruit."

An aching pause smothers the room.

"These two made it into the spring, Verette," Torch rasps. "If they can do it again, we can destroy the tree, take the apple ourselves, and keep it from Enver until he yields the throne."

Verette fails to hide her flinch, and starts gathering empty mugs instead. "It's an option. I'll think about it. If you're back, that means Leona's ready, right?"

"All set in your normal rendezvous point." Torch's voice has become carefully neutral, which tells Eugene exactly whom the well-trodden debate has been with.

"Then we need to get going." Verette deposits the mugs in a sink and heads for her cloak. "Fitzherbert, Rapunzel, Minister Cressien, we're going to meet Leona, who will ferry us out to the pleasure barge. We'll need to keep quiet once again until we reach her, but it's a short walk."

Eugene barely has time to push back from the table before

Verette is hustling them out. The walk to meet Leona is just as swift and silent.

They reach a shallow little cove where only one skiff waits, half in the water, half on a thin strip of black sand. Solena—no, Leona—stands beside it, face tight and alight all at once. It eases when Eugene steps out of the mists.

"Eugene," she croaks.

He strides over, wraps her in a hug, and mumbles, "Why on earth do they keep using clove hitches?"

"Don't have time for sentiment," Leona says gruffly, but doesn't pull away for a long moment and swipes obstinately at her eyes after she does. "The barge should be rounding the west cliffs right about now. Verette, help me with the boat."

They pile into the skiff, Cressien looking none too pleased and more than a little seasick as they push off. Leona makes Eugene help her row and puts Rapunzel in charge of keeping the boat's lantern dry as they drift out of the cove.

The pleasure barge drifts around the mouth of the cove a few minutes later, its lanterns glowing like clusters of stars. Eugene and Leona row the skiff right up beside it, and crew members quickly help them all climb aboard—all save Leona.

"We'll talk soon, Eugene," Leona promises. Then she hooks the lantern on her walking stick, balances it on the skiff's sides, and pushes off, back toward the cove.

"Rapunzel, let's go get your double so you can change back." Verette hurries off, Rapunzel trotting after her, slightly bemused.

"Is it me," Eugene says to the air, "or does she not seem all that eager to depose her father?"

Cressien is already heading for the side of the barge; Eugene thinks it's the nausea, not disdain, making him terse. "She may not have much of a choice. But speaking of choices . . . you put yourself at enormous risk today."

"That's what I'm here for, isn't it?" Eugene can hear the bitter note in his voice.

Now it *is* disdain making Cressien terse. "Explain yourself."

"I mean, you're a minister, and Rapunzel is the *princess*—"

"That's very interesting," Cressien seethes unconvincingly as he anchors himself by the railing, "but I want to know why *you*, as a member of our delegation, believe your purpose here is to be expendable."

Eugene's breath gutters. It's one thing to brood on the admission, another to say it out loud. "I—I'm just being realistic," he manages. "You said it yourself: The ink's still wet on my pardon. I nearly hanged in the palace courtyard. The nobility are never going to like me, even if I try." He runs a hand through his hair. "I'm a commoner and a thief, and apparently my parents tried to overthrow a monarchy. That's not exactly husband material for a princess. I just figured it was only a matter of time before I was asked to . . . move along."

Cressien pinches the bridge of his nose. "Did the king or queen ever say as much?" There's an awkward pause. "I didn't think so. And you know *why* I didn't think so, you absolute buffoon?"

"Hurtful and unnecessary," grumbles Eugene.

"Because *I am a commoner*," Cressien erupts. "I was born to small-town cobblers. I attended state-run schools and went to an advanced academy on state-provided grants, and I know dozens of commoners just like me who serve in the kingdom's highest offices at the pleasure of a king and queen who saw their potential, not their rank."

"And how many of you have a criminal record?" Eugene can't help firing back.

Cressien shakes his head. "You need to understand that Their Majesties see that as their own failure of policy, not your failure of character. They have no intention of getting rid of you, and *trust* that I asked. They simply don't know what to *do* with you."

Eugene is struggling to process. "What is that supposed to mean?"

"Do you have any idea what diplomatic concessions we could extract from other countries if a marriage treaty were on the table—"

"The other part," Eugene cuts in. "About what to do with me."

Cressien makes a vague gesture at Eugene's entire, well, self. "You and Princess Rapunzel are clearly devoted to each other. Their Majesties will always welcome you in the palace, but they aren't sure what office to give to you as a member of the household."

"To make me respectable." Eugene scowls.

Cressien looks more annoyed than ever. "*To give you independence.* They don't want you feeling as if your livelihood depends on their good graces. And, loath as I am to say it, I do see areas where a man of your talents might thrive."

That knocks the wind out of Eugene's sails. "You do?"

It's Cressien's turn to scowl, like he's eating a vegetable he particularly abhors. "Our spymaster is seeking an apprentice. She reports to me, and regrettably, I would be willing to recommend you for the position if you wish it. But *only* if you cease acting so recklessly."

Apprentice . . . spymaster?

Eugene has to admit it has a nice ring to it. But it's not just a title; it's a future. A way to stay in Rapunzel's life, yes—*and* a way to make his own.

"I . . . think I'd really like that," he says slowly.

Cressien nods, impassive as ever, but he's running a thumb over his bare ring finger again. "This is not a professional recommendation, but . . . a personal one. Tell Princess Rapunzel about how you felt. Difficult conversations only get more difficult the longer you wait to have them."

Eugene swallows.

Before he can muster an answer, Verette's voice sails across the deck: "Fitzherbert. Your turn to change."

Part Three

Starfall

Seventeen

Rapunzel

This time, Rapunzel paces around the barge's salon not with anxiety, but excitement.

She's back in her violet gown, and strictly speaking, she knows she should be exhausted from the late hour and the agitation, terrified to set foot back onto an island where even the ground itself is spying on them, furious at the deception, and sad for Verette.

But Rapunzel's mind is already whirring with ways to help the People's Council, stringing together half-formed plans and taking inventory of the tools at hand. It feels like whenever she had to engineer her own way to the highest reaches of the tower, like finding where she dropped a stitch in her knitting, like charting the stars and spotting the patterns for herself.

A problem can be *solved.* Enver has Astera locked in place, frozen in time. Cut him off from the tree, and you can move him from the throne. Get the People's Council into the Starlight Spring, and they can figure out how to get rid of the tree. Find an opening, a diversion to keep Enver occupied, and you can get the People's Council into the Starlight Spring.

And that's what's keeping Rapunzel pacing around the salon now, a perpetual motion machine fueled by the sheer exhilaration of problem-solving.

At least . . . until there's a crash from Verette's cabin.

Rapunzel hurries over and knocks on the door, which swings open. Verette was supposed to be changing back into her own fine gown inside. She's managed the gown, but now she's crouched by the closet full of verettes Rapunzel saw earlier. A crate inside has overturned, scattering the charms over the cabin floor.

"Here, let me." Rapunzel sets her satchel on the desk and starts gathering the ones that landed the farthest away. "These are the verettes Asterans have given you, right?"

"Yes." Verette's voice is unexpectedly hoarse. When Rapunzel glances over her shoulder, she realizes the closet isn't just crammed full of the charms, it's actively overflowing.

For the first time, it occurs to her that it can't be convenient keeping them all on a barge like this.

"You look like you're running out of room," Rapunzel says carefully. "Do you not want your father to see?"

Verette stares at her, wavering between denial and surrender—a struggle Rapunzel knows all too well.

Then she sits on a wooden chest with a long sigh and starts taking the moth ornaments out of her hair. "A few years ago, Father threw away all the verettes people had given me. He said it was just clutter. I didn't know why he did it."

Rapunzel's hands tighten on the charms.

Verette continues, "It was right after my first coming of age ceremony. I'd been so excited and nervous to become queen, and then it just—didn't happen. He said I should be grateful I got such an amazing party, but that it was too soon for anything else, and then a few days later, all the verettes were gone." She swallows. "And then the next day he gave me this barge, and said I was old enough to have my own."

Rapunzel remembers every night she lay in her bed in Gothel's tower, promising herself, *I'll leave tomorrow, I'll go see the world for myself and nothing will keep me here.*

And every morning she woke up and found a clumsy flower Gothel drew on the chore list she left behind. Or a pan of burnt muffins ("This is why you do the baking, Flower") waiting on the oven. Or a new bolt of fabric—never quite enough to make a whole new dress, but Rapunzel always got creative piecing hers together.

It was all part of Gothel's prison; Rapunzel knows that now. But there was a reason she reached for her mother when she fell.

Rapunzel reaches into her satchel and pulls out Pascal, who blinks sleepily in her palm. "This is my best friend, Pascal. My—Gothel, the woman who pretended to be my mother, she gave him to me for my seventh birthday. But anytime I talked back, or asked a question she didn't like, she'd threaten to take him away and leave him in the woods." Rapunzel sits on a crate. "The first lie I ever told her was that he'd run away, and he hid in the tower with me until I left. I'm still afraid to tell my real parents about him, even though I know they're different. I'm just . . . scared."

"I would be too." Verette lifts a finger for Pascal to inspect. "I . . . I don't even know how old I really am, because of him. I don't think anyone does, besides him. I was older than eighteen when he allowed the first coming of age ceremony, and then he just kept saying they weren't real ones, they didn't count, and . . . no one could stand against him, so it just became normal." Her eyes well up. "I shouldn't want to give him another chance. I *know* better."

"My real parents are—wonderful," Rapunzel says haltingly. "They work hard for the kingdom, everyone loves them, and they've been so kind to me. But." Something's building inside of her, a seed long buried in the earth, finally pushing sprouts aboveground. "I've been trying so hard not to see Gothel in them that I only saw them as perfect. And it made me feel scared when *I* wasn't perfect. But I know they love me as I am, and I love them even if—if I think—they don't get everything right. I mean, Eugene stole a piece of jewelry and almost got executed for it under their law—without a trial! We could make another tiara, but there will never be anyone else like Eugene." The words spill out faster and faster. "Gothel only ever wanted to use me, and now everyone wants me to take it easy and settle into being a princess, but I feel like I'm *meant* to help people. Like I'm supposed to appreciate the good my parents have done, and still . . ."

"Do better," Verette finishes. "Were you—scared, leaving your tower?"

That's the easiest answer for Rapunzel all night. She smiles softly. "It's always terrifying when your dream comes true. But Eugene says the good part is, you get to go find a new one."

"I want to see the starlight fountains run again," Verette says fiercely. "I want to help Astera move forward. I . . . I want to see *your* kingdom." She wavers a moment. "And my father is never going to let any of us go."

Rapunzel passes her the verette charms she's picked up, simple hemp and clay to silk cord and gold bead, every one a blessing from the people of Astera, every one a dream in Verette's shaking hands.

"I think," Rapunzel tells her, "you're old enough to decide that for yourself."

✧ ✧ ✧

Minister Cressien finds Rapunzel in the palace gardens the next morning, ostensibly doing a floral study of a cluster of lily and aster. Secretly, she's also counting the guard patrols and how often they pass, because this particular bend of the garden lies en route to the entrance to the Starlight Spring.

And for once, Pascal isn't hiding, instead gleefully sunbathing on the warm stone bench beside her pastel sticks.

For a few moments, Minister Cressien watches her push yellow ochre across the page. Part of Rapunzel is bracing for a remark about the pigments on her hands, the absence of her shoes. Instead he says, "You have a unique style, Your Highness."

Rapunzel looks up. "You can call me Rapunzel, you know."

"I would rather not," he says—but with no trace of rebuke. "It serves us both to remember that this is my job, Your Highness. That said . . . as minister of diplomatic affairs, I've seen the continent's finest art collections, from portraits of monarchs to scenes of legendary battles. Your style differs from the . . . traditional schools." His gaze flicks down briefly to her bare feet, in case Rapunzel was not sufficiently aware he was shifting into metaphor. "It draws on both realism and elements of folk art, styles that appeal to commoners and nobility alike. Unconventional. But I believe it has its own strengths."

"Thank you," Rapunzel says. "But you were right. I wanted to show my parents I could help them, and I rushed into this before I was ready. It must have been really upsetting to feel like I was underestimating how hard your work is."

Cressien's head inclines. "I appreciate that, Your Highness. Nevertheless, it *is* my job to help prepare you to engage with the rest of the world, and to provide accurate and unbiased information to your parents. Your mother merely wished me to keep her informed on your general safety and well-being, nothing more. Upon reflection, I suspect that my personal troubles may have influenced me to be unjustly severe in my reports. You deserved a fair assessment, one I failed to provide due to no fault of your own."

"Do you want to talk about it?" Rapunzel asks.

He shakes his head. "I appreciate that as well, Your Highness, but no. But if I may . . . I understand the desire to be helpful, and I applaud it. However."

"It can be exploited." Rapunzel scrubs a swath of gray over the flowers.

"Well, yes," he agrees, "but I don't believe I need to tell you that. Your mother likes to remind me that there is more in me, more to my life, than my service to the kingdom. I don't believe I really listened to her until too late. You should know that the day you returned, your parents . . . well, they came alive again, in a way I never thought I'd see in my lifetime. It must be difficult for you, adjusting to losing your magic, but please understand that that was a wound only you—not the sundrop flower, *you*—could heal."

Rapunzel's sketchbook page wobbles and blurs. A drop splashes over the corner. Cressien wordlessly offers her an immaculate handkerchief, not even flinching at the streaks her pastel-dusty fingers leave.

"Thank you," she says coarsely.

"Of course, Your Highness," Cressien says. Then, clearly itching to change the subject, he gestures to Pascal sprawled on the stone bench. "Who is this? I believe I've seen him in your company before."

"Pascal," Rapunzel answers, a bit nervous. "We've been friends for years. I—I haven't told my parents about him yet, so please don't put it in a report?"

"I don't know that reports are making it out of here anyway,"

Cressien drawls, "but may I ask why not? Their Majesties are very fond of animals."

Rapunzel raises a shoulder. "How many princesses have chameleon friends?"

"Fewer than have cats or dogs," he allows. "So perhaps you're the first. I know a kingdom where the queen collects ceramic ducks. Another where the most powerful duke bathes weekly in elderflower vinegar. Princess Verette is unusually fiendish for pickled foods, did you notice? And if your shoes are hurting you, the answer is to find shoes that don't. You have good instincts, Your Highness, and a different perspective. One your parents will always welcome. No one wants to force you to be someone you're not. Our job is to assist you in finding the way *you* want to be a princess."

Rapunzel looks at her floral study. "Like my art style?"

"I believe the saying is 'Know the rules so you can break the rules.'" Cressien clasps his hands behind his back; Rapunzel suspects it's so he doesn't have to reclaim the soggy, pigment-smeared kerchief. The hourly bells begin to toll. "Our job is also to hold you to your itinerary," he remarks. "Your tour of the royal university will begin in an hour. Additionally, you are addressing the council tomorrow, and I wished to offer a review of your speech."

"Oh," Rapunzel says sheepishly. "Was I supposed to write that down?"

Cressien glances heavenward and, with the faintest ghost of a wry smile, sighs, "We'll draft it this evening. Together."

EIGHTEEN

EUGENE

Two days later, Eugene isn't sure if it's tradition or precaution that sees them celebrating Verette's birthday in the grand audience hall instead of the ballroom. Notably, this time he can feel the stares of many, *many* guards, especially every time he wanders by the refreshment tables.

The audience hall itself is another architectural marvel, with columns and vaulted ceilings carved like luminous geysers raining pearly stars, bedecked in garlands of white and blue flowers that shine vibrantly against midnight silk drapes and golden trim. Great diamond-paned windows climb nearly to the roof, and doors to private verandas have been propped open to let the early evening breeze glide over the stone. And it's needed—even though the hall is massive, it's jam-packed with dignitaries, many of whom are lined up to approach the dais at the head of the hall.

Eugene and Rapunzel are currently parked in chairs on the dais's right side, watching as citizen after citizen pledges deeds in honor of Verette. King Enver hovers just over her left shoulder, the empty throne bristling at both of their backs a few yards away.

"I've gotta say," Eugene mutters out of the corner of his mouth, "'I will save the Starlight Spring' is a pretty hard vow to beat."

"It's not a contest," Rapunzel whispers back with the beatific smile of someone who has absolutely trounced the competition. Then she blinks. "Look at the king's hands."

". . . to paint a public mural in your honor," a slight man is saying at the head of the line, "the most extraordinary the island has ever seen. All blessings to the queen to come."

Enver stands with his hands linked behind his back, and only Rapunzel, Eugene, and his guards can see them briefly clench.

Then the man Eugene is assuming to be a painter—otherwise that mural is going to be extraordinary for very different reasons—does something unexpected.

He taps below his left eye, then his right, then his chin. Just as Eugene and Rapunzel did when they met Verette.

Furtive murmurs skitter through the room as he bows and walks away.

"I thought that was just old-fashioned," Rapunzel says under her breath.

Eugene watches Enver's hands curling once more into fists. "It is. It's the old way to greet a monarch."

The next person to step up is wearing bracelets subtly evoking verette charms. The one after that has moon eye moths embroidered into their collar. Rings, tassels, even cuff links—they flash on more and more people pledging their deeds. And they're almost always an indicator that the oath maker will refer to Verette as "the queen to come."

It brings Eugene no small degree of bittersweet triumph to see Enver's knuckles turn whiter and whiter.

They've spent the last two days planning with the People's Council for tonight, and if Enver is somehow aware, he's done a better job of hiding it than he's hiding his annoyance now. Still . . . the palace only has one audience hall.

It may be tradition, or it may be Enver sending a message; either way, Eugene is keenly aware that they're celebrating in the room where his parents' deaths were ordered, with the man who ordered them.

Andreas Herbert. Marietta Fitz. It's like double vision, the way he hears the names, and the way he knows he *should* hear them. Printers. Authors. Revolutionaries. *Gone.*

In another world, maybe he would have grown up here, knowing their faces, their voices, running down these cobblestone streets and playing Flynnigan Rider. And he'd never give up his life now—but until now, he didn't know it was possible to mourn the one you never got to live.

Marietta Fitz. Andreas Herbert. And the Eugene Fitzherbert who should have been raised on starlight here.

He can add every one of them to what Enver owes.

The pledges continue for another half hour, and both Eugene and Rapunzel are happy to get up and stretch when they're done. Ordinarily this is when Eugene would expect a banquet before the evening continued with the issuing of invitations, but apparently Asteran custom dictates everyone graze from the refreshment tables throughout the night instead of gathering for a sit-down meal. It makes for a convenient excuse to station himself by a cheese tray—the fountain seems to be deliberately retired—as Rapunzel makes her circuit around the room, and Minister Cressien and Councilor Teophine attempt *not* to look at him.

Right now, Sulian is smuggling a handful of operatives into the palace's tunnel system. And if this night goes the way Verette's hoping, the way Eugene's dubbed Plan B, the stable master will wind up smuggling them right back out.

But if it goes the way everyone else suspects it will, then they'll switch to Plan A. (For Apple. The order's a little confusing.)

It doesn't take long for Hughes to find him in the crowd. "His Majesty would like a word, young Fitzherbert."

"Does he now." Eugene only sounds a *little* insincere. It's partially because overall, he'd rate his interactions with Enver three out of ten at best. Primarily, it's because Verette, Rapunzel, and Hughes have all waged an oblique but coordinated campaign the last couple of days to make Enver think he owes Eugene an apology.

They only need a few minutes. Then the first obstacle to Plan A will be removed.

Hughes leads him away from the refreshments, muttering, "He's speaking with Councilor Persevault in his office. I believe you're familiar with both the councilor and the office."

"Just doing my future job," Eugene replies. "Did you know Cressien wants me to apprentice to the spymaster?"

"I know when Enver discovered the missing letters, he had every servant and guard searched for ties to the People's Dagger," Hughes says through his teeth, "so perhaps this apprenticeship will grant you a more thoughtful perspective."

Eugene feels a stab of guilt as they head into the royal wing. "Did anyone get in trouble?"

"No one was arrested," Hughes says. "But some were dismissed for *extremely* tenuous connections, likely to discourage any staff from risking associations with the group."

Eugene feels more than a stab of guilt at that. The prospect of the apprenticeship almost feels too good to be true. (Stay with the girl he loves? Check. Use his very specific skill set to protect her and their home? Check. Presumptively decent pay? Cash *or* check, thank you.) And Cressien wouldn't offer his recommendation lightly.

But if Eugene cost innocent people their jobs . . .

Hughes clears his throat. "It was better than if you'd left no sign of a culprit. The king would still be tearing the castle apart looking for the messages." His voice catches a bit. "Your uncle, however, would have planted something to implicate Councilor Persevault."

Then he holds a hand up, the "silent" gesture the People's Council agreed on. As they round the corner, Eugene sees two guards stationed at the entrance to the king's quarters.

Hughes doesn't speak again until they reach the king's office. The door is firmly shut, the voices inside low and muffled. It doesn't sound like they're close to wrapping it up.

Hughes confirms: "They may be at it a while. We'll wait here."

"Got it." Eugene posts up by Hughes's side.

Since the ball, Eugene has learned more than he'd ever dreamed about his parents, though that's still mostly scraps and fragments, pieced together as best he can. People like Sulian and Torch knew them from their time with the People's Dagger, and Sol—no, *Leona*—and Ruvon knew them as the queen's friends.

But there's one void that no one can help him fill quite as well as Hughes. Eugene debates with himself a long moment, makes sure they're out of earshot of any guards, then takes the plunge. "Can . . . can I ask about my uncle?"

Hughes briefly closes his eyes. "What do you wish to know?"

"Anything," Eugene says.

For a moment he thinks Hughes will refuse. But then he says, "You're more like your father than your uncle. But . . . there are similarities."

"Really?" Eugene can't help sounding almost like a little kid.

Hughes nods. "He was clever, funny. Resourceful. Irreverent. Occasionally hardheaded. *Frequently* boneheaded." A shallow smile digs at the corner of his mouth. "You know, he and your father used to play 'Flynnigan Rider' when they were little boys. People tend to underestimate the power of the stories we tell our children, and the stories children tell themselves. Andreas and Marietta saw something more than just adventures. They saw a dream that was possible because Flynnigan Rider never has to worry about his health or his money. They wrote it into the book because they believed better things were possible for all of Astera. And according to your uncle Eugene, they especially wanted that dream for you."

Before Eugene can process this, the office door swings open.

"Fitzherbert," Enver calls. "Just who I was looking for."

Councilor Persevault gives him a particularly nasty look as he shoves past.

Eugene swallows and walks into the office. It's not as dim as when he broke in a few nights ago, but beyond the wall of windows lies only periwinkle twilight and the scattered glimmer of lanterns in the city below.

Enver shuts the door behind him.

"It occurs to me," Enver says, "that I've neglected to speak to you, when you must be in a very difficult position."

Because you murdered my father and drove my mother into exile? Eugene keeps that to himself. He has one very specific job to accomplish here, and he can't squander all the work that put him in this room.

Then Enver surprises him: "A position that, perhaps, only I understand."

"Your Majesty?" Eugene braces himself on the back of an armchair. If this is Enver's apology, he's coming at it from a bizarre angle.

Enver paces over to his desk and casually shuffles some papers. "It's not easy being a royal consort, is it? Of course you love the girl, but it's different to love a queen. To know no matter how hard we work, we will always come second—for the country, second to the queen, and for the queen, second to her country. I was a duke, and I still never felt good enough. It must be a thousand times worse for you, coming from an orphanage."

Eugene would like to deny it.

He would also like to have spent the last six weeks *not* convinced Rapunzel's parents were waiting for an opportunity to send him packing.

"I don't know what to say," he answers truthfully.

Enver sets the papers down—oddly. Almost fanning them out.

As if he's hiding something beneath them.

"I just want you to know that you belong in Astera as much as I do, and you will always have a place with us." Astonishingly, Enver strides over and clasps his shoulder. "And despite your parents . . . here, at least, you can rise to be your queen's equal. Just like me."

Unbidden, Hughes's words echo back to Eugene: *They believed better things were possible for all of Astera.*

So, too, do Cressien's: *The king and queen saw their potential, not their rank.*

His parents dreamed of lifting everyone. And Enver—growing the apple tree, attacking the council and the People's Dagger, closing the Starlight Spring, keeping Astera on a leash and dangling the hope of Verette's reign just out of reach—Enver has only ever climbed for himself.

Someone like that could never be satisfied with anything less than the only crown in a kingdom.

That's not Eugene's dream. Or his parents'.

And he has it on good authority there's a new life already waiting for him—as an apprentice spymaster.

Maybe it's time to apply himself to the job.

Enver has spent this whole conversation trying to get Eugene to identify with him. *Just like me. It's not easy, is it? We will always come second.* Maybe he'll give up more information if Eugene plays along.

Maybe he'll let Eugene get close enough to the desk to see what's under the papers.

Eugene butters his face with humility and gratitude. "You really think I could be like you? I mean—I never believed an orphan like me could actually be important. I'm just some guy, you know?"

What he's really asking is *Why are you suddenly trying to convince me to stay in Astera?*

"Nonsense! With hard work and dedication, a lad like you

could go far in a kingdom like this." Enver straightens up, and then—he winces. One hand strays to his burgundy doublet for a moment before he seemingly shakes it off. "I could see you contributing a great deal, in fact."

Eugene rubs the back of his neck and wanders over to the windows, really laying on the "simple little guy" act. "I don't know . . . I really don't want to split up with Rapunzel."

What he's asking now is *Are you after me, or both of us?*

He hears the shift in Enver's voice, the veneer of fake sympathy. "That is certainly a challenge . . . I'd never want to choose between my homeland and my heart."

"I don't know that I can," Eugene fibs. He shuffles a little further, angling himself so the desk is halfway between him and the office door.

Enver decides to push even harder. "Well, if you decide to spend more time in Astera, perhaps you'll come up with a way around that challenge. Long-distance relationships aren't for everyone."

Eugene can't tell if that's a condolence or a threat.

A bell rings to mark the hour, and Enver starts. "Oh, bother, I've lost track of time. They're going to start the invitations any minute now. We'd best be off."

"Of course." Eugene bows and heads for the door, passing the desk on the way.

He can't make out much beneath the array of papers, but it looks like there's a . . . map? A red ink line arcs across the pale blue of a sea, its arrowhead terminating on a familiar coastline labeled *Kourenne.*

Does Enver mean to follow them back home?

Eugene keeps the confusion off his face until he's exited the office and bowed to the king, who rattles off orders to Hughes before striding away.

Hughes hangs back a moment. "Everything in order, Fitzherbert?"

Eugene makes sure, once again, that no one's watching. Then he swiftly passes Hughes a heavy iron key.

Enver's key to the entrance of the Starlight Spring.

After all, Eugene didn't need an apology, not really. He just needed an opening to pick the king's pocket.

"All in order," he says smugly—then sobers. "But there's a map on his desk, under his papers. I think it shows a sea route back to our kingdom. And when I came in, he tried to hide it."

Hughes's face tightens. "Perhaps he means to send Princess Verette back with you."

"Or actually pass on the throne and return with us himself," Eugene suggests. "Or maybe he wants to do a kingdom swap? Is that a thing people do?"

That only seems to trouble the chamberlain more. He stows the iron key in a pocket. "We need to get this to Councilor Teophine right away," Hughes breathes through his teeth. "No matter what the king is up to, I'm certain we're going to need it."

Hughes leads them back to the audience hall and vanishes into the crowd; Eugene does the same, though he's weaving his way over to Rapunzel. She beams when she sees him, and excuses herself from a knot of hoity-toity bureaucrats. When he reaches her, she whispers, "We have a problem."

That wasn't what Eugene expected to hear. "What?"

Her hands have been linked behind her back. She furtively whips one around. Pascal is huddled on her wrist, blending seamlessly into her lilac sleeve.

"*Somebody* decided to stow away on my dress again," Rapunzel grits through a sunny smile. "And I won't have a chance to take him back to my room."

"Maybe he can fend for himself," Eugene suggests. Rapunzel scowls, and he throws up his hands. "Pascal *did* trip Gothel so she fell off the tower. I'm just saying, when the chips are down, that frog has the instincts of a stone-cold killer."

Pascal blinks at him, somehow imbuing the movement with a myriad of implications, all of them sinister.

Eugene relents. "I'll drop him off when we head out."

"*Thank* you." Rapunzel tucks Pascal into the crook of her elbow. "How did it go with the king?"

"Weird," Eugene says, muffling the words in a canapé he snagged on his way across the hall. "Successful but weird. He was hinting that I should stay in Astera."

Rapunzel's face drops. "What? *Why?*"

"No clue," Eugene says. "He also has a sea route charted out to follow us home, I think."

Rapunzel's nose wrinkles as she thinks. "The tree takes years to grow each apple, so even if he's eating them, he could have traveled in between . . . so if he wanted to leave, why wait until *now*?" Then her head tilts. She looks up at Eugene. "Wait . . . do you *want* to stay here?"

The prospect of honesty has only grown more daunting after all these weeks—but didn't Cressien warn him it would never get easier? Eugene takes a deep breath. "The funny thing is . . . I've been expecting your parents to ask me to leave. I mean, they'd be nice about it, but at the end of the day, I know I'm not who most people, let alone royalty, want courting their daughter."

"Did they say something to you?" Rapunzel demands.

"Also funny, Cressien asked almost exactly that. And then he told me how wrong I was. And he might have gotten me a new job." Eugene doesn't realize he's nervously wadding up the half-eaten canapé in a napkin until it's too late. "Point is, I was afraid there wasn't a place for me in the palace in the long run. And now . . . I feel like it's exactly where I could belong."

Rapunzel's smile returns again, bright as the sun. She plucks the canapé catastrophe from his grasp, tosses it with impressive aim into a nearby decorative urn, and then takes his hands in hers. "Good, because I think I'm starting to feel like I belong too. But I wouldn't without you."

For a moment, Eugene forgets about everything but the relief of having a path under his feet again, and the girl he'd climb a thousand towers for there for the journey.

Then she huffs a laugh and nudges him. "Speaking of Cressien . . . I wonder if he's going to try to get us to stay here longer, too."

Eugene follows her gaze to the minister, who's almost a little *too* engrossed in debate with . . . Hughes? If he strains, he can pick out fragments of the exchange, and Eugene can say with confidence that it's the first time he's heard anyone flirt over things like export fees and cargo regulations. "Good for him. Didn't your mother say something about him and his husband splitting?"

"I think so."

Eugene cups his cheek. "This may be the most romantic diplomatic summit I've ever witnessed."

Rapunzel cocks her head to the side. "How many *have* you witnessed?"

Before he has to answer that, there's a commotion on the dais. Verette, rigid, steps to the side as Enver plants himself in her previous spot before the throne.

Rumbles rise from the guests, who have already started queueing up for the issuing of invitations. Eugene's jaw clenches. If this is so unusual—maybe—maybe Verette was right, maybe he's pushing Eugene to stay so she has allies, maybe this is it—

The hush that falls over the hall says he's not the only one dangling in anticipation.

"My esteemed guests," Enver begins, spreading his hands, "I wanted to take a moment to share a few words about my remarkable daughter. I'm so proud to have raised such a strong, lovely, and intelligent young woman, and I am confident she will be the leader Astera needs . . ." He turns to Verette, who presses her lips into a tight smile. ". . . when the time is right."

Rapunzel audibly sucks in a breath.

"And like all of you, I very much look forward to that day's arrival," Enver blithely carries on as a crackling tension rips through the hall. "For many years now, I've watched her grow. . . ."

He's keeping the throne. Again. Even if Eugene couldn't tell from the avoidance in Enver's words, he can see it written plain as day on the faces around them.

And, most alarmingly, on Verette's as well.

Behind the mask of demure politesse, through the droning, empty praise, her cheeks burn, her eyes glittering with unshed tears.

Then Verette does the unexpected. She brushes past Enver, down the steps, into the parting crowd, as her father's voice falters. Not once does she look back, marching in a perfect, unwavering line, until she's left the hall entirely.

Eugene can't believe he ever even hoped he could be the son of this king.

Murmurs boil over as Enver says, unsteady for the first time, "She—she wasn't feeling well earlier—must be an upset stomach."

Eugene glances back at him to find the king brushing his own belly with a stiff smile. It fractures into a lightning-fast flinch: Enver's lips part briefly, his eyes unfocused—and then he gathers himself once more.

"Teophine," Enver says shortly, jerking his chin in the direction Verette went. Councilor Teophine bows and weaves her way through the attendees.

Rapunzel quickly passes Pascal over to Eugene, then announces loudly, "I'll go with her." Before Enver can object, she's already fallen into step with Councilor Teophine, nearly out of the hall.

Eugene swallows. That was the signal; Plan B has officially been scrapped.

Plan A-for-Apple is in motion.

Enver's words turn forcedly smooth. "Please, everyone, keep enjoying yourselves. We'll do the invitations later, if Verette's up to it. Thank you all for joining us tonight."

Then he hurries off the dais.

Eugene's eyes narrow. He's watching Enver's hands again, because that's where he betrayed himself before.

And this time, Eugene would swear that on the king's fingertips, he can see a smudge of . . . red.

The memory slides like cold steel into his gut. A knife. Pain exploding below his ribs. Crashing to the stone floor of Gothel's tower.

His own shaking hand, stained with the same vivid red.

And another memory, this from just a few days ago, returns: Enver reaching for the same place on his stomach when he thought the People's Dagger had crashed the reception ball.

And another: Sulian saying *Torch swears it was all planned. That she got him in the belly.*

And another: Teophine saying the starlight water alone isn't enough to heal a mortal wound.

It finally snaps into place.

Enver and Eugene have something in common after all: a killing blow they never should have survived. But Eugene's healed for good.

Enver's didn't.

The apples aren't just keeping him young, like Gothel.

They're keeping the king alive.

Just then, Eugene has one more realization, perhaps even more dangerous: Pascal is nowhere to be found.

Nineteen

Rapunzel

Rapunzel pulls her gray cloak tighter against the chill of the night as Verette fumbles with the door to the Starlight Spring. The heavy iron key has gone on a journey tonight, passing first from Hughes to Teophine, then from Teophine to Verette once they'd both left the hall.

"Got enough light?" Leona whispers, nudging her lantern closer. Its flame wobbles in place, a vivid cornflower blue thanks to some sort of chemical compound in the oil. (Rapunzel asked. And then she made Leona promise to write the particulars down for her later.)

"I just—*there*." The door swings open, and all three women hurry into the passageway.

NINETEEN

Rapunzel pulls the door shut behind them, and the lock automatically resets as it latches. Enver should be too preoccupied to eavesdrop on them through the roots as long as the party lasts, but that's not the only deadline they have to meet. "How much time do we have?"

Leona squints at the lantern. "We're to meet the others at the fork in half an hour. The coloring agent will have fully burned off by then, so once the light's pink, we need to hustle."

Rapunzel nods, then looks to Verette. "I can take song duty first."

"No, you've been here before. You focus on leading the way." Verette draws a breath, then starts quietly humming the lullaby. Roots ignite up and down the walls of the path, even brighter and farther than they did for Rapunzel. So long as Verette's controlling them, the roots can't betray them to Enver.

Rapunzel starts down the passageway. Originally she and Verette had planned to split up, with Verette going for the harbor to cause a diversion and Rapunzel going with the group headed for what they've been calling the starcloud tree. Leona herself had raised one very salient logistical issue, though:

"So as long as one of you hums the song, the roots can't alert Enver. What if you have to stop?"

Which is why both of them are here now. Even Verette storming out of her own party early was part of Plan A-for-Apple; she and Rapunzel just had time to change into plain shirts and breeches and the gray cloaks while Councilor Teophine returned to tell Enver Verette had run off to her party barge again.

In truth, somewhere far above, Councilor Teophine, Minister Cressien, and Hughes are combining their efforts to keep King Enver fully distracted while Verette, Rapunzel, and Leona figure out what he's planning with an entire secret fleet. In half an hour, the second group of Sulian, Eugene, Ruvon, and Torch will enter the passages after Eugene picks the lock, and Rapunzel's team will double back to meet them before they all head for the tree.

Then Verette will take them to have a very firm talk with her father, and if all goes well, the price of the Asteran throne will be a single apple.

Rapunzel heads right at the fork, watching the roots shudder as they pass. In the past few days of testing, they've only done that for Verette, but by now Rapunzel can almost *feel* them in the walls, not entirely unlike the strands of her golden hair. There's no sensation to them, just an awareness, the way she knew whenever a lock had snagged on a chair leg or slipped out of a tie.

(Former) Councilor Ruvon's best theory has stuck with her—that even though the sundrop's power is gone, it left its mark on her. "After all," he said two days before, "even as we lost the effects of our starlight, no one's hair *reverted* all these years. Magic like that changes us. And what is a star but a more distant sun?"

It lights their way far better than the lantern now. When they get close to the entrance of the hidden harbor, Rapunzel holds a hand up, and Verette's humming pauses. There's no sound echoing back this time besides the faint creak of ship timbers and breaking waves.

"All clear," she whispers. They sneak through the opening and crouch at the top of the ramp; the glimmering roots are much scarcer here, running only through the cave's rock ceiling above. "I don't think they like salt water."

"Good." Leona peers down to the moored ships. Her face tightens. "What the devil . . . ?"

"What's wrong?" Rapunzel asks under her breath, following the light of a single guard as he moves down the docks. She doesn't see any lookouts, but then again, considering the number of soldiers patrolling above tonight, Enver may have diverted all his forces to security for the party they're missing.

Leona's scowling ferociously. "Those are all warships. And look, they're being loaded—that's why all the gangways are down. This is an armada. And it's going to sail this week. What is my brother *doing*?"

"What is my *father* doing?" Verette echoes.

"There, that's the flagship, right?" Rapunzel points to the largest of the fleet, which isn't just flying the Asteran flag, but also a dark red flag depicting crossed swords and a compass with the needle pointing west.

"*My* old flagship," Leona says darkly.

"Eugene saw a map on Enver's desk earlier tonight marked with a route to our kingdom. If we can sneak aboard and find the captain's cabin, we can see if they've charted the same course." Rapunzel finds Verette and Leona staring at her. She shrugs. "I asked our ship's captain a lot of questions on the way here."

Leona checks the lantern. The flame's a vivid royal purple. "We still have time if we move quickly. And unmooring the flagship would be a decent diversion."

They wait until the lone guard's loop reaches the near end of the dock, then head down the ramp and hide behind the provision stash as he makes another round. Once his back is turned again, they follow as quietly as they can, then bolt up the flagship's gangplank.

"This way." Leona leads them past rows of cannons to the stern, occasionally shaking her head and muttering about her brother Erwan's shoddy upkeep. The groaning boards swallow the sound of her walking stick, but Rapunzel glances over the railing and finds the light of the guard's own lantern has gone still. She ducks. After a moment, the bobbing glow on the water says he's resumed his route.

Rapunzel's stomach nonetheless knots with unease.

She follows the others into the captain's cabin. "Let's be fast. I think the guard's suspicious."

Leona's already studying a map on a large mahogany table. "Good news, bad news. Good news: We know where they're going. Bad news: You're right, it's Kourenne."

This might be the most upset Rapunzel has ever been about being correct. "Do we know why?"

"We're still looking." Verette shuts a desk drawer. "At least

Councilor Persevault knows better than to leave the orders out in the open."

Rapunzel kneels by a chest beside the desk and tries the lid. It's locked. "Do you see a key anywhere?"

"Wait." Leona thumps over and reaches for a compass set into the head of the desk. It sinks into the wood halfway with an audible click. A panel pops out from the wall behind it as she flashes a wolfish grin. "Didn't bother changing it at all, the lazy sod. There's your key."

Verette reaches into the compartment and passes the key to Rapunzel, then pulls out a tightly rolled parchment as well. She holds it up to the violet lantern light to read, and her face drops. As Rapunzel unlocks the trunk, Verette begins to read aloud.

"'Greetings to Their Honorable Majesties of Kourenne. I, Erwan Persevault, Councilor of the West and Master of Seas, bear this message on behalf of His Majesty, King Enver of Astera. Your daughter, Princess Rapunzel, and her consort, Eugene Fitzherbert, are now in our custody, and your minister of diplomacy will remain a hostage on my flagship. If you wish to see any of them again, you must cede to Astera the territory containing the former location of the sundrop flower, and allow us unrestricted access to it. To ensure your compliance, the princess and her consort will remain in Astera until at least a decade has passed. Furthermore, our fleet will intercept any vessels coming or going from Kourenne until you agree to our demands. We hope Their Majesties will act with the wisdom and prudence they are known for.'" The parchment trembles in Verette's hand. "Why—why would he—?"

"For this," Rapunzel says numbly, staring into the open chest.

Rows of tiny jars are carefully packed in sawdust, each one containing a single dark glassy seed with pearly light flickering in its heart.

Apple seeds.

"Councilor Teophine said some people think the sundrop magic was in the ground, and the flower just concentrated it," Rapunzel says. "Now the Starlight Spring's been tapped out, he wants to plant even more trees there and hold me hostage until they bear apples. That's why he was trying to convince Eugene to stay—he knows I wouldn't fight as hard to leave if Eugene wouldn't go with me."

Enver knows she's only *just* started to see the rest of the world. That she only *just* found her family again.

That she spent eighteen years in a prison disguised as a home.

And now, he's trying to make his home into a prison for her.

For a moment, there's only the rush of seawater below, the soft groan of the swaying ship, and a hiss from the lantern.

Finally Verette breathes, "He was never going to let me take the throne."

Rapunzel looks up to find Verette's eyes fixed on the jars. Leona sets a hand on her shoulder. "Your Highness—"

"He never even considered it. He just wanted a pretext to lure Rapunzel here—he *used* us—"

NINETEEN

A faint, strange tinkling begins to emanate from the chest. The seeds are shaking, almost dancing in their jars.

Then something tickles at the back of Rapunzel's skull. She picks up a jar, brow furrowing, and watches the starlight pulse in its depths. She'd almost swear she can sense—*roots*?

A clamor rises from the docks outside. Rapunzel pushes herself up and moves to the window. "Look—!"

Sailors march down the planks, rolling carts of cannonballs and barrels of blasting powder.

"Explosives are loaded last," Leona hisses over her shoulder. "They're launching *tonight*."

"You've some nerve showing your face here, Leona." A bulky silhouette blocks the door, then steps inside. Lavender light washes in the details of Erwan Persevault. "Should have known I'd find you when the watchman told me three rats snuck on board."

"Erwan," Leona says coldly. "You've done a lousy job with my ship. Suppose you'll have to steal someone else's and try again."

Erwan lunges for her, swinging a meaty fist. She pivots out of the way and does a quick little thrust with her walking stick that sends him crashing to the floor. Then she uses it to crack him in the jaw.

"You're lucky I don't have time to deal you worse," Leona snarls, and blows a strand of her short hair away from her face. "You're doubly lucky I'll ask the queen to spare you the gallows."

Erwan sneers, "Spare this." His boot smashes into her bad knee. As Leona staggers back with a cry, he rolls to his feet—

And the jars in the chest burst. Rapunzel throws herself backward, shaking off the shattered glass, and finds shining roots swarming over Erwan.

Verette's hand is outstretched, her braid burning for the first time with starlight.

The roots slam Erwan into the floorboards again and again until he's stunned, then coil around him until he's bound and gagged.

"Good work," Leona grits out. "Now let's go before someone comes looking."

"Give me a second—I think I'm getting it—" Verette twists her hand. Tendrils sprout from another seed and grow into a brace for Leona's knee.

Rapunzel grabs the parchment with Enver's orders and folds it into a pocket, along with a handful of seeds. "Come on!"

They help Leona down the gangplank as fast as they can, then hide behind a pile of crates, out of sight of the sailors still loading the ships. The path back up to the tunnel stretches long and is much, much too exposed. "We need a distraction," Leona whispers.

"I need a seed," Verette says. Rapunzel fishes one out. Verette takes it, tosses it over her shoulder, and crumples her face with concentration.

Rapunzel peeks around the edge of the crates toward where the seed landed, and sees a tangled ball of roots burst into life. It discreetly rolls up behind a stack of barrels and yanks a bottom one free, sending the whole pyramid tumbling down. Shouts of dismay ring through the cavern.

"Now," Verette forces out. Starlight kindles in her braid again as the root brace on Leona's knee sprouts more and more strands. They split off and weave into a stool of sorts with clusters of spiderlike legs. Sweat beads her brow. "Let's go."

The walking roots bear Leona up the ramp as Rapunzel and Verette hurry after. The three of them have just crested the final incline when the tendrils finally give out, and Rapunzel and Verette each sling one of Leona's arms over a shoulder and half carry her the rest of the way.

They finally reach the tunnel, then sag against a wall to catch their breath. "We can't," Rapunzel wheezes, "let the ships leave."

"How can we do that without hurting the sailors?" Verette wipes her damp face. "It's not their fault they're caught up in this."

"Sink 'em with the roots," Leona grunts.

Verette shakes her head. "They can't go through salt water."

Rapunzel is just straightening up when a shape emerges from the dark. She gasps—

"It's me!" Eugene hisses, hurrying into their lantern's magenta light.

"But we're supposed to meet at the fork," Rapunzel says, confused. "Is everything all right?"

"We might need a change of plan." Eugene looks at the ground, then back up at them, uncertain. "Verette . . . you should know the real reason why your father needs the apple."

TWENTY

EUGENE

"I don't understand." Verette's voice bounces off the stone walls with a treacherous wobble.

Eugene shifts uncomfortably; the only other sound is Rapunzel's soft humming to maintain their control of the roots. They've moved farther down the passage to avoid drawing notice from the underground harbor. The glowing roots in the walls give plenty of light to see by—almost too much, in fact, as he can tell from the stubborn jut of Verette's chin that the problem is she doesn't *want* to understand.

He tries again. "Torch wounded your father during the massacre twenty years ago. He's bleeding from the same place right now. The apples may be stronger than the water, but I don't think he's ever fully healed. It's not just about staying young, it's about staying alive."

Rapunzel raises her hand.

Verette purses her lips, and the roots surge with light. "I think I've got the hang of it now. We don't need to keep humming."

"Gothel—" Rapunzel's voice cracks. "When my hair was cut and the magic left, all of the aging she'd delayed came back at once. Maybe the king's wound comes back like that too, but slowly."

"So if we destroy the tree, Enver dies with it." Leona's dry tone implies an additional *everyone wins.*

Verette's fists clench.

Leona cocks her head. "Are you all square with that, Your Majesty?"

"It's fine." Verette's face hardens. "Maybe—maybe we can grow him edible plants in a container watered from the Starlight Spring. Or make preserves with spring water. Or something. I don't know, I'll—I'll figure it out." She looks over her shoulder. "But we *have* to stop the fleet. And I think I know how. We just have to be stealthy."

"We don't have long before Enver notices none of us have come back to the party," Eugene points out. "This could be our only shot at the apple."

Leona nods, grim. "He can lose the ships and still keep the throne. You need the apple to force him to yield."

"Then we split up," Rapunzel says. "I'll take Leona and get

the second group through the roots and into the spring, if you and Verette can stop the fleet."

Eugene's chest tightens. He'd rather sacrifice another cheese fountain than send Rapunzel off on her own, but she *is* still the girl who played chess against herself for years. "I can do that."

Verette catches Rapunzel's sleeve. "Can you give me the rest of the seeds?

Rapunzel passes them over. Then she steps closer to Eugene and stands on her tiptoes for a swift, anxious kiss. "Be careful," she tells him as his hands settle on her shoulders.

"Is that a royal command?"

Her eyes flash. "You know what? Yes."

"You know how good I am at following orders," he jokes, "but maybe I'll make an exception this time."

Leona clears her throat.

"Fine, fine, we're going." Eugene releases Rapunzel, then adds with more sincerity than he usually allows, "You be careful, too."

He tries to quell the churning of his gut as best he can as Rapunzel slings Leona's arm over her shoulders and sets off, humming under her breath.

Eugene turns to Verette. "All right. So how are we stopping the ships?"

Verette starts jogging down the tunnel. "We can't hurt the sailors, and salt water kills the roots, so I can't sink them from below." Her voice drops as they near the entrance back into the underground harbor, which is a lot noisier than Eugene remembers. "So if we can't sink them, we stop . . ." Her voice trails off as she looks down into the cavern.

Eugene peers through the entrance at a chaotic scene; sailors crawl all over the ships, either searching or loading what looks like some serious ordnance, as a red-faced and disheveled Erwan storms onto the docks, bellowing.

"He's *supposed* to be tied up," Verette sputters, "he—he's going to warn Father—"

Eugene grabs her elbow. "So we skip the sneaking and cut to the chase."

Verette sucks in a breath, then points to the opening of the cavern, where the ships will leave. "If I can block *that* with roots, even from the waterline up, it should hold them in."

Eugene scans the area. One watch station on either side of the cave mouth, most attention on Erwan. "Doable," he says. "How do we stop Erwan?"

"You take this seed to the closest watch station." Verette hands him a very bizarre-looking apple seed and points. "I'll go to the far one and seal the tunnel exits on my way. He can't tell my father anything if he can't get out, either."

"Devious," Eugene says approvingly. Now, in light of everything, he's pretty sure Enver's being his father would have been the worst possible outcome . . . but he can't lie, he wouldn't have hated having Verette for a sister. "Ready?"

"Ready," Verette says.

They rush through the door. Roots spike through the ground and weave crude bars across the gap behind them. As they barrel down the path, Eugene sees Verette throw another seed, which bursts into a ball of roots that swells to nearly the size of a horse—then shifts into the *form* of a horse in time for her to jump onto its back and ride it down the docks.

Belatedly, Eugene realizes Maximus could likely have handled the fleet on his own. Though arguably with less consideration for loss of life. Eugene makes a note to detour to the stables once they get out.

While Verette is distracting everyone with some wild and unorthodox uses of foliage, Eugene hares off for his designated watch station. There are only two soldiers there, and both of them are fixated on the princess currently closing off the other exit with gnarled roots. This makes it remarkably easy for Eugene to sneak up behind the first man, take his spear, and knock him out with it. By the time the second guard has figured out what's going on, he is unfortunately too late to duck a solid whack to the chin from the spear butt.

Eugene fishes out the seed and drops it on the ground. A moment later, he sees Verette ride up to the watch station on the opposite side of the cavern's mouth, at which point the soldiers on duty there have a very unique and immobilizing experience with tree roots that will hopefully never be repeated in their lifetime.

The ground rumbles beneath his feet. He stumbles back as tendrils burst from the seed and sink into the rock, then climb and spread up to the lip of the cavern's mouth and flourish into a giant net of root and vine, meeting with a second web growing from Verette's side. In seconds, the opening has been completely blocked off.

Eugene can see Verette grinning with open relief all the way across the water. He opens his mouth to shout a congratulations—

And thunder blasts through the cavern. Eugene throws his hands over his ringing ears, staggering in place. Another boom follows, then another.

When his watering eyes clear enough, he sees the net now hanging by shreds, rent by great burning holes.

Smoke trails from the flagship's cannons. From the scurry of movement in the galleys, Eugene is sure they're already reloading.

Verette sways on her feet, reaching for the roots. They twitch and shudder, but the feeble sprouts aren't going to hold up to a second round of cannon fire.

Footsteps rumble toward Eugene. His takeover of the watch station hasn't gone unnoticed, and Erwan's soldiers have figured out he's an easier target than the princess who can sic roots on them.

Hot desperation rises in his throat. He *told* Rapunzel he could handle this—he can't let her down, but all he has is the spear in his sweating hands—

His eyes land on an unlit camp stove set up for the cold night watches beside a couple of low stools.

And the cast-iron skillet propped against the stone wall a few feet away.

The weight of the frying pan handle feels *spectacular* in his grip as the spear clatters to the ground.

Eugene hefts the skillet, squares up to the oncoming soldiers, and gets ready to cook.

Twenty-One

Rapunzel

"My water screw!"

Ruvon's lament rings through the great root-bound cave as Rapunzel leads the group inside the Starlight Spring, still humming. Leona leans on his arm, and Torch and Sulian bring up the rear, but Ruvon is clearly the most distraught of them all.

He jabs a finger at the starcloud tree's silvery trunk, where the giant spiraling blades still jut through. "We angled it to draw out the water closest to the stardrop. Enver must have planted this infernal tree right over it after the final Fountain Festival, when the reservoir was low."

Rapunzel's found that as long as she keeps the lullaby's tune, the words don't matter, which is why she half sings, "The stardrop is still intact?"

Ruvon makes a face she now understands to mean he's distilling a fifty-page report to a few sentences. "We're . . . not certain. Starlight seems to emanate from a point below where the tree is now, but we never tampered with it even before Enver restricted access to the spring."

"Let's get this over with," Torch bites out. A coil of rope bounces on her shoulder as she strides down the stairs and across the flat root-webbed silt, headed for the tree. As Rapunzel follows, the shimmer of nearby roots brightens, starlight tracing down myriad fibers. "It's time for Enver to give up the throne like he promised."

"And to stop holding the promise over Verette," Rapunzel fits awkwardly into the song.

"It's more than just the throne." Master Sulian hasn't said much this whole walk, but his eyes are as sharp as an old knife that's been held to the grindstone a long, long time. "Teophine and I have watched her in this palace these last two decades. She never kept friends long—they always outgrew her, with Enver making her drink starlight every morning. He had every portrait of Queen Gaelle locked away. Anyone who mentioned her to the princess fell out of favor or lost their job." Sulian swallows. "Torch, Ruvon, and Leona have lived in hiding for twenty years. All of Astera lost our chance at normal lives, thanks to him. And now we know it was all so he could survive the massacre *he* planned. We're all ready for a change."

"Little help here?" Torch calls back.

Rapunzel finds starlight pooling under her feet as she comes to stand by Torch. "What do you need?"

Torch scowls up at the lone apple. Even though it's dangling from the lowest bough, it's still yards and yards out of reach. Years of calculating the loops of her hair tell Rapunzel the rope on Torch's shoulder is also inadequate. "Can you do anything to get it closer?"

Rapunzel studies the tree, placing a hand on one massive glowing root arch. Verette could probably do something, considering how she wielded the roots before.

And what is starlight but the light of a distant sun?

When Rapunzel closes her eyes, she can feel the magic coursing through the tree. It—it's not hers. Not her power, not her sunlight.

But it's close enough.

She thinks of the last day in the tower, of Eugene growing cold in her arms, of how desperately she feared that chill. How she reached for the sunlight, and despite everything, it answered her call.

She thinks of Third Street Hospital. Of the chief engineer of the Northeast Secondary Sunmill. Of a closet full of verettes.

And she reaches for the starlight.

Leaves rustle, the fibers of the wood almost like strands of hair, rays of sunlight, threads of starlight, bending for her. By the time she opens her eyes, the bough has descended, the apple now dangling only a few feet from her face.

It looks even stranger up close, lighter freckles dancing over its pale, crystalline periwinkle skin with the rainbow gleams of a prism.

Still singing, Rapunzel reaches up and breaks the apple off the tree.

A rush of starlight swells below her like a tidal wave, as if without the apple draining it, it's free to flow. Not only does light blaze from the roots, but the dirt, the stone, even the residue on the walls, all of it comes alive with stardust, until Rapunzel's eyes water. For the first time, little embers of sundrop gold dart through the iridescence.

Maybe she can do more than pick an apple.

She hands the apple to Torch, then stretches out a hand toward the tree.

The starcloud tree shudders from tip to trunk. Indigo leaves flutter down from the branches pressed against the spring's ceiling, each as translucent as the apple. With a crack, one of the largest roots jerks from the ground, and the brightest flare of starlight yet bursts out from somewhere deep below the tree—

Then Enver's voice roars in her skull: *"NO!"*

The root slams back into place, the light guttering out. Rapunzel only barely manages to keep singing between her gasps for breath.

Ruvon's voice echoes through the cavern. "If we release the sunmill above, the water screw should turn and help pry up the tree!"

Twenty-One

"Wouldn't this whole contraption just be stuck?" Leona asks.

"Obviously not, darling. The mill sails' crystals have been storing up energy from the sun for twenty years," Ruvon retorts. "If the water screw weren't already beyond repair, I'd never recommend it. The amount of force alone . . ." When he's met with blank stares, he snaps, "Am I the *only* one who did the reading on sunmills?"

Another pulse of light sears down the roots, a cold silver this time.

Rapunzel jerks back, voice wavering as the magic begins to *drag*—

And then even the largest roots begin to thrash.

Chaos erupts everywhere.

Torch shouts *"It's Enver!"* as cracks split down the walls of the spring.

The ground collapses under their feet. Gnarled roots whip around them all, yanking them up, up, toward a ceiling being ripped open by a thousand shining tendrils. They chew a tunnel through solid rock, and for a moment, all Rapunzel knows is the crash of breaking stone, muffled cries, the slither of roots, and the jostle and bang whenever she's dragged too close to the wall.

Then the sound of shattering limestone changes to the glassier crack of marble, and they're unceremoniously shoved up onto the floor of—the audience hall.

The roots jerk Rapunzel to her feet, alongside Leona, Sulian,

Ruvon, and finally, Torch. Gasps sweep the already rattled hall.

From all appearances, most of the evening went according to plan, the party seemingly on the verge of winding down before Enver ripped them through the floor—right under the refreshment tables, judging by the mess of food and linens scattered around the crude gaping gash. Most of the guests are bunched up against the walls now, Cressien and Teophine among them, taut with horror. Hughes is hiding his dismay, but his throat bobs as he waits at Enver's elbow.

And Enver—well, that's where things went wrong.

Because just like the roots, the tree, and the spring, Enver's veins are blazing with starlight.

Rapunzel tries to hum around the root jammed between her teeth as a gag. But even if it didn't come out strangled, Enver's command over the starlight is unshakable.

The ground trembles once more, spreading fractures through the tiles. Then another figure is hauled through the floor, tangled in roots.

Verette.

And there is no sign of Eugene.

Rapunzel's heart freezes.

Where—where is Eugene?

"Verette." The king walks slowly, frostily down the steps of the dais, trailed by Hughes. "What do you think you're *doing*?"

"Why don't you go first, *Father*?" Verette shoots back. She's the only one of their captive group to not have a root jammed between her teeth. The tendrils around her twitch and sputter with little flares of light as she tries vainly to break free. "Why don't you tell everyone about the apple tree you planted in the Starlight Spring? How it's been draining all the starlight from Astera for decades, just so you can eat its fruit and prolong your life. Or how you planned to hold Rapunzel hostage to force her kingdom to let you plant another one." Her chin lifts, eyes burning. "Tell them, Father. Tell them there was no poison in the spring. The only poison in the palace has been *you*."

Hughes keeps pacing around the prisoners, but Enver stops in front of Verette. His smile is slow and as bitter as wine soured to vinegar. "I see . . . I'm afraid you're just exaggerating again, sweetheart. I understand you're upset with me, but this just proves you're not ready to be queen yet."

Rapunzel shifts and hears a papery crinkle at her hip. She looks down and sees a thin stripe of parchment peeking out of her pocket.

Enver's demands for her parents.

And he's too busy grandstanding at Verette to pay attention to her.

"I did plant a tree by the spring," Enver's saying, "oh, twenty-five years ago? I thought if the fruit concentrated the starlight, it might be able to save your mother."

Rapunzel snags the edge of the parchment and slips it free, then adjusts her angle so it's hidden behind her back. As Hughes passes, she feels the sheet tugged from her hand.

Enver's still going. "It didn't bear fruit in time to save her.

If you found anything strange or problematic in the Starlight Spring, it could only be the work of *your* friends, the People's Dagger."

Gasps rain through the hall at the name.

Rapunzel, however, feels like a strand of hair just snagged on a splintered board. Something about that doesn't add up. Still, no one else seems to have picked up on it yet, the other captives' faces all balancing fear and fury.

Then it clicks.

The only other time she felt this kind of horrified disgust was when she looked at Gothel and asked, *Should I even call you that?*

Rapunzel makes a decision, then, one she knows is going to be very unpleasant but worth the payoff. She bites down on the root.

Unsurprisingly, it's tough and woody, and her teeth ache as they dig in—but she can feel the beginnings of a notch.

Enver's brow furrows. He starts to turn to Rapunzel.

And Councilor Teophine's voice rings out as she reads off the parchment in her hands: "'Greetings to Their Honorable Majesties of Kourenne. I, Erwan Persevault, Councilor of the West and Master of Seas, bear this message on behalf of His Majesty, King Enver of Astera—'"

"Stop her," Enver barks out.

No one moves.

"'Your daughter, Princess Rapunzel, and her consort, Eugene Fitzherbert, are now in our custody,'" Teophine continues, " 'and your minister of diplomacy will remain a hostage on my flagship—' "

"I said *STOP HER*," bellows Enver.

A man with a guard captain's sash strides over to Councilor Teophine and tears the parchment from her hand.

Then he scans the words. He looks up at the king, stricken, and doesn't fight at all when Teophine takes the declaration back.

" 'If you wish to see any of them again, you must cede to Astera the territory containing the former location of the sundrop flower, and allow us unrestricted access to it. To ensure your compliance, the princess and her consort will remain in Astera until at least a decade has passed,' " she finishes grimly. "What were you saying about exaggeration, Your Majesty?"

"This isn't the Night of the Poisoned Dagger, Father," Verette spits out. "There are too many witnesses this time. You can't slaughter us all and save yourself with some lie about traitors again."

"That—that's preposterous," Enver blusters. Rapunzel can see desperation tightening a winch in him as he searches the crowd for allies. "You don't expect anyone to believe this, do you?"

The last of the root tears free in Rapunzel's teeth. She coughs it out with a muffled *"pleh,"* then raises her voice. "How did you save yourself?"

"What?" Enver's erratic stare lands on her.

And Rapunzel knows she's struck true when the king's fingers graze his stomach.

"The Night of the Poisoned Dagger, you should have died from your stomach wound. You're still bleeding right now." Red flashes as the king tries to hide his hand behind his back—but there are witnesses on every side now, and the ones behind him stare and point. "You said the apple wasn't ready in time to save the queen, and she died that night, too. So how did you save yourself?"

A terrible look breaks across Verette's face as she, too, makes the connection.

"It wasn't that serious," Enver sputters, even as an undeniable wet gleam slicks his red doublet. "I just drank from the Starlight Spring—"

"You said they poisoned it!" someone shouts from the crowd.

"I-I had some in reserve for the queen," Enver lies. "I've been fine with just the starlight water—" His eyes graze a window, and something shifts in his face, moving from near panic to triumph. A broad, relieved smile breaks like porcelain as he laughs, "And it doesn't matter anymore! It's done! There's nothing that can be done to stop it!"

Rapunzel follows his gaze to a window overlooking the island's edge.

Warship sails jab into the horizon like thorns.

They didn't stop the fleet after all.

And now they're going to return to her mother and tell her

Rapunzel couldn't keep the one promise she made: to come back.

A hush falls over the hall, sickened and awful.

It makes the explosion that engulfs the flagship all the louder.

Another crash follows as a fireball swallows a warship whole. And another, and another, tearing ship after ship apart.

In seconds, all that's left of Enver's armada is charred rib-cage hulls and fire on the waves.

Twenty-Two

Eugene

All things considered, Eugene would have to rate destroying a fleet with its own munitions a solid ten out of ten. And admittedly, Verette made it easier by clearing any sailors who had not already cleared themselves from the ships. The trickiest part for him, really, was making sure the powder kegs wouldn't light until the ships made it out of the harbor.

And, about five minutes from now, explaining to Leona that he just blew up her flagship.

But that's a problem for future Eugene. Right now, Eugene is infinitely more concerned with getting back to Rapunzel, and the one part of this plan that hasn't worked out so well is figuring out exactly *where* she is. He has a hunch it's wherever Verette got dragged off to; when Verette sensed Enver fighting for control of the roots, they decided to let him take her just to buy time for the ships.

Which is why he's taking a page out of Verette's book. Specifically, the horse page.

When he runs into the stables, he finds Maximus already standing over the shattered ruins of his stall door, nostrils flaring. He tosses his head and snorts at Eugene as if to say, *About time.*

"Sorry, *I* was busy committing grand acts of sabotage," Eugene says airily as he grabs a fistful of Max's mane and swings onto his back. "Let's go get our girl."

Maximus takes off, careening past palace guards who look like they're having about the weirdest night of their careers. It takes a couple halls and corners for Eugene to realize they're bearing toward the audience hall.

Of course.

A man like Enver will always want an audience.

Eugene slides off Maximus when they reach the doors; the chaos inside says it'll be easier to go on foot. "Keep an eye on our backs."

Max snorts again and starts snapping his teeth at the nearby guards.

Eugene pushes his way through the wreckage and the frightened crowds, toward the blindingly bright mass of roots at the dais, just as the first explosion rocks the hall.

Shouts and gasps burst through the air, alongside the orange glow blooming from the western windows. When the thunder fades, Verette's voice pierces through: "*How*, exactly, did you save yourself, Father? You never answered."

"It was starlight water, that's all!" Enver blusters, the most unraveled Eugene's ever heard him.

Eugene staggers into the open just as Hughes says, "Then you don't need this."

He's standing by Cressien and Teophine, holding the starlight apple aloft for all to see.

Enver goes still.

"Are you really going to stand here," Hughes accuses, shaking, "and say you executed Eugene Fitz for nothing?"

"All your seeds went with that fleet." Leona seems to have chewed through her gag. "I'd be very careful with that last apple, if I were you."

The king hasn't moved—except for his darting eyes.

And then desperation makes a devil of him.

He turns on Hughes, his roots lashing out, stiffening to razor-sharp spears—

There's a flurry, a cry, a sickening thud. The apple hits the ground.

Hughes staggers back, aghast.

And Cressien, who pushed him out of the way, looks down at the roots impaling his own stomach with a mixture of disbelief and indignation.

"Oh," he says unevenly, "that's not how I thought this would go at all."

TWENTY-TWO

He slumps as the roots jerk loose. Hughes catches him and lowers him to the floor with Teophine's help. The only sound Eugene registers is Rapunzel's scream.

A juicy crunch splits through the air. Silver light pulses down every root, emanating from King Enver, who breathes deep before taking another fervent bite from the apple now clenched in his fist. Starlight runs like tears into his beard. With every chew he stands straighter, the roots shivering with power.

But he's not the only one who's using their teeth.

Verette's wrenched her rootbound hands up to her face. She bites into the gnarled, shining root, tears a mouthful free, and swallows.

An opalescent glow darts through her bonds. The raw root isn't as bright with starlight as the apple, but nevertheless, the tendrils binding her shiver—then peel away.

"You killed her," Verette snarls. "The People's Dagger didn't touch Mama that night. She was just sick! You could have split the apple and saved both your lives! You let her die so you could have the apple all"—a root thick around as a man bursts through the floor—*"for"*—it clumsily sweeps at Enver—*"YOURSELF!"*

All the binding roots slacken, then surge with starlight and swarm to Verette. Enver reflexively takes a step back, swinging the apple away from her.

A tiny green figure crawls into view under the king's cloak, planted on his shoulder. And with focused, deadly precision, Pascal's tongue strikes the apple out of Enver's hand, then whips it to Rapunzel, towing Pascal himself along.

The moment she grabs the apple and Pascal, roots shove through the floor, walling them off from Enver and Verette.

Hands grab both Eugene and Rapunzel by the shoulders—Ruvon and Sulian, pushing them toward the nearest exit. Sulian shouts, "Take the apple and *run*!"

"But Cressien—" Rapunzel protests.

"You have to get to your ship," Ruvon urges as stripes of light flare through the root wall. "We'll keep Enver distracted. Get into open water, where the roots can't reach you, and destroy the apple. He won't stop until there's nothing left to chase."

Rapunzel pushes the apple toward him instead. "Can't this heal Cressien?"

"It wasn't enough to permanently restore the king," Ruvon says with a grimace. "Even if Verette can hold him back, we'll need to take any opening we can get to tear down the tree and cut him off. But . . ."

No more tree, no more apples. No more time.

Enver's voice booms through the hall: *"Stop FIGHTING me!"*

It's been over a month, but Eugene can still hear Gothel hissing the exact same words. From the look on Rapunzel's face, she remembers it just as terribly well.

"I can't just—" Rapunzel's voice catches. A silver root bursts through the ground by their feet, and they all stagger back. As Eugene steadies her, she looks up at him, wordlessly asking.

Eugene braces himself, then tells Ruvon and Sulian, "You're not getting rid of us that easily."

Ruvon's scowl deepens, but Sulian, for once, softens with a pained smile. "You sound like your parents."

"Wait—" Rapunzel lights up like a lantern. "The palace sunmill. You said starting it up could weaken the tree. If Cressien can hold on—"

"*Perhaps* that could give Verette a fighting chance." Ruvon takes the apple and cuts an offensively neat slice, considering he's using a knife pilfered from the refreshment wreckage. "This may keep your minister with us for now. You'll have to reconnect the main shaft and release the brake wheel, which is located—"

"Behind the sails," Rapunzel finishes as he passes the apple back. "I *did* do the reading."

"Then go, and may the stars' favor follow." Sulian starts to turn. Eugene grabs the stable master's arm as one last bolt of inspiration strikes.

"Maximus," Eugene says. "With the white coat. You want to distract Enver? Give that horse a sword."

Twenty-Three

Rapunzel

"LOOK WHAT YOU MADE ME DO!"

Rapunzel can't hold back a flinch as Enver's voice chases her and Eugene down a corridor, audible even over a crash that rocks the audience hall. It's not the fear, though all of this is nerve-wracking. It's how long it took to see what was right in front of her face. It's how maybe, on some level, she *did* see it—she just wanted it to be different this time. It's what Eugene puts into words as they careen into a garden:

"He sounds like Gothel," he says, disturbed.

Rapunzel spins until she finds the sails of the palace sun-mill over the rooftops, and heads for the archway in the right direction. "I guess I thought she was, well, unique. But the way he talks to Verette—it's almost the same, isn't it? It's just a pattern any awful person can use."

They emerge into the courtyard of the dormant sunmill as confused birdsong breaks overhead. For a moment, Rapunzel's just as confused. It should be late, well past sundown, yet a pearly glow is turning the palace grounds nearly as bright as day.

"Where is that light coming from?" Eugene searches for the source while fishing in a pocket for his lockpicks.

"Not sure," Rapunzel starts as they reach the sunmill's doors. She gives them a futile rattle; sure enough, they're locked. Eugene kneels by the keyhole and gets to work. Pascal buzzes a warning in her ear. She looks back and finds cracks darting over the stones of the courtyard, racing toward them. Silvery light jams through the fractures, the roots tickling at the edge of her awareness. "Enver's found us, hurry!"

Eugene twitches the picks, his words strained through gritted teeth. "He's gotta be following the apple. If we see a way to destroy it—" He breaks off as the lock clicks. Something in the catch of his voice tells her that's not the only reason he paused, though.

Roots explode from the ground, thrashing toward them, only to jerk to a halt as a more prismatic light flares over the silver. "It's Verette," Rapunzel realizes aloud. "She's fighting—"

Before she can finish, another tangle of roots erupts near them, heading for a ladder on the side of the sunmill. The coils snarl around it and, with a horrible squeal, rip it to pieces, flinging them into the air as shrieking gulls wheel away. Rapunzel stares, bewildered. Why would Enver go for a *ladder*—

Eugene yanks Rapunzel through the doors and slams them shut, turning the lock. Then, through the dim, he points to the apple. "If it gets bad, *you* could try eating this. I'd do it myself, but . . . the starlight doesn't know me the way it knows you."

Rapunzel stares at what's left of the apple glowing in her hand. The slice for Cressien didn't take much, but Enver's own savage bites claimed nearly half, his teeth marks dug even into the seedy core.

It's the kind of power people would lie for, kidnap children for, kill innocents for. The kind of power that others will do anything to use.

"If it gets bad," she evades, and turns to look for the machinery. Surprisingly, it's not as dark as she expected, but for disconcerting reasons: More cracks have spiderwebbed the empty basin of the Great Starlight Fountain, and silvery light juts up from below and illuminates the interior almost enough to see by. The marble statue's eyes fall on her with an air of judgment.

"We're right over the spring," Eugene notes, frowning as a fragment of the basin rattles and falls out of sight. Another spear of silvery light breaks through the void. "Why isn't he using the roots there to stop us?"

Rapunzel waves a hand in a broad circle and heads for

the jumble of gears and shafts at the far end of the sunmill's ground level. "Everything he's doing is destabilizing the ground under the palace, especially here. I bet the roots are the only thing holding up the fountain basin right now. The starcloud tree *might* survive the fountain caving in. It won't survive the sunmill also coming down."

Eugene shudders. "There goes my plan to camp out here. How do we get this thing moving again?"

"When a sunmill isn't operating, the main shaft is raised so it doesn't turn the water screw by accident." Rapunzel reaches the machinery and starts hunting around, holding up the apple to see better by its muted glow. "There should be something like a crank or a lever to lower it around here somewhere."

"I thought you said you did the reading!"

"I went on a tour!" Rapunzel retorts, a bit sheepish. "It's close enough!" She spots a rusty crank wheel the size of a tabletop, pockets the apple, and gives one of two handles a push. A wretched groan ricochets off the sunmill's walls, which brighten a little more. A faint, rocky thud tells Rapunzel more of the fountain basin has fallen into the spring. Dust billows down from the support beams overhead, catching even more of the starlight, but the shaft has barely moved. When she drags on it again, it lets out a disgruntled creak and refuses to budge.

Eugene grabs the other handle. "Think this was meant for two. Clockwise?"

"Clockwise," she guesses with a veneer of confidence. "On

three—one, two, *three*—" The wheel grinds into reluctant motion, then picks up speed as a massive iron rod begins to descend. "Steady, it'll throw off the gears if it falls too hard—"

There's a bone-shaking judder—from the doors behind them.

Enver won't disturb the roots holding up the spring, but those aren't the only ones he can use.

Eugene just lets out a grunt of aggravation as he wrenches the crank wheel. "*This*—guy. Can't he—give it—a *rest?*"

The main shaft finally drops into place in another great spurred wheel. "There! Now we just have to get . . ." Rapunzel stops.

"What is it?" Eugene steps back and wipes his brow.

"We have to get up to the brake wheel," she says slowly. "It's behind where all the sails connect at the top of the sunmill. But . . . Enver tore down the ladder outside." She looks at the walls and finds only barren stone. "I don't think there's one in here."

Another splintering bang shakes the doors.

Rapunzel takes a deep breath, then reaches for the apple. Eugene catches her hand.

"You don't have to do this if you don't want to," he says softly. "I—I can try to climb up, or something."

The walls grow brighter as another slab of the fountain basin falls away. Eugene's throat moves as he swallows. Rapunzel doesn't have to say it; they can both see there's no time.

"I just—" she whispers, "I'm just scared it might—change

me. Make me more like Enver. I don't want to be used again, but I still really, really want to be *useful*. My hair had this incredible power, but the only good thing it ever really did was save you. And I don't know if I could have cut it off myself."

Eugene doesn't answer right away. Then he folds his hands around hers. "This is about . . . the gallows, isn't it?"

The next crash frays with breaking boards, even if the doors still stand.

Rapunzel's throat burns as she nods. "I love my parents, but what they almost did to you was wrong. And the same power they have, Enver has, and look what it did to *him*. How can I be sure I'll be different?"

"You make sure there are always people who can tell you no," Eugene says bluntly. "If people say there's a better way, you hear them out. Your hair didn't make you a better or worse person, just different." He lifts their twined fingers and, even sticky with apple juice and smudged with rust, presses a kiss to her knuckles. "Sunshine, I loved you before the whole princess thing. I loved you with your hair, and even more without it. And whoever you'll be in a minute from now, a week, a decade . . . I know I'll love her most of all."

For a moment, the world falls away, and it's just her and him, and the way he can always make her feel like she's stepping into the sun. Rapunzel's whisper is ragged. "You're always going to be my dream, Eugene."

The ground trembles, the hinges of the sunmill doors screaming as the wood starts to give way.

She frees a hand, pulls the apple out of her pocket, and bites down.

It tastes like—an ordinary apple.

Then it tastes like frost on a December morning.

Then it tastes like the honey candy Gothel brought her when she was seven, and then the mint plant she grew on the windowsill, and then the salt air of the sea at midnight.

Starlight runs down her throat, kindling every bone.

She can feel the roots writhing at the door like hundreds of fingers. She can feel the utter exhaustion of the starcloud tree below, forced to grow roots far deeper than it was ever meant to, to bear fruit long after it wanted only to return to the earth. She can sense Enver and Verette's struggle in the audience hall, like an arm wrestling match with a thousand arms.

This far away, and with Enver this distracted, it only takes a push to drive him from the doors.

She opens her eyes and discovers that the roots have frozen in place over the wooden wreckage. A soft, buttery glow washes over them—not the daylit blaze of the sun, but the golden glimmer of the morning star.

"Huh," says Rapunzel.

She can sense the starlight in the apple's remains, concentrated into dangerous potency. It feels . . . malleable, the way the sunlight used to, when she pushed it out and into a wound.

She cups the apple in her hands. Then she takes a breath and imagines drawing out the starlight, letting it drain into her bones.

In moments, she's left with a plain, mostly eaten apple, its skin dull, its flesh starting to brown.

"Enver won't be finishing that," she says with grim satisfaction. "Come on."

She can weave the starlight to her will easily enough, but the roots unfortunately prove more of a challenge. Even though she can sense them clearly, moving them feels like trying to pick up a mug with a pair of tongs. As she and Eugene approach the doorway, the tendrils jerk back in an ungainly tumble, nowhere near how they behaved under Enver's adept control.

And even with Verette fighting him, Rapunzel can still feel the shift in his attention as silver like mercury surges through the network of roots, bound for them.

They have to get to the brake wheel before he does.

Rapunzel makes an awkward yanking gesture. It calls a burly, thick root up through the earth, one standing as tall as the doorway and with plenty more length in reserve. "Grab on," she tells Eugene. Once they've both got a solid grip, she reaches for the starlight in her bones and draws the root upward.

It rockets them into the air like a string pulled tight, stretching higher and higher past the glittering sails. Amazingly, Rapunzel can *smell* the sunlight waiting for release in the crystal panes, even if it's not the form she knows.

Then she makes the mistake of looking down.

Silver tendrils are swarming up the sides of the sunmill, racing them for the top.

Eugene sees them and says a very crude word. When she stares, he says defensively, "I learned it from Cressien."

Their root arcs toward the heart of the sails, where their beams all meet and affix to the brake wheel's shaft. The shaft itself runs horizontally into a little covered hutch at the top of the sunmill to protect the gears from the elements, and a narrow walkway runs around it for maintenance workers. Rapunzel swings down onto the walkway, with Eugene a heartbeat behind her.

The bottom two sails creak and rattle. Enver's roots have curved away from the walls—and knotted around the edges of the sails like a heavy silver fringe, immobilizing them in a giant X.

There's no doubt about it. He's not chasing the apple anymore—he's caught on to their plan. Even if they release the brake wheel, the sails won't activate and the water screw won't turn. She can feel the weight of the dragging roots—

Inspiration strikes. She rushes to the brake wheel's hutch and throws it open. A heavy steel bar has the brake wheel locked in place, but this time, the release lever is clear as day. She points to it. "Eugene, on my signal, you pull this, okay?"

"As Her Highness wishes," he says with a grin, and Rapunzel realizes—even with every awful thing that's happened, she's smiling too.

It's not the starlight lighting her bones; it's not trading seventy feet of hair for thousands of filaments of roots. It's that she's solving problems, keeping her word, *doing* things again, because that's the kind of princess she wants to be. This is what she left the tower for. And even when the starlight fades, no one can take that from her.

Rapunzel crouches at the edge of the ledge. The roots pull on the bottom left and right sails, and she can sense Enver's control in every fiber. She can use that. In fact, she ventures little feints at the starlight in the roots just to goad him into tightening his grip.

The trick is Enver's trying to stop the sails entirely, and Rapunzel only needs one.

"Now!" she shouts, and brute-force *shoves* her way into the roots—but only those holding the left sail. They curl back from the sail, shivering. Enver doesn't follow suit fast enough with his roots dragging on the right, and as the brake wheel releases with a clanking jolt, the silver roots pull the right sail down—kick-starting the sunmill into motion.

A shudder runs through the stones. The sails pick up speed, years of stored sunlight humming with glee. Enver's roots are nowhere near strong enough to stop them now, and the sail tears them from the ground like so many feeble lichens.

Rapunzel can feel the starcloud tree far below, as the tension of the water screw strains to turn even through the wood of the trunk. It's lived longer, larger than so many of its kind, grown where it was never meant to thrive.

And the tree—the tree is tired.

"Look," Eugene says as he helps her back to her feet. He points beyond the sails, and she remembers this isn't just the top of the sunmill—it's the highest point in the kingdom, with a view to match.

Below them, all of Astera is ablaze with starlight.

The roots lace nearly every inch of open ground she can see, fanning out all the way down to the shore and shining even through the dirt and stone. It's what's turning night to day, wild and sprawling. Tiny figures like ants spill out into the streets to stare as flocks of birds swoop and cry.

And as the water screw grinds into the tree . . . the light flickers.

For a blink of an eye, Enver's control on the roots slips.

Then they thrash with the panicked ferocity of a cornered animal.

"We have to get back and help—" Rapunzel starts, only to see the root that lifted them up here turn cold with silver. It reels back. "Watch out!"

Eugene grabs her waist and swings her out of the way as the root whips toward them and slams into the ledge inches away. They stumble back, his hands firm on her sides. "How are we getting down?"

A sail sweeps past them, moving fast enough now to trail a breeze behind it. Rapunzel squints at it, thinking. "On the count of three?"

"You know I love how your mind works, but there are *zero* handholds on those," Eugene starts.

A crack and boom sounds from the audience hall. From here, they have a terribly clear view of more silver roots punching through the roof, ripping holes into the shingles.

At the same time, the root reels back, waiting for a gap between sails to strike, and Rapunzel makes an executive decision: She threads her arm through Eugene's and yells, *"Three!"*

They leap as the root crashes down again and shatters the ledge where they stood. The sail's iron frame shakes with their impact, yards and yards of crystals jingling a discordant melody. Rapunzel scrambles for a grip but lets it loosen when the sail dips into its downward arc, and slides down to the very end—where a cluster of fraying tendrils still dangles listlessly. They wake at a touch of gold, and as Eugene skids down to join her, she tosses one to him, then wraps her fists around another and swings off the end of the sail.

The broken courtyard careens too far beneath them, even though their root-ropes frantically grow to close the gap—fifty feet—thirty—ten—

Rapunzel lets go and hits the ground running. Eugene lands with an *oof* behind her, and together they sprint back for the audience hall. The rest of the palace is in chaos, the corridors clogged with fleeing servants, Enver's guards fighting other soldiers with verettes pinned on their chests like medals, roots flickering with pearl and silver and fleeting gold as they pass. Around one corner, they see Maximus absolutely obliterating a very perplexed squad of guards, while Leona and Sulian and Torch nab anyone who squeaks by. Down another hallway, Teophine and Ruvon are evacuating staff and guests.

The ruined hall, when they stumble into it, is nearly unrecognizable. Mangled decorations and upended tables are strewn like shipwrecks in a sea of rubble, broken glass, and twitching roots scattered over the cracked floor. Hughes and Cressien shelter behind a heap of debris, sweat glittering on Cressien's face as he sits against Hughes's shoulder, his eyes closed. Enver and Verette are still locked in struggle in a cage of roots.

Rapunzel rushes to Cressien's side and drops to her knees. "I'm here," she tells him as he cracks an eye open. "I—I think I know how to fix this, if you can hang on a little longer."

"Certainly not running away anytime soon," he breathes with a wince. "Need to bill Enver for this waistcoat."

"If we make it out of this, I'll mend it for you," Rapunzel promises, and pushes herself back up. Cressien only huffs something that might be a laugh, an unfortunate testament to how much blood he's already lost. Ruvon said the apple could only buy him time, and as the tree is weakening . . .

The whole hall flickers and dims—then floods with starlight once more as Enver lets out a guttural, furious yell. "Do you really want me to die, Verette? Is that what you want?"

"No! I want—"

"Just because I wouldn't give you the throne before you're ready, you want me to die," Enver accuses.

It's time to end this. Rapunzel turns to Eugene. "Can you stay with them?"

"Of course." He squeezes her shoulder.

She strides toward the writhing cage of roots, anger rising in her throat. Gothel used to blame her the same way when she was upset, and now—Rapunzel has outgrown it.

That pale gold starlight washes over the roots. She tears the cage open, roaring, *"ENOUGH!"*

Enver and Verette gawk at her. He sputters, "But—how—"

"Your apple's gone," Rapunzel tells him. "Your tree is dying. It's time to let go."

Enver reels back. This close, Rapunzel can see a strange texture stealing over his skin, almost like . . . tree bark.

"No," he insists. "This isn't how this was supposed to be. You were supposed to heal me—if *you* hadn't given up the sundrop's power, you could have saved me for good and I could have brought the tree down myself. The ships were only supposed to be a last resort, but *you* pushed me to this!"

He wants to guilt her, to make her feel like it's her fault he *has* to hold her prisoner.

Rapunzel spent eighteen years playing that game against a much, much better player.

She refuses the bait. "I think I can try to heal you now. But only if you give your word—"

"I don't need it!" he interrupts, drawing himself up as if being taller somehow makes that true. "You'd know better if you just listened to me! We can take turns—I'll kill the tree here once the one's grown in Kourenne, let the Starlight Spring recover, then cut down the tree in your kingdom and plant one back here! It can be a cycle!"

"Crop rotation is not an excuse for invading another country," Eugene calls from behind the rubble heap.

"He's right." Verette reaches out a hand. "Father, please. You're going too far—not just with the plan, with this magic. *Look* at yourself."

Now, the rough streaks of bark gnarling into his skin are unmistakable . . . as is the pewter gleam.

"You have to stop," Verette urges.

Enver stares at her. A bitter resentment builds up behind his eyes, twisting his face with rage. "I did *everything* for you," he hisses. "I am your father. You don't tell *me*"—his hands flex, even with leaves budding at the knuckles—*"what I can"*—silvery starlight burns down every limb, acid bright—*"AND CANNOT DO!"*

The starlight is slipping from Rapunzel's control. Even with her and Verette both fighting, years of sustaining himself on the apples have made the starlight part of him in a way they can't match, the evidence written in the veins blistering over his skin but not theirs. Out of the corner of her eye, she can see the more distant roots curling and shriveling as he strips the starlight out of them.

A hand lands on her shoulder.

"This doesn't look good," Eugene says in her ear. "And I hate to say it, but Cressien's not looking good either."

They're running out of time.

Rapunzel thinks of the starcloud tree being torn up in the spring. How it lit up brightest of all at a song. How she shoved Enver from the roots before, when—

When his attention was split.

"I have an idea," she whispers to Eugene, "but we need to break his concentration."

He looks up at the ceiling, mouth tilting, and says, "Give me twenty seconds."

"We can find some other way to keep your wound healed," Verette pleads to her father, hand still outstretched. "It doesn't have to be like this. But you have to let go. You have to let us *both* do what we've promised."

Enver meets her gaze for a long, long moment. It's a chance he didn't earn, one last try to save him from himself, save them all from him.

"It's killing you," Verette breathes. "Please, Papa. Just let go."

Rapunzel feels the shift—

Of Enver's drag on the starlight tightening.

"Not yet," he gasps. Pale blue leaves sprout from his fingertips. "Not ready—*not yet*—"

He turns to the throne.

Eugene taps Rapunzel's elbow. "I need a boost to the roof."

She takes a deep breath and focuses on one more heavyweight root, summoning it up through the floor in a torrent of pale gold. Eugene grabs on to it, an odd lump swinging over his shoulder—a tablecloth gathered into a makeshift bag.

Enver's voice thunders through the broken hall, brittle but steady, laced with pain and triumph. "This is still my kingdom! I am its master and its ruler!"

When he lifts a foot, roots trail like a beard from his boot sole.

Rapunzel pushes her way through the squirming masses of tendrils on the ground and reaches Verette's side. The other princess's face is streaked with tears and grime. She gives Rapunzel a look of pure astonishment when Rapunzel takes her hand.

Rapunzel opens her mouth, thinks of the sun as one more star, and begins to sing the lullaby.

Enver has decades of stolen starlight in his veins. But the song, like their memories of sunshine and lost mothers, lives deep in their bones, where even the roots can't reach.

Verette's breaking voice joins in. And this time, the starlight answers to *their* call, not the king's.

Enver is fighting still, even harder than the tree fought before, chasing after every scrap of light and magic and digging in. "You will *not* take my place," he grits out, lurching onto the dais. "It's mine! The throne is *mine*! I am *still in control*!" Leaves flush and bristle at his cuffs, while pewter bark hardens over his face. *"I will not be moved! If I can't have it, no one will!"*

He hurls himself into the rootbound chair and grips the armrests hard enough to splinter, glaring balefully as shoots tear through his bloodstained waistcoat and lock him into place.

Rapunzel sees the difference, clearer than ever:

Verette has walked the highest and lowest streets in Astera, sat by sickbeds, sung to children, crawled through sewers, built a coalition to guide their future. And Enver . . . Rapunzel realizes she only ever saw him leave the palace for a tour.

It's the difference between someone who wants to lead, and someone who simply wants to rule.

"Actions make a monarch," Rapunzel tells him as Verette keeps singing, "not a throne. If you haven't learned that, you're not ready to be king."

Enver glowers at her, wordless with outrage, clinging to the starlight and the throne simply so no one else can have them.

And over the song and the rumble of roots and clamor of fighting, she hears something else: a maelstrom descending on beak and wing.

A flapping noise precedes the soft patter of a shower of—*bread?* Rolls, breadsticks, tiny bits of toast, they all rain on Enver from above.

Of all the possible challengers to the Asteran throne, the last thing anyone probably anticipated was a flock of relentless seagulls.

They swoop down on Enver, who can't even lift his arms to bat them away. Verette's voice falters, but Enver's grip on the starlight evaporates. Suddenly it's all rushing to Rapunzel in a sweeping tide, and all she can do is lead it—not to her bones, not to the spring, but to the man dying in a strange palace in a strange land, here only because someone invited a princess in over her head.

A princess's powers may still be new to her, but if there's one thing Rapunzel will always know how to do, it's heal someone.

Drop by drop, spark by spark, she guides the starlight from weary roots and wilting leaves and splinters of a warping trunk. She sends it into Cressien, closing the wounds in a way Enver never could, until his heart beats steady, his breath comes easy, and the pain is only a memory.

When the starlight has done its work, she turns and finds

the roots no longer burning with silver, or opal gleam, or mellow gold. They're dulling to plain gray stone.

And Enver is fading with them.

Verette stands in front of the throne, tears running down her cheeks. "Papa, we just wanted to help. Why didn't you let go?"

A distant, defeated smile only barely flexes his lips. He breathes, "Make me proud."

And then—

The starlight is gone, and only the stone is left.

Verette sways on the spot. Rapunzel steps closer and braces her elbow, trying to think of anything to say that is big enough for something like this.

Footsteps crunch over the broken stone. Hughes comes to Verette's other side, looking almost as lost as she does. He wraps an arm around her shoulders. Then he gathers himself.

"Your mother is with the stars," he says raggedly. "And as one of the few who knew her, I swear—Gaelle has always, *always* been proud."

Twenty-Four

Eugene

A week later, Eugene notes with no small degree of dismay that the seagulls have yet to fully move on.

Fortunately, they largely congregate around the remains of the audience hall, and most of the flock he brought down on Enver has left. But even now, on their last day in Astera, the shrilling of the gulls still follows him and Rapunzel out into a familiar sunlit courtyard.

Like most of the palace, the sunmill is laced in the stone roots of what once was the starcloud tree. The sails creak and tilt occasionally with the breeze, but the waterworks are motionless; Ruvon is working with Councilor Laroux to salvage as much of the apparatus as they can. The logistics of the

Great Starlight Fountain, however, have also changed with the landscape.

The fountain's basin outlasted Enver by only a few minutes. When it collapsed, it took a large swath of the courtyard with it, leaving a yawning sinkhole where the spring's cavern once was. The rim has been roped off, with only a few ladders dangling down into the pit, but that won't last for long.

There have been many hard choices this week, decisions of what to salvage in the palace and what to let go. Eugene and Rapunzel have helped everywhere they can, whether by picking the locks on the queen's chambers or helping shelter citizens whose homes were swallowed by roots. Verette, however, has been simply and unmovably clear about one key decision: The Starlight Spring was torn open, and it's staying that way.

Eugene and Rapunzel find her at a table set up near the lip of the sinkhole, huddled over sheets of parchment with Ruvon and Councilor Laroux. ". . . and if we add a support column below this shelf, that should stabilize—oh, you're here!"

"We'll keep working, Your Majesty," Councilor Laroux says.

Verette tenses briefly, as she has every time someone's called her "majesty" in the last week, but just says, "Thank you."

"Still weird?" Eugene asks as she walks over.

"Still weird," Verette confirms. She's not dressed like the queens in storybooks, but in a laborer's breeches and shirt, the only sign of rank a plain silver circlet over her long braid.

"I'm still not used to 'highness,' and it's been a month and a half," Rapunzel says. "I guess it just takes time. But anyway, what did you need help with?"

Twenty-Four

"I actually wanted to show you something. Come on." Verette beckons them to the rim.

Eugene frowns. "If this is an assassination attempt, frankly, it could use a little more polish."

"That's how you know I'm not really trying," Verette says cheerfully. She ducks under the rope fence and heads for a ladder.

Eugene and Rapunzel follow her down into the chaotic morass of broken stone and petrified roots. Even what was exposed mud is now coated in pale dust. The former starcloud tree sits like a bizarre statue in the corner, the trunk splintered and twisted around the gash the water screw left as it pulled it up, roots and all. The network of roots itself makes a strange webbed dome of stone tendrils under the tree, lit from within by a soft glow. Ruvon did say the tree was planted over where the stardrop fell, and now it's finally exposed.

"Look at this." Verette kneels at a low patch in the rubble.

Eugene looks down as Rapunzel sucks in a breath. What he thought was dust on the ground—shivers. The reflection of a wheeling seagull darts through it. He crouches and dips a finger in.

He only gets one knuckle deep before grazing the mud, but when he lifts his hand, the drops of water gleam like pearls.

"It's coming back already?" Rapunzel's voice squeaks with excitement.

"Like you said, it just takes time." Verette stands. "But I wanted you to see before you leave tomorrow. And . . . I may have another surprise before you go."

✧ ✧ ✧

Verette does not tell them what that is, only sending them to go pack before Rapunzel can run off to help hold a ladder for a repair crew or grab a broom and sweep up glass. She's come alive in an entirely new way the past week, lending a hand wherever she can but letting Eugene and Cressien steer her away from burning the candle at both ends.

That is, when Cressien hasn't been . . . distracted.

As Rapunzel and Eugene approach the guest wing, Eugene sees through the open door of the parlor that it's already occupied. Never before would he have considered Cressien a man capable of lounging, but the minister looks positively at ease on the parlor sofa, smiling as Hughes passes him a cup of tea and sits beside him.

Eugene promptly steers himself and Rapunzel back into the hall outside the guest wing, then says under his breath, "I think we can give them some privacy."

"Agreed." Rapunzel's mouth twists as they lean against the wall. "Especially since it's their last day together for a while. I *did* offer to talk to my parents for him, but . . ."

Eugene doesn't have to ask; both Cressien and Hughes love their kingdoms too much to abandon them. "I guess we'll just have to force them to take a *lot* of vacations. But that reminds me—there's something else I wanted to settle before we head back." He ducks his head. "We didn't really have time to mull it over back in the sunmill, but how do you feel about Sunshine?"

"Er . . . generally favorable?" Rapunzel blinks. "I mean, I like rainy days too."

Eugene stifles a laugh and whispers, "No, I mean—as your official nickname."

Rapunzel just stares at him, and this time, he doesn't think it's a lack of comprehension.

"You hate it," Eugene says nervously.

But Rapunzel's whole face is lighting up, brighter than the dawn. "I *love* it. It's perfect."

"Really?" His grin nearly matches hers.

"Really," she says.

There's a sudden crash from the guest parlor. Rapunzel rushes in, Eugene on her heels as she blurts out, "Is everything okay?"

Cressien and Hughes are mopping tea off the parlor's low table, an overturned teacup the clear culprit. Hughes scrambles to his feet, Cressien a second behind him, neither forgoing so much as a scrap of decorum. "Good afternoon, Your Highness. We were just . . ."

Hughes falters, clearly coming up empty for excuses. It's really a miracle he didn't get caught all these years, but then again, from the way he and Cressien are both acting, Eugene also suspects it's been a long time since either of them was in puppy love.

"Crocheting," Cressien croaks. "We were . . . crocheting."

Eugene lets out a dramatic gasp. "No—don't tell me you were considering *smooching* in here. No boyfriends until you're eighteen—we discussed this!"

"We did?" Rapunzel makes a face.

"I'm leaving." Hughes gives him a sour look and heads for the door. Then he stops. "Actually, Fitzherbert, I, er. I was sent to track you down. Councilor Persevault would like to speak with you before you go. I believe she's currently in Queen Gaelle's library."

"I'll stay here and pack," Rapunzel tells him. "Take your time."

Eugene kisses her cheek. "You're my favorite."

He heads off, splitting ways with Hughes as they pass the audience hall. For now, it's the one part of the palace that hasn't been touched since the night Enver locked himself into the throne. Verette left the choice to the People's Council, and the consensus was that a place like that ought to remain only as a memorial to what was lost, and a testament to the price of losing it. Eventually, the rubble will be cleared; then there'll be a plaque left to testify to the truth of the Night of the Poisoned Dagger and the lives lost to Enver's folly . . . and Enver himself, as a warning to those who would outstay their welcome on a throne.

As a council, the group claimed it will be addressed last because the living take priority, and that has been true. But as Verette's friends, they have all seen her eyes fill with tears when they pass the king's statue. It's not unlike the look Rapunzel used to get anytime anyone mentioned Gothel.

A portrait of Queen Gaelle has replaced Enver's in the royal wing, and as Eugene passes it, he can see the resemblance to Verette. It's not shocking at all that there's more of Gaelle than Enver in her.

Twenty-Four

The queen's chambers have been aired out repeatedly, but they still *feel* intrinsically dusty, the library most of all. Leona is peering into a chest of short, wide drawers, and as he comes to a halt at her side, she pulls out a chart—no, a *map*.

"A*ha*," she huffs with satisfaction. "Did you know, one of the first things Enver banned was maps of anywhere but Astera? They were all locked up or burned. You want to keep people on an island, you make sure they don't know where else to go. But Gaelle, she always loved collecting them. Your Minister Cressien's agreed to bring some of our cartographers to Kourenne to catch up, but these are a good start."

"Cressien thought maybe Enver banned *The Tales of Flynnigan Rider* because it encouraged kids to leave," Eugene says, studying the next map in the drawer.

Leona makes a *tch* sound. "That, and spite. He always felt like your parents should have been more grateful. Like Gaelle liked them more than him." She points to a shelf where there's a dust-filled void between tomes. "There, that's where your copy of *Flynnigan Rider* came from. Gaelle got the very first binding of it, and she was so excited, she embossed her insignia upside down inside. When Marietta and I made it all the way here on the Night of the Poisoned Dagger, the queen was on her deathbed. She insisted we take it. Marietta could barely stand to look at it on the ship to Kourenne."

Eugene tells himself it's the dust thickening his throat. "What were her last months like?"

"She tried," Leona says bluntly. "She tried to be happy and stay for you, but she was . . . fading. Always flinching at shadows, afraid Enver had followed her across the sea, calling for your father in her sleep. When she took ill, her last request was for me to make sure you got that book, that it was meant for you. A week later, the hospital sent word that we'd lost her."

The silence sits heavy in the little library for a long, long moment.

"I really wish I could have known them," Eugene finally says.

"I wish you could have, too. You deserved to grow up climbing the walls of the printshop, and they deserved to know their son. We all deserved better." Leona rolls up the maps, tucks them under an arm, and closes the drawer. "You'll always be welcome in Astera, as long as I'm Master of Seas. And I *expect* to see more of you, especially since you've taken up with the princess of our newest allied nation. But for what it's worth . . ." She motions to her cane the way she used to in the orphanage, and Eugene automatically passes it over.

"You can't really picture me in a printshop, huh," Eugene says with a rueful grin.

Leona shakes her head with an answering, albeit more wry, grin and heads for the door. "Can't picture you with gray hair. Now, if you buy me a *very* strong drink . . . I'll tell you the stories your parents never wanted to reach the light of day."

Eugene laughs. "With what money?"

Leona stops in her tracks, staring at him. "Oh, stars help me, we need to go to the administration center, *right now.* No one told you about the royalties."

TWENTY-FOUR

Morning light casts the harbor in pale gold, almost the same as the starlight Rapunzel held, as they gather by the royal galleon. Compared to just a fortnight ago, the assembled company is mostly the same, but the mood distinctly different: Rapunzel is bouncing on her toes; Cressien is marginally less tightly wound. Eugene has the fresh glow of a man who has just inherited his parents' substantial accumulated royalties, *with interest*, and is going to make some very reckless financial decisions once they figure out the currency exchange rates. Verette and the rest of the People's Council are also in good spirits, despite the early hour and the necessity of farewells.

"I believe," Verette says with a merry kind of formality, "that our hospitality was lacking during your visit. I wish to make it up to you all." She reaches into a satchel slung over her simple indigo gown and pulls out an oddly mismatched stack of paper, then hands it to Eugene. It's been loosely stitched together in crude thread, and on the very top page are scrawled handwritten letters: *The Tales of Flynnigan Rider.*

"I found it among my mother's belongings," Verette says. "I believe it's the first draft."

The manuscript shakes in his hands. He can see two dueling sets of handwriting in a string of names: *Marion Andrews?* A. M. Fitzherbert? *Eugene Rothar?* Then: *A. DREW ROTHAR*.

He can't picture their faces, but he can imagine them at the counter of Herbert & Fitz, laughing and brainstorming over this very list, the same way he and Rapunzel joke and chat as she paints in her old nursery.

"Thank you" doesn't feel like enough, but it's all he can say.

Rapunzel rubs his back as Verette gives him a pained, knowing smile. "You're welcome. Minister Cressien, I confess your gift is a bit . . . sideways. We have an opening now for an ambassador to Kourenne, who will be sent to your kingdom next week." She turns to Hughes and extends her hand. "Congratulations on your promotion."

Hughes's jaw drops.

"I'm going to miss you," Verette says quietly, "more than I know how to say, but . . . it's time we all try something new."

Hughes's eyes glisten; Cressien beams from ear to ear. Hughes shakes Verette's hand, then pulls her into an embrace. Even Eugene is getting a little choked up. "Can I borrow your hanky?" he whispers to Rapunzel . . . just as she finishes mopping up her own face by blowing her nose. "Actually, I'm good."

"For Princess Rapunzel," Verette says, "I must first apologize that our original invitation turned out to be issued in bad faith. I would like to extend an invitation of my own, for your entire party to attend the Fountain Festival in one year's time."

"I accept," Rapunzel says, hiding her hanky behind her back as Eugene pretends not to see. "And I also wish to extend you an invitation to visit us on *my* birthday, so you can see the floating lanterns."

"I also accept. But that would leave me once again in your debt . . . if not for these." Verette looks behind her and motions to a guard. They come forward, bearing a bushel basket heaped full of something white and strangely shaped—

"THE SHELLS," Rapunzel gasps. "You—you remembered—is it okay?"

"We have more verai than we will ever need," Verette says firmly. "They may not be as iridescent now, but I suppose that means you'll just have to come back when the shells start washing ashore full of starlight."

Rapunzel doesn't bother with a handshake; she lunges right at Verette and wraps her in a hug. "I guess I will."

It takes them the better part of an hour to weigh anchor and embark, but they leave the harbor with an escort from the Asteran navy, Leona perched at the bow of the foremost ship. Eugene makes his way to the stern and watches until she and Astera both sink behind the waves.

It's strange, leaving a place that could have been home. That was home to the life he should have had, to the people who wanted him. He doesn't know who he would have been under Enver's rule, if he would have changed their odds for the better or followed his parents and uncle into an early grave. Part of him will always miss that life.

He turns and finds Rapunzel at the bow, laughing with Cressien, the breeze tugging at her hair as she keeps a firm grip on her sketchbook.

And Eugene knows that if his parents could see him now, they'd be happy, even if Astera isn't his home. Everything they wanted for him, he has: a girl he's madly in love with. A job that will let him use his skills for good. A future he's proud to chase.

(And the outrageously ample inheritance doesn't hurt either.)

It's not just their dream he's living, but his own.

He pulls his own battered copy of *The Tales of Flynnigan Rider* from his satchel. The inside cover creaks as it falls open.

Eugene pauses.

Something's . . . off.

He's never taken the time to really study the endpapers before. They're soft cream marbled with pale silver, the Asteran royal seal embossed inside. There's nothing odd about that. Right?

He flips to the back. The endpaper there is clearly one sheet, folded in the middle, one half making the very last page of the book and the other half glued to the back cover, the standard method. When he turns again to the front . . .

It's clear as day. The marbling pattern is flipped on the inside cover. The embossed seal is right side up.

Leona said yesterday the royal insignia should be upside down.

Someone cut the endpaper down the seam and pasted it back wrong.

Eugene's brow furrows. He takes a knife from—well, a gentleman never tells—and carefully slides it along the edges of the endpaper, slicing through the lines of glue. Then he peels back the sheet, exposing the raw board of the cover.

Thunderstruck hope rises in his chest.

Beneath the endpaper, framed in wobbling paste lines, are scrawled two ragged words:

FIND ME.

Epilogue

"I've submitted my final report, Your Highness."

Rapunzel, who has been absorbed in sketching out the mural she'll start probably the instant they get home, looks up.

Cressien is leaning against the railing of the bow. He's already been more at ease this past week, and the prospect of Hughes moving to their kingdom has him positively sparkling, which manifests in Cressien as a slight upward tilt at the corner of his lips.

"I'm glad," Rapunzel says tentatively. She tugs on Pascal's coat as he clings to the railing beside her. "Now you can relax. Is it still a wasted effort to ask you to call me Rapunzel?"

"It is," he confirms with a faint tinge of humor. "While the circumstances were less than ideal, I'm relieved I had the opportunity to review my previous reports and . . . recalibrate. Of course, I was in no way biased by your saving my life."

"Of course," Rapunzel says with a very feeble attempt at gravitas.

Cressien's eyes crinkle, only for a moment, but Rapunzel counts that as a win. "I am looking forward to continuing our work together."

"Me too," she says honestly. "I've been thinking a lot about the kind of princess I want to be. I want to *do* things. I want to make people's lives better."

Cressien nods, thoughtful.

"I—" Rapunzel hesitates, staring at her sketch. Sometimes the best thing for a painting is a big, bold stroke. "I don't want us to execute anyone anymore. I-I think we should stop. *Especially* without a trial. We almost lost Eugene, and if we could lose someone like him, who else have we already lost? And I don't think everyone will make the best use of a second chance, but . . . execution shouldn't be the first and only option anymore."

To her immense surprise, Cressien says, "I think that would be a strong beginning, Your Highness."

Rapunzel nearly pitches her sketchbook into the sea in excitement. *"Really?"*

"I would be honored to help you propose it when we return."

She gives him a sly look. "Are you sure you aren't going to be distracted?"

"I may be a little distracted," he allows. "I thought I was prepared to attempt a long-distance relationship, but I went through seventeen drafts of a romantic letter last night alone, every one rubbish."

"I'm sure they weren't that bad," Rapunzel laughs.

"I used 'moon' as a simile in five consecutive sentences. Unintentionally."

Pascal lets out a dismal *bihrrrr.*

Rapunzel tilts her head. "We all have our own unique styles?"

That gets a raised eyebrow out of him, which seems to indicate, *Well played.* He pushes off from the rail. "Fitzherbert is approaching. I believe I'm going to go attempt draft eighteen before the seasickness claims me."

As he wobbles away, Rapunzel realizes that despite the wind, and the chill of the sea, and the reality that her hair can't have grown more than a quarter of an inch . . . her neck isn't cold anymore.

If there's anything she learned from the brief time she commanded starlight, it's that she didn't miss her magic. She didn't miss her hair.

She's missed being the girl who took herself out of the tower. And it turns out that the best part is, now she gets to help other people leave theirs.

Eugene strides toward her, practically bouncing on his

toes. In his hands is his copy of *The Tales of Flynnigan Rider.* "Sunshine, you're not going to believe this."

Rapunzel can taste it in the spray of the ocean, feel it in the sun on her face, hear it in the rise of Eugene's voice: Another adventure is knocking at the window.

She smiles and says, "Show me."